Rea[illegible] bout

The Tattoo

"A book about the 'sins of the fathers'... A gritty, troubling book and he's done it well. The issues he raises are key to Hawaii today and for future generations."

—*The Honolulu Advertiser*

"Unforgettable...If McKinney's ultimate achievement is his portrayal of Hawaiian culture in a way that mainland Americans—those who've never seen, nor ever will, anything but the touristy side of Hawai'i—can identify with, then the ultimate failure belongs to the mainland American publishing houses for ignoring the book for so long."

—*San Antonio Current*

"The other Hawai'i, the one tourists never get to see."

—*Ian MacMillan*

"McKinney excels in his descriptions of the Hawaiian landscape...In Ken Hideyoshi, McKinney has created a character both gritty and complex."

—*Small Spiral Notebook*

"Rough-and-tumble, rife with fully drawn badass characters and plenty of action, McKinney's novel is powerful and strong."

—*Time Out Chicago*

The Queen of Tears

"McKinney vividly recreates Seoul during the Korean War from the beat-up cars made of beer cans to the affluent homes lined with fish ponds and grape vines.... It's a technically skillful achievement in a story deceptively disguised as a slim, fast read."

—*Honolulu Weekly*

"McKinney's portrait of a besieged woman within a multicultural, multigenerational family saga poignantly and powerfully dramatizes the troubles women face, the pan-Asian melting pot of Hawaiian culture, and the conflicts inherent in Americanization."

—*Booklist*

"McKinney demonstrates a talent for restraint and tight pacing."

—*Publishers Weekly*

"[An] interesting case of Korean, Korean American, and Hawaiian characters.... [McKinney] has a keen eye for details of places and people. The storyline is well developed.... McKinney is pitch-perfect on the social and racial climate of Hawaiians, Asians, immigrants, mixed-bloods, and whites.... The frequent dialogues are crisp and pointed."

—*Korean Quarterly*

"...highly readable, carefully detailed and nuanced, flowingly plotted, and populated with complex, authentic local characters."

—*Honolulu Weekly*

Bolohead Row

"McKinney is exceptionally skilled at imagining compelling characters, who worm their way into the consciousness of even reluctant readers.... If his aim is to provoke self-righteous middle-class Islanders into awareness and understanding of the folks who populate ***Bolohead Row,*** he succeeds. [It] is well written and potentially very important for its ability to reflect..."

—*The Honolulu Advertiser*

"With ***Bolohead Row,*** McKinney officially establishes himself as the state's young breakout writer, and singlehandedly creates the genre of hardboiled Honolulu fiction."

—*Honolulu Weekly*

"What makes this book work is McKinney's "talk story" approach. He allows the reader to "sit down" and listen as Charlie tells us about his struggles. Through his journey—which includes drugs, violence and even murder—he begins to find a way to let go of the "game" and start concentrating on "life."

—*Hawaii Magazine*

List of Characters

Banyan Mott—Husband, father, community college professor, his life unravels when he purchases a home in Mililani Mauka. All is not what it seems in this picturesque suburban subdivision. Is his new home really haunted or is he losing his mind?

Kai Krill—former owner of Banyan's Mauka house. After her husband's untimely death, she and her teenage son end up in a Wai'anae Coast homeless encampment among drug addicts, the mentally ill, and families desperately trying to hold it together.

Josh Krill—A freshman at Wai'anae High, he simultaneously faces his father's demise, homelessness, and adolescence. Will he be able to survive the dramatic turn of events?

John Krill—Kai's husband, Josh's father. He welds sheets of steel onto a Komatsu bulldozer and tries to flatten Mililani Mauka. No one knows why.

Police Officer "Dan the Man"—one of the police officers on the scene at John Krill's rampage through Mililani Mauka, he has to shoot John Krill. Lonely, and considered one of Honolulu's unluckiest cops, he spends most of his time at home hand-crafting medieval weapons and armor until he becomes Josh's guardian angel and surrogate father.

Caley Mott—Banyan's wife, a nurse at Queen's Hospital. With its soccer parks, barbeques, and friendly neighbors, Mililani Mauka is right up her alley. Unfortunately, she suspects her husband is going insane as their marriage unravels.

The Luapele Street Posse—One's a firefighting steroid monger. Another has a daughter competing in a nationally televised talent show. The Posse is a group of friends who live in a Mililani Mauka culdesac where they watch each other's children ride bicycles, never talking about the secrets they keep behind their automatic garages and wooden colonial doors.

mililani

MAUKA

Other books by

Chris McKinney

The Tattoo

The Queen of Tears

Bolohead Row

mililani MAUKA

Chris McKinney

Mutual Publishing

Author's Note:
The following story is fictional and does not depict any actual person or event. Any resemblance to actual incidents, or actual persons living or dead, is coincidental.

ISBN-10: 1-56647-869-3
ISBN-13: 978-1-56647-869-4

Library of Congress Cataloging-in-Publication Data

McKinney, Chris.
Mililani Mauka / Chris McKinney.
p. cm.
ISBN 1-56647-869-3 (alk. paper)
1. Honolulu (Hawai)--Fiction. 2. Domestic fiction. I. Title.
PS3613.C5623M56 2009
813'.6--dc22
2009006681

Cover photos (tent) by Marcin Pwainski, dreamstime.com; (house) by Ian Gillespie
Cover design by Jane Gillespie
Page design by Leo Gonzalez

First Printing, May 2009

Mutual Publishing, LLC
1215 Center Street, Suite 210
Honolulu, Hawaii 96816
Ph: (808) 732-1709
Fax: (808) 734-4094
e-mail: info@mutualpublishing.com
www.mutualpublishing.com

Printed in Taiwan

For ***Mika***

Acknowledgments

I'd like to thank the following people for their valuable contributions:

Gavan Daws, the Fukuda family, John Heckathorn, Karen Lofstrom, Matthew Martin, Barry Menikoff, Karen Palmer, Pamela Simon, Michelle White

Special thanks to Bennett Hymer.

Table of Contents

Prologue

It begins in silence, about six AM, darkness giving way to coral-shadowed clouds that shock the sky. The engine starts up, shakes with a choking, hacking early morning diesel cough, steadies itself, and a black shape rumbles off the trailer, out from under the blue tarp. Onto Luapele St., past new houses that do not look exactly alike but were built with the same parts. Left on Pahoehoe, two-story houses here, one skewered with a flagpole, Old Glory hanging limp. A woman out walking her dogs stands and stares; her three sand-colored Pom-Chis, mutt-mixture Pomeranian-Chihuahua, yap and skitter and tangle their leashes and show their little teeth. Right onto Mehe'ula. Two joggers stop short at the curb, a man and woman in matching spandex shorts and green University of Hawai'i plastic visors. The thing blows exhaust in their faces and rolls on, going the wrong way, into the early bird traffic heading for Honolulu. Cars brake and honk; a few flash high beams. The thing jumps the gutter and guns into pine trees on the nature strip. Three blocks down, at the Mililani Mauka Fire Station, a man coming out for his first smoke of the day hears the splintering whumps and an engine growling. He turns to look, his jaw drops, he loses his cigarette and runs back inside.

The thing slows, pauses, rotates. The driver looks through his periscope at the Castle & Cooke Real Estate Center. It has white flags all around it, saying START LIVING. He sights on the main office, built out of the same parts as the houses. He smiles and puts his foot down. The flagpoles snap like matchsticks.

He has spent four months of nights and weekends welding sheets of half-inch steel over his Komatsu bulldozer, two layers, sandwiched with concrete.

He aims at the front wall with the big corporate logo, and, hardly trying, punches a hole in it. He reverses, comes on again, doubles the size of the hole, and rolls over the rubble into the sales area, treads crunching desks, computers, scale models of subdivisions. He punches an exit hole in the back wall, one-two, and swings back onto Mehe'ula, along the medial strip, taking out the Mililani, All-American Town, est. 1986 lava-rock plaque.

He hears sirens, checks his periscope, sees a blockade coming up—sawhorse barricades, cops in flak vests, straddle-legged, handguns gripped double handed. He puts his foot down. They scatter. Someone yells from a bullhorn. He flips a police car, another, and flattens them both. Bullets ping off the steel plates, nothing to him, just fingernails tapping on an empty glass. A cop runs around behind, manages to scramble up and drop a duffel bag over the periscope. The dozer jerks and flails, like a bull ride at quarter speed. The cop scrabbles and drops off, the duffel shakes loose.

The driver sights Mililani Town Center—Kentucky Fried Chicken, Star Market, McDonalds Express. The police cars are trailing him, but hanging back. He sees people lining the street, families, mommies holding babies, daddies hoisting kids on their shoulders. He thinks of his wife and his son, all the times he dragged them to Walmart, the Halloween candy and costumes, the Christmas decorations, the wire snowman wrapped in a string of red and green light bulbs, his boy's first bicycle, the chopper look, mock gas tank with flames and all. He can see the Komatsu reflected in the Walmart window, the steel plates, the periscope looking back at him. He is crying now. He guns the engine and plows forward, ripping through the aisles of reasonably priced goods.

He cuts the engine in the electronics section, listens to the silence, reaches down to his boot top, and takes out a .22 caliber pistol. He unbolts the hatch and waits. Hushed voices, pattering footsteps. The bang of a riot gun. A tear gas cartridge cracks against an air vent and starts smoking. More riot gun cracks. Choking now, he bursts through the hatch, trying to fan mist out of his face, gun still in hand. Rubber bullets pelt him. He rolls off the dozer and falls into more smoke, broken metal shelves, and cracked plasma television screens.

"Gun!"

He stands and fires. They fire back. Two rounds rip through his chest, knocking him on his back.

Four cops approach, guns drawn. A tall one grabs the .22 and tosses it away. A short one holsters his gun and drops to his knees.

"Sorry," says John Krill, coughing up blood. Then he looks up. "My boy."

The wounded cop rips open John's shirt and sighs. John stares up at the flickering florescent lights as the frantic voice of the policeman fades.

I. A Menehune Named John

1

Mililani is on O'ahu, but it doesn't look like Hawai'i. There are no beaches, no lū'aus, no waterfalls. Here, the tops of pineapples don't stab through rust-colored soil. It's a new town, Mililani Mauka, the northside, new houses, quiet streets, an ordinance prohibiting the sale of alcoholic beverages. Then there's Mililani Town, the southside, newish houses but not as new, quiet streets but not as quiet, three grocery stores, one liquor store, a pizza place, and a bar/burger joint—the only places that sell alcohol. Mililani is not Hawaiian. It's a place where all the parents think their kids are GT—Gifted and Talented. It's more American than anything else.

So it makes sense that Banyan Mott finds himself here. He comes from a typical American family—one of three children, all of whom fell short of their parent's lofty dreams—his older brother, Dexter, not a neurosurgeon at Queen's Hospital, but a butcher at a Korean market; his sister, Tammy, not a downtown lawyer, but an uptown hair colorist for Mane Salon, or maybe it's Shear Salon—the establishment's name always mute on the tip of Banyan's tongue; and Banyan the artist, he's so artistic, they'd say, a framed photograph of a ten-year-old Banyan receiving an art award in front of the state capitol—now he's an English professor at Honolulu Community College, where public school graduates who can't identify subjects and verbs in sentences reign supreme.

Banyan had lived in town, in Honolulu, rented a 2/1 duplex with his wife, a registered nurse, and two-year-old kid, but he was tired of getting robbed by crystal meth addicts—his car three times, his house twice, so he finally gave in to his wife, accepted the down payment from his in-laws, and bought a house in Mililani Mauka, on Luapele St., a two-story 3/2 1400-square-foot home with central air, for $500,000 at 6.3% interest. His daughter was feverish the day they completed the move, and he felt as if he spent that $500,000, cheap for Mililani Mauka—hallelujah for foreclosures—more for the central air than anything else.

His daughter sleeps in her own room for the first time, in a converted crib among boxes. She pushes her head up to one corner and sucks on her thumb. His wife is in the kitchen unpacking boxes. She is wearing a knee-brace, which strikes him as funny-looking, like a ballet dancer wearing a football helmet. "What's with the knee brace?" he asks.

"Nothing," she says.

He decides to drive around Mililani Town to get his bearings. He passes the construction site of the new Castle and Cooke Real Estate Center, then Mililani Town Center—a sign that says Wal-Mart will be up in another week—he turns right.

He heads toward Foodland, drives by a pink-and-baby-blue three-story apartment building that lists units in the classifieds as townhouses for sale. Recreation centers and parks with jungle gyms ... Banyan cannot drive a mile without passing one. He thinks he has just seen all of Mililani. He finds himself wanting to breathe heavily into a brown paper bag.

He heads back to Luapele Street. Pine trees have already been replanted. Banyan knows all about the action that took place here seven months earlier. Not many people missed the footage of that bulldozer rolling over trees, buildings, and police cars. Like other viewers, he cheered that bulldozer on without knowing why. The pine trees are back up; damp soil surrounds the base of the new trees. It seems to Banyan that

Mililani has an octopus-like quality to it—cut off an arm, and it will grow right back.

He gets back home, to the house which, as far as he knows, is the first house in all of Mililani Mauka with a history.

Caley, his wife, is unwrapping dishes from newspaper with the caution and precision of a grandmother who recycles festive wrapping paper. "How was your trip?" she asks.

"Explain mortgage insurance to me again."

"Don't start."

"They're afraid we can't afford the mortgage, so they charge us $400 more a month?"

Caley ignores him. Banyan picks up the discarded newspaper off the kitchen floor. "It's small," he says. "Nice, but small. Soccer to our heart's content."

"It's not like we're on another island. By the way, don't throw away that newspaper. I'm saving it."

"What the hell for?"

She ignores the question. "I like it. It's quiet. It'll be a great place to raise Raimi."

Banyan resists the urge to crumple the newspaper in a ball and throw it at his wife. For half a year she laid her siege, firing trebuchets that lobbed toxically optimistic concepts like "housing prices will never come down" and "Mauka is the perfect place to raise a child." After all of this, if his daughter grows up to be a crack whore, Banyan may have to kill her.

He checks on Raimi, and grumbles to himself that his wife didn't leave the night-light on. He considers that maybe night-lights are more for parents than children, and as long as his kid is not in complete darkness, she will never stop breathing. He plugs in the light. Raimi's head is jammed into a corner, and her legs are tucked up under her butt. He feels her head. She's cold, so he shakes her, anticipating movement. She rolls over, eyes still closed, arms extended over her head like a ref signaling a touchdown. She's two, and he still fears SIDS.

Raimi sleeps for eleven hours straight that night for the first time in her life. She wakes up smiling with no fever. The apparent medicinal qualities of suburbia reassure Banyan about the move and gigantic mortgage. She is not crying, so he heads downstairs to grab her a metallic pouch of juice guaranteed to have 100% of the RDA for Vitamin C. As he leaves the room, his peripheral vision catches sight of a miniature man, stocky, sitting cross-legged at the foot of the crib. Banyan thinks ***smurf,*** but he does not recall a non-blue Afro, goatee, beer belly smurf. The little man is playing with Raimi's building blocks. Banyan spins around. The ghost is gone.

2

Sixteen miles of homeless. That's what the paper says. The leeward coast, the west, downwind side of the island, where several years ago rent used to be a few hundred bucks a month. Now it's up to about a thousand. It's where the homeless, mostly native Hawaiians, sit like hardened oil in a pot of water—the police come and turn up the temperature at one of the roughly dozen beachfront parks, the water boils, the oil spreads, the temperature cools, and the oil congeals, not in the exact same spot, but it's still all there in the pot. It takes a helluva lot of heat to make oil evaporate. When the median price of a single-family home soared over $600,000 on Oahu, so did the number of encampments along the Wai'anae Coast. Brown people living in tents and under tarps—business as usual.

But Josh Krill isn't thinking about all of that. He is crouching on the oceanside of Farrington Highway, hand over his brow, watching a shirtless man with a stiff dog carcass cradled in his arms march into the sea. The surf beats on the man's bearded face as he pushes the floating corpse toward the horizon. He swims back to shore. The waves push the dog back to the sand. The man picks the dog up again and this time swims farther out. A small crowd gathers. Josh joins them.

The man with the dead dog is at this for a half an hour before he gets caught in the current. Josh, now on his tiptoes, has a hard time spotting him over the small breakers. A yellow fire department jet ski appears and tows the man in. The dog is gone. An exasperated firefighter questions the bearded man. Burial at sea, the man says as his round body, starved for oxygen, expands and contracts. Burial at sea. The firefighter shakes his head. Fucking homeless, he mutters.

The firefighter escorts the man up to Farrington Highway, where an ambulance waits. A woman with enormous, dark arms raises one, smoothing out the dimple on her elbow, and extends her middle finger.

Josh heads back to the campsite. He passes a blue tarp attached to a broken-down van. A woman under the tarp washes clothes in a red cooler as three of her children, all girls, try to do homework at a fold-out table cluttered with canned goods. The wind blows at their paper as they try to write. One of the girls places a can of Spam on a corner of her paper and smirks, satisfied. Another tosses a book in the sand. Without looking up, the mother says, "Read in the van."

"It's too hot," the girl replies. She is not more than twelve.

Josh walks on, past other camps like this one, some consisting of a single tent, polyester-and-mesh domed roofs rattling in the wind. Other, bigger camps are surrounded by pretend property markers of chicken wire, beach rocks, or driftwood; these are laid out like a makeshift home interior—kitchen with a propane tank, canned goods, and grill in one corner; table with plastic Wal-Mart chairs in another; tent containing sleeping bags in another. A dog tied to a tree at one of the bigger camps snatches at drying clothes hanging from branches. Tee shirts spread like scarecrows' torsos, fluttering in the wind.

Josh and his mom occupy a spot by this camp, comforted by the constant barking of the tied up dog. They have an eight-by-eight tent and a canopy his dad bought at Sports Authority. Josh goes to the tent and drags out his bicycle, a yellow mountain bike, a gift from his father last Christmas. He untangles the rubber-sleeved chain from the spokes, frame, and crank.

The liquor store across Farrington Highway does not have a bike rack, so Josh weaves the chain through his bike. An unmarked police cruiser slows then speeds up. An old Hawaiian man sits on a milk crate out front, cutting an empty beer can in half with the tab. Josh walks into the store. He strolls through the aisles, passing canned goods, not really shopping, just killing time. He stops at the pork and beans, picks up a can and studies the film of dust on the top. His father was a big fan of pork and beans cooked with bacon, onions, Tabasco, and red Redondo's hot dogs. He wipes off the dust with his shirt and puts the can back.

The only things he's interested in buying are some blue slush from the ancient Icee machine and some Copenhagen. He tells the Korean woman he is buying it for his uncle. The woman sells him both without question, and Josh puts the round can of Copenhagen in the back pocket of his denim shorts, and sips on his Icee. The old Hawaiian man has finished cutting his beer can in half, and is spitting tobacco in it. He lights a cigarette. His teeth appear to be mostly gone; all that are left are sharp stubs, dark and jagged like lava rocks.

Two shirtless boys are checking out Josh's bike. One straddles it, a cheap, half-chewed cigar pressed firmly between his chapped lips. He is like a half-assed, destitute, teenaged Polynesian Capone, hair slicked back with seawater. Josh sucks in his stomach and recalls the tough-guy movies and Discovery Channel documentaries on prison life he's seen. The secret is to act tough and not back down. The boy with the cigar gets off and lays the bike down. "Nice bike," he says. "Where you went get um?"

Josh kneels. He balances his Icee on the rough asphalt and works the combination of his lock. "None of your fuckin' business, fat ass," he says.

The boys don't say anything. Josh's hands tremble, and the lock takes longer than usual to remove. He is trying to watch the boys and take the chain out of the spokes at the same time. Once the chain is out, the boy with the cigar kicks the side of Josh's face. So much for the Discovery Channel secret.

By the time he's on his feet, the Korean woman is yelling that she has called the police. The two boys ride away. The one on the handle bars holds with his fingertips an afro pick planted in his hair, while cigar smoke trails them. The pair looks like the first guys trying to invent the airplane.

Josh eyes the dark-toothed man sitting on the milk crate, the one who seems to be trying to discover whether lip or lung cancer is easier to get. The man spits in the can and says, "Welcome to Wai'anae."

Josh sprints toward the thieves, and for the first time in his life understands the hate that drove his father to flatten Mililani Mauka.

3

Honolulu Community College occupies a square of land boxed in by the freeway; also in the box: car dealerships, a strip mall with a Korean bar, a tattoo shop, a Subway, and an H & R Block. There's also a canal with brown water. At 9:45 AM, Kai searches for parking along the canal, suspecting, after circling the box a half dozen times, that she will be late for her first class. She should have gone to Leeward Community College, she thinks, but this is the one with the cosmetology program.

The view on campus does little to help her cling to the romantic notion of going back to school at thirty-five. Two tall buildings, several one- and two-story ones. They all look as if they were built during different decades, starting in 1940, but were all painted a sickly salmon color during the 1970s. Her first class is in one of the tall buildings, so she takes the elevator, noting that it only stops at floors one, three, and five. She gets off at five, surprised to find herself facing a stairwell that is actually floor five-and-a-half. Confused, she steps into the stairwell and looks up, then down. She shrugs and chooses down.

The fifth floor itself isn't so bad. It's age-worn and florescent lit. Cool air and eighteen-year-olds stream down the hall. The door to room 505 is closed, so Kai softly knocks.

A narrow-shouldered man wearing jeans, an untucked white suit shirt, and a stud in his nose, opens the door. The length of his eyelashes shocks her. Pretty, she thinks.

She steps in, eyes down. She was hardly expecting a pipe-smoking, tweed-jacket-wearing English professor, considering this is Kalihi, not New Haven, but this guy looks as if he came straight out of an exclusive nightclub or Japanese graphic novel. Cartoon blue hair would probably match him.

The classroom is standard—blackboard, chairs with little desks attached to them, just like when she was in high school. Most of the faces are young, but she is grateful when she spots a couple of students with graying hair. One is a white woman with two arthritic thumb braces wrapped around her wrists. Of course, the entire back row is occupied, mostly with too-cool-for-school guys leaning their baseball-capped heads against the wall, so Kai is forced to take a seat in the front. The professor passes out papers and asks that everyone call him Banyan. Banyan owns her house now. When she saw his name in the Schedule of Classes, she could not resist signing up for his English 100.

His jeans look ironed. She wonders if he has a wife who's an ironing freak. She watches him as he tells them that every semester, on the first day of class, he assigns an in-class writing sample exercise. She digs his night club look. She imagines he can dance. She wonders if he's gay.

They are to spend the remainder of the time writing an essay on what they feel are the most important things in their lives, with the exception of family, friends, or God. He says that writing on something silly like the importance of electric toothbrushes or shampoo with conditioner is preferable to topics he's read a million times. The class laughs uncomfortably, a laugh of manners. He says it's not a graded assignment, but he wants to know where the class is on grammar. The word "grammar" shakes Kai up a bit, like hearing about the nutritional value of Brussels sprouts, or liver and onions. Banyan asks if anyone has any questions. No one answers, so he begins writing in his gradebook. Kai starts with a title: "My Husband Ran Over Mililani Mauka With a Bulldozer So Now I'm Homeless and All I Got Is This Lousy Tee Shirt."

She decides the title is too long, so she scratches it out, making sure every letter is covered in ink, then she writes, "This Ain't No Romeo and Juliet." She is aware of the fact that "ain't" is slang and a contraction to boot, but hopes she's forgiven since it shows that she knows the title of a Shakespeare play. She's been in enough schools to know that every English professor's brain floods with serotonin at the mention of William Shakespeare.

The classroom empties as student after student finishes the essay. Kai is one of the last to hand hers in, exhilarated that she is basically telling Banyan, "Hi, I'm the one who lived in that house of yours before my husband went nuts and flattened Mililani." She feels a little like a stalker as she hugs her books, peers at his eyebrows, wonders if he plucks, and walks out of class.

She's self-conscious about her lack of a backpack. In her day, kids either carried their books by hand or wore backpacks on a single shoulder. Now, the kids wear backpacks as if they are campers. She still has Psychology 100 and Chemistry 55—The Fundamentals of Cosmetic Chemistry—before she has to go to work. Her decision to take psychology has nothing to do with a desire for self-discovery or an exploration of her husband's psychosis. She knows why he went nuts, and feels guilty as hell for being a part of it. Kai just wants to start school with her strongest subjects.

4

As Banyan races along the canal, hoping he will miss the three o' clock traffic back to Mililani, he wonders how his life made a turn to the surreal. The visions of the menehune, what he thought of as a smurf ghost the first day, have become more frequent, especially after he realized that Hawai'i doesn't have smurfs or leprechauns or Puck or Oberon or even kappa—little Japanese water sprites with monkey heads, turtle bodies, and webbed limbs—evil sons of bitches that suck out the livers of cattle and children through their anuses. Hawai'i has menehune, so that's what he was seeing, as if identifying it was an invite to come over any time, and now some crazy lady is stalking him because he bought her home. The worst of it is, from what he's seen so far, she's his most promising student.

The freeway is packed. Two freeways, each three to four lanes wide, merge into a single highway going west toward Pearl City, Waipahu, Mililani, and Wai'anae. Thousands of cars roll to suburbia and country on arguably the worst-conceived freeway in the United States. He's thinking of the menehune, how last week he worked up the courage to look directly at it and saw that it was wearing a "Kiss Me, I'm Tahitian" tank-top, with a big red lip design and all.

Banyan doesn't believe in ghosts, but there it is, every night for the last few weeks, a mini-man with a tank top and grey sweats patrolling his house in the middle of the night. Sometimes it hovers over Raimi's bed, which Banyan moved to the master bedroom against the extreme protests of his wife, and sometimes it stands in the bedroom doorway, elbow leaning against the doorframe, like a guy trying to pick up women at a club. He once caught it sitting on the toilet doing sudoku. It does not talk, and when Banyan closes his eyes really tight, and then opens them, the menehune disappears. He knows there is only one explanation—he is losing his mind. As his car inches forward on the freeway, he searches for the silver lining and locates it. At least the ghost wears contemporary clothing—Mililani Mauka isn't old enough to have little guys running around with ti leaf skirts and haku leis. He **is** losing his mind, but there is logic to his imagination.

Mililani is in Central O'ahu, about a thousand feet above sea level, so the air gets noticeably cooler as Banyan nears home. He is approaching his favorite part of the day, when he gets home and his daughter smiles and yells, "Hi Daddy!" She sprints to him, he bends forward, she wraps her skinny arms around his neck as he hoists her up, and she immediately goes for the stud in his nose. Then, after that initial moment of elation, he has to plop down on the carpet with her and play. He holds a yellow game piece from Candyland while Raimi holds a plastic girl with purple hair, a toy from a McDonald's Happy Meal, and the two say hi to each other for what seems like a thousand times. Sometimes they jump or fall down or suddenly go upside down, but mostly they just say hi to each other. She is two, and the thought of having another child wears him out. His older brother, Dexter, swears to the virtues of having two children close together in age, children who can occupy each other's time, but Dexter is a nine-to-fiver, and only really sees his kids maybe three hours a day.

Banyan opens the door and is welcomed with great enthusiasm by Raimi. His wife, Caley, folds plastic shopping bags in perfect squares and stores them in a large, lidded plastic container under the kitchen sink. He sits on the sofa, an orange sectional with green and blue pillows, and Raimi hands him a little figurine of Swiper from ***Dora the Explorer***. Raimi will be doing the voice of Mr. Potatohead on this day, only Mr. Potatohead is looking a bit Dali-esque—his lips are on the top of his head, and his eyes are plugged into his arm socket. As Banyan says, "Hi Mr. Potatohead," he wonders if Raimi ever saw the menehune, and if so, would she even be scared? Would she think that he's a big toy?

Banyan alternates talking to Mr. Potatohead and his wife. "How was your day?"

Caley ignores him, which means Raimi was bad today.

"Hi Swiper!"

"Hi Mr. Potatohead!"

Caley finishes folding the last bag. "Okay, can you watch her? I have to get ready for work."

"No problem."

Caley runs up the staircase like she's just been let out for recess.

"Daddy, Daddy, look Mr. Potatohead upside-down!"

"Be careful, Mr. Potatohead!"

"Did you put gas in the car?" Caley yells from upstairs.

"No, sorry, I forgot. I was trying to beat traffic." Both conversations are about as interesting to Banyan as faculty committee meetings.

"Great, I might be late for work."

"Hi Swiper!"

Anal-retentive haole bitch; how about I kick your other knee in so you can wear two dumb-looking braces? Maybe shave thirty minutes off your narcissistic make-up ritual. The thought shames him. It's not that he hates his wife, but he has come to understand that for some reason his marriage makes for a self-contained rage that is easy to tap into. He'd like to ask someone if this is normal, but the friends that he hardly sees anymore avoid conversations about their spouses as if it's a matter of national security. But they love to talk about their kids. "Hi Swiper! Hi Swiper!" Raimi says, her tone increasingly desperate.

"Hi Mr. Potatohead!"

They only have one car, a Volvo station wagon shaped like a sports car, and it has about as much interior space as a four-cylinder from Japan. Banyan goes to campus three days a week, and Caley works for twelve hours, three nights a week, at the Queen's Hospital emergency room. "Oh, look what we got in the mail today," she says, tossing him an envelope from upstairs. He catches it noting that it's cut perfectly across the top. "Okay, gonna get ready."

The letter is from the MTA—Mililani Town Association. Banyan is an English professor, but struggles through the legal language. Raimi walks to the kitchen and squats over the tile. "Come, Daddy, come Daddy."

"Give me a minute, sweetie."

She cries. The letter informs Banyan that the cement block wall surrounding his property is two-and-a-half feet too high and must be brought down. He knew it was coming—the warning was part of the property purchase packet, but he is surprised that it comes so fast. "Wanna go outside, sweetie?"

"Outside, outside," Raimi sings, improvising her own notes.

The wall is basic, hollow concrete blocks stacked up to about a foot over his head. It surrounds the entire 3,500-

square-foot lot, except for the driveway. The aluminum mailbox is cemented into the wall, and there is no clearance for a red flag. Caley has already put a "Mott" label on the box. The woman loves labels.

Banyan is no expert, but the wall seems relatively new, maybe a couple years old. Each row is perfect. It reminds him of Legos, of perfect model homes made of popsicle sticks, and of Caley. The job of chopping off two-and-a-half feet seems impossible. "Come, sweetie," he says to Raimi. They go into the garage where he grabs his sledge hammer and a lawn chair.

Banyan folds the chair out for Raimi and puts it by the car. He looks at the wall, thinks twice, and scoots the chair even further away. "Now stay there, sweetie."

The wall is too tall, but he swings down with the hammer anyway. He misses, loses his grip, and the hammer hits the driveway. The hammer bounces once, and Banyan jumps out of the way. "Ha ha, Daddy silly!" Raimi says.

He picks up the hammer, embarrassed, feeling more like an English professor than ever before. He decides to swing sideways, like a lumberjack. The hammer is not heavy—six pounds—but all of the weight is in its head. Banyan lets anger flow to his arms, and he swings.

The hammer glances against the wall, then sails out of his hands. He cringes as it heads toward Raimi, is relieved as it flies over her, but cringes again when it lands on the hood of his car. He runs to his daughter and scoops her up. The car alarm blares, headlights flashing, the sound of a duck under extreme duress. Raimi laughs.

"Daddy silly!"

As his wife swings the door open, Banyan is positive that there's some kind of symbolic lesson to what just happened, but he's not sure what it is. He carries Raimi to the wall and is proud that a piece the size of Raimi's fist is missing five blocks up. It reminds him of a jail-break story, the kind where the protagonist digs a hole in the wall of his cell a crumb at a time. "There is no way you're doing this yourself," Caley says.

"Don't worry. For some reason, I'm feeling satisfied."

People from places with snow will laugh, but Mililani gets cold at night—by Hawai'i's standards. It's about sixty-two degrees, and Raimi, who lasted in her converted crib a good week, has the top of her head crammed into Banyan's ribs. Banyan moves her onto the pillow next to him and grimaces as he lurches out of bed, rolling over a pile of unread student writing samples.

He has been having a tough time sleeping since they moved (seeing menehunes will do that to a guy), and now after two swings of a hammer, his back is killing him. Since high school, he knew he was destined to enter an occupation where air conditioning, a computer, a swivel chair, and acoustic tiles sealed over his head would be in the cards. He picks up the scattered writing samples, tries to read one, but after spotting a comma splice, a two misspelled words, and a subject-verb agreement error in the first sentence, he tosses the stack on the floor, stomping on the pile once before heading downstairs.

Caley sleeps on the orange sectional. The sun peeks through the dark sky, poking dull light through the window. The light hits her dirty blond hair, but her face, which is covered with freckles, is still in shadow. Her bony feet are crammed between sofa cushions. He pulls the blanket down over her feet and picks up a pink plastic cup off the toy-train table. A ring of burgundy residue sticks to the bottom of the cup. He puts the cup into the sink, relieved that he has not seen the menehune yet.

He wants to go outside and survey the damage to his hood. He clicks the garage door open, but instead of looking at the car, he walks to the wall. The baby fist-sized dent is gone. Did he really make a chip in the concrete? As he tries to remember if the event was true or a dream, a voice from behind, humming the Commodores' "Night Shift" speaks. "If you think, after all the shit I went through for this wall, I'm going to let you break it down, you're fuckin' crazy, dude."

Crazy. Ain't that the truth. Banyan doesn't turn around, but stands still, like a man being approached by a grizzly from behind. A garage door opens across the street, and a man steps out to grab the newspaper on his driveway. He looks at Banyan and waves. Embarrassment being an effective cure for fear, Banyan waves, rubs the wall, then turns around and goes back inside.

5

Josh is a half-mile away from the store. He is crying hard now, hyperventilating, in front of a lot where used baby bouncers, children's bicycles, and lawn mowers are being sold. The first time you swim on your own, the first time you ride a bike, the first time you kiss a girl—Josh is experiencing another memorable first—the first time you want to die. A siren blares louder and louder as an unmarked police car nears. It's the same one Josh spotted earlier when he was wrapping the chain around his bike.

The two recognize each other. It's one of the cops who showed up his father's funeral. "Krill?" the officer asks.

"Yea."

"Jesus Christ, what the hell happened to you?"

Josh stares at his reflection in the tint of the rear driver's side window. His forehead is lumpy, and two dried rivers of blood circle his upper lip like a mustache, then converge to run down his neck, all the way to the front of his tee shirt. The soles of his feet sting. He's apparently lost his slippers. "Hold on," the officer says and opens the trunk. "Jesus, I don't really have anything back here." He pulls out a white kitchen garbage bag and dumps out the contents—a pair of black cleated shoes, a paperback, a canister of racquet balls, and a pink towel with a bit of car grease on it. He hands the towel to Josh, who is not quite sure what to do with it. "So what the hell happened?" the officer asks.

"Some guys stole my bike at the store up there."

"Goddamn. Come. Let's get you home. Ah shit, let me get my first aid kit. Look at your goddamn feet."

Josh sits on the driver's side, door open, feet sticking out as the officer pulls glass out with tweezers. Sudden radio static and pain make it hard for Josh to sit still. "Doesn't look like you'll need stitches," the officer says, "but I should call this in and fill out a report."

"Please don't," Josh says, staring at the officer's sidearm.

The cop looks at his watch, as if the time of day has some influence over the decision he is making. He works on Josh's feet.

After several minutes of soft cursing and brow-wiping, Josh's feet are wrapped sloppily in gauze, like two Christmas presents from an unmarried uncle. "Well, let's get you home, and your mom can decide what to do."

"She's gonna be at work."

"You live on the beach, right?"

Josh looks down, thinking, yea, I must look homeless right about now. He points across Farrington Highway toward the ocean. "God damn," the cop says. "Tell you what. I live close. You can hang at my house or something."

"What's your first name again, Krill?"

"Joshua. Josh."

The officer stands up and extends his hand. "My man, another local boy with a regular name. I'm Daniel, Danny, Dan, Officer Dan the Man. Your folks named you well. No Airplane or Apple or some shit."

"My mom wanted to name me Pollux. Dad said over his dead body."

"Jesus Christ, good man. It's like I told you that day. A guy plows through a Wal-Mart with a bulldozer, don't think any less of him. He's still your dad, took care of you, gave you a goddamn good name. Right? Not like he killed anyone."

Except himself. "Yea, I guess."

Josh and Officer Dan get in the car and drive. A drizzle starts, and Dan turns on the wipers. The wipers smudge salty grit on the windshield, making it hard to see where they are going.

Dan's house is several miles east in Nānākuli, before the three towers of Hawaiian Electric Company power plant and the landfill, but close enough to the Ko 'Olina hotel and marina area that Josh can see the seventeen-story J.W. Marriott Ihilani Resort and Spa along the coast. He imagines a comic book force field around the resort area, a dome that protects it from the homelessness, drugs and violence just a mile down the road.

Dan's house is at the end of a short road that approaches a dark brown, almost black mountain that is vegetated blond—a brush fire waiting to happen. The entire street is old house, renovated house, old house, renovated house. Josh's dad used to talk about it all the time, how the Wai'anae Coast, where he and Josh's mom grew up, was going to be gentrified by mainland baby boomers looking for a rustic place to retire. One house is beige with white trim, a garage door with little glass windows lined up across it. The neighboring house is a one-story rectangle sitting on short stilts. It's a primer color capped with a graying asphalt roof. A sagging chain link fence circles it, a "Beware of dog" sign dangling by a corner.

Dan's house is one of the renovated ones, but it's a work in progress. The roof is new blue ceramic Spanish-style tile, but the wooden walls are only sanded; jalousie windows with a few missing louvers reveal what must be a fifty-year-old house. The driveway is smooth concrete. Dan stops in front of his new garage door.

"Let's get you a clean shirt," he says.

Josh does not really want to go in, but he feels lost, and those who are lost rarely sit still. He follows Dan through the door, wondering how to avoid dirtying the gauze on his feet, but shrugs, and walks in anyway. He's surprised to see that this is a house that seems to lack walls. The kitchen is off to the right, a marble island the single thing separating it from what Josh can only label the big room. The middle of the big room has a circular sofa, and a suit of chainmail armor draped over a wooden mannequin, arms straight out like a cross. The walls are stained wood paneling, one side adorned with both wooden and metal medieval weapons, the other with framed inspirational posters. One shows a man dangling from the edge of a snowy cliff. It says, "Perseverance: What the mind can conceive and believe, it can achieve." There is no television, which is the only thing Josh marks as not-so-hot. Otherwise, it's like the coolest living room he's ever seen.

"Here, a tee shirt." Dan tosses it to Josh then goes to the wall Josh is staring at. He pulls a tonfa off it, a police baton, but this one looks more like a Japanese antique.

"I made this out of ashwood," he says. "You know, a boy never becomes a man until he's made something out of wood. Properly trained, you can really jack somebody up with this."

"Do you think I'll ever get my bike back?" asks Josh.

"Let's see what we can do." Dan sticks the tonfa through a loop on his belt.

There are no sidewalks along the Wai'anae Coast. Dirt, gravel, and wild grass recede from the asphalt of Farrington

Highway and turn into the front yards of homes. One house has a web of wires streaming from it, wires that connect to the telephone pole. In the next yard over, a tied up Shar-pei with a black leather collar struggles to untangle itself from the branches of thorny bougainvilleas. Dan and Josh approach the liquor store. Josh is no longer angry, only afraid to see the two boys again.

Sure enough, there they are. One has a tee shirt tied around his head like a do-rag, the other wipes down Josh's bicycle with a torn piece of denim. There are three other boys as well. They all look the same: thugs in training. One of them is smoking a cigarette, sees the approaching cruiser, and takes off running. Dan accelerates, then hits the brakes, coming to a stop beside the four remaining boys. He sticks his head out of the window. "Any of you fuckers try to run, I swear I will fuckin' run you down," he says. He winks at Josh. "Sorry for the profanity, buddy. Some of these animals, it's like the only language they understand." He talks to Josh and seems unconcerned that the four boys might run while he's taking his time getting out of the car. "So what we got here, a gang or something?"

The boys look at the ground. One spits on the bike and the others hold in giggles. Dan puts his thumb and index finger around the spitter's chin and lifts his head. He slaps the boy across the face, hard, not like a starlet slapping her co-star in a melodramatic way, but a short, fast slap, connecting more with the bottom of the palm than fingers. The boy drops to his knees. One boy seems shocked, while the other two take small steps back, never taking their eyes from the ground. "Fuck you," the boy on the ground screams. "I going tell my dad!"

"Man, a tough guy, just like I thought," Dan says. "Josh, come out here for a minute." By now the Korean storeowner is standing out front, smiling, and an old Monte Carlo slowly approaches then speeds off. Most of the passing cars don't slow as they race down Farrington Highway. Josh wants to take off himself, but he gets out of the car, waddles over with gauze on his feet, and stares at broken glass.

"Hear the tough guy over here?" Dan, not smiling, stares at Josh until he lifts his eyes. Dan looks back at the fallen boy. "Let me tell you something, motherfucker. You in a gang? Maybe daddy's in a gang? Maybe your cousins or uncles or some shit?" Dan pulls out his badge. "See this? This is my gang's color. This is our sign. And I'll tell you something, you little shit, we are the biggest, baddest motherfuckin' gang in the state. I can drive down the freeway and people slow down for me. Can your daddy make that happen? I could make your daddy disappear, and you couldn't do shit about it."

The boy stands up, teeth clenched from holding in sobs. Another car approaches, slows, then speeds off. Dan takes out the tonfa from his belt. Josh feels like throwing up. "I think I better go home now. It's getting late," he says.

"Hold on, Josh, we'll head off in a minute." Dan points the tonfa at the car driving away, as if the weapon is a teaching tool. "You see that? That happen when your daddy is in front of the store? Okay, so here's the situation. The kid gets his bike back. The kid is untouchable now, and I'll tell you why. I just made him an honorary member of my gang. This means, you see him here, you see him at school, you see him anywhere, and you do anything to him, you are declaring war on my gang. My gang hits back, and when we fuckin' hit, let me tell you, your goddamn breadfruit-eating great grandpa back in Samoa feels it. Got it?"

All the boys nod. "You boys just witnessed power. You want power? Is power cool? Go to school or some shit, because the only guys who can do shit to me are either people in my gang of high rank or a bunch of suit-wearing motherfuckers in the state capitol. That's power. You guys are just pissants. Now get out of here, before I stop being nice and haul your asses to jail."

The boys load the bike into Dan's trunk and tie it down with bungee. Josh feels guilty, like he's the one who's stealing now. After the bike is secure, the boys jog up the road together like a pack of wild dogs. After they feel they are a safe distance away, they slow to a strut and stick their bare chests out, never turning back.

Dan says, "Listen, Josh, I'm still on duty, so not really sure what to do here. When does your mom get back?"

"She works till late. I'll be okay though. I should do homework or something." Josh is nervous about the white lie. Unlike the private junior high he attended, after just one day, his freshman year at Wai'anae High seems like an academic joke. Most of his classes don't even permit him to bring a textbook home, much less write notes in the margins, something the private school had told him was helpful.

"Show me where you're camping at least, so I can keep tabs."

Camping—that's what his mom called it the day they packed up their stuff in her '89 Sentra. That was four months ago, three months after his dad had gone nuts. He wonders how his mother's first day of school went, and hopes she's having just as bad a day as he's having.

They hit the road. They pass a woman holding up a sign announcing that she will sell her home to the highest bidder. Then they pull into a parking lot that's like a hospice for cars made in the 1980s. Josh gets out and walks to the driver's side to say thanks.

Dan sticks his arm out of the window. "Here's my card, Josh. Anything you need, let me know. I'm off tomorrow. Hell, I'll come pick you up from school or something. We can do something."

Josh is afraid to say no. He gets the feeling that Dan blurted the idea out without really thinking it through since he's quiet now.

"I'll come get you." Dan stares out of his windshield, eyes stuck on a windowless van. Dirty bedsheets hang like drapes in place of glass. "What a fuckin' shame," says Dan. He drives off, and his tires shoot up gravel and sand in his Ford Taurus's wheel well.

Josh is not sure where his revulsion at Dan's pity comes from, but it makes him tremble. He walks out to the sand and sits, unwrapping the two sloppy puffs of gauze from his feet. The crappy thing is, hang out with a cop tomorrow afternoon—why not? He has nothing better to do. Hell, maybe Dan will buy him new slippers or something. Unlike his mother, who probably blew the emergency slipper fund on college textbooks.

He takes the Copenhagen out from his back pocket and flicks his wrist, his finger snapping on the plastic container, packing the tobacco. He opens it, removes a pinch, and inserts the grains between cheek and gum. Josh spits in the sand, creates bubbling brown valleys, and listens to the ocean while a man screams at his son, something about ants, roaches, rats, and eating shredded cheddar cheese in the tent.

6

Number 126 negative thing about being homeless: you don't have a private place to get yourself off. Kai wanders the beach envying skebe old men, the kind who have no reservations about ogling Catholic school girls on the bus and jerking themselves off. An orgasm, anything that feels good, would hit the spot.

She creeps through dry kiawe, searching for empty cans and bottles, tempted to squat in the brush, put her hand in her pants, and go at it. She conjures images of the men she's been with. No. She imagines celebrities, limos, and hotel suites, but she's so far removed from that world, it's all pretty unimaginable. There's Banyan, followed by a twinge that heats her ears. She shakes her head like a dog just dunked in water. A beer can. She pours out what appears to be spit then tosses it in the garbage bag. Five cans, three bottles total. She sits in the brush and cries.

Four boys run toward her, one hurdling overhead. "Fire!" he says.

Kai stands up, walks toward where the boys came from, and feels the heat of the brushfire. A woman comes at her, dragging a collapsed tent over the brush, tearing the vinyl. Kai gets out of the way then heads for the smoke.

Two tents in the middle of the blaze, a propane tank nearby. She steps back at the sight of the tank, stops, and finds herself wanting to walk right up to the contained gas and give it a hug. Her son is practically an adult. She can't possibly ruin his life any more than she already has. She likes the smell of smoldering kiawe, like she just stumbled on a giant barbeque. Why not walk into the smoke and dig in?

Sirens approach. Kai runs away, not wanting to get blamed for starting the fire.

A mile up, bits of chalky sand stick to Kai's feet and legs. She approaches the surf with far more caution than she did the brush fire, stepping over cloudy glass shards dulled by pounding surf. She rinses off and heads up to Farrington Highway, passing a bushel of dead flowers left for yet another victim of a traffic fatality. She waits at the traffic light, then crosses the highway and walks into KFC.

The pimply kid behind the register glares at Kai as she enters. She ignores him, puts the garbage bag on the ground, takes off her backpack, and pulls out paper and pen. She has an essay due tomorrow. She'll need to type it out at the computer lab on campus before class.

"Excuse me," the cashier says. "I don't mind you coming in here, but don't bring your rubbish."

Kai lifts the plastic bag, which leaks out mystery liquid. She apologizes to the kid and takes the bag outside, leaving it by the door.

"You can't leave it there either," the kid says.

Kai writes, trying to ignore him.

"Don't make me call the cops," the kid says.

All of the customers are watching Kai now, too. As Kai stands, a woman pulls her three-year-old closer to her. The boy smiles, a mouthful of metal caps. He sips his soda, watching Kai.

Kai packs up her stuff and walks out. She picks up her bag of cans and bottles and whips it over the hedge. She ducks as the bag tumbles in the middle of the highway. Car breaks screech as she scurries through the strip mall parking lot, hiding behind parked cars. She squats behind a dumpster, breathing hard. She reaches up and grabs the dumpster railing to pull herself up and peek at the highway. A syrupy slime sticks to her hands. She looks in the dumpster—bloated trash bags, empty green beer bottles, and a dead pigeon, no eyes.

Kai wants to throw her books and notepad in the bin and walk away. Instead, she heads for the nearest liquor store.

Two hours later, she sits on the sand, drunk, pretending she's a sunbathing guest at a beach front resort being served by a waiter named Pablo. She passes out.

When she wakes up, her son Josh, who is wearing old gardening gloves, cautiously drags her up the beach by one arm, like she's decomposing giant box jellyfish that needs to be moved because it's stinking up the shoreline.

7

For Banyan Mott, the Sunday before Labor Day used to be the day his family did an overnight campout at Ala

Moana Beach Park to prepare for the next day. Checklist: a large canopy propped up and held together by aluminum poles, lawn chairs, and steaks on ice. The next day, beers at 10 AM, friends, a volleyball net, and a couple of cool-down sessions in waters polluted by tourists' sunblock. As he sits in the barber chair at Fantastic Sam's, staring at the grey plastic ceiling fan with burning, sleepless eyes, he does not really long to be at Ala Moana Beach Park; in fact, he is glad he is not there. But he does not want to be here either, and it occurs to him that depression is being unsatisfied with where you are, but thinking there's no place you'd rather be. The thought dulls the image of the beach and makes him want to do something drastic. "You know what, I want a flat top," he tells the barber. His long brown curls tumble from his shoulders.

He had dropped Caley and Raimi off for the day at his mother-in-law's house, so he knows it's just him and the menehune John Krill when he gets home. He presses the remote garage-door opener, and John is sitting on a white plastic chair, feet crossed and resting on Raimi's blue, red, and yellow toy plastic shopping cart. Feeling braver after getting his new severe haircut, Banyan decides he will not give the ghost the silent treatment anymore. Besides, it's talk to the ghost or read personal narrative essays depicting fender benders, drunken high school graduation parties, or boyfriends and girlfriends who make teenage hearts flutter.

Banyan gets out of his car and pulls another plastic chair from the stack, closes the garage door, and sits next to John, who is eating a banana and singing "God Bless the Child." Eating a banana and singing—it's a neat ventriloquist's trick. "I take it only I can see and hear you?"

"Yep. Just like in the movies."

"Not here to mess with my kid?"

"Nope, I just don't wanna see the wall come down."

"You obviously weren't a midget when you were alive. What happened?"

"God made me short. He knows we hate being short."

"What's he look like anyway? God."

"The old-school artists pretty much got it right. He looks like Lawrence Olivier as Zeus in ***Clash of the Titans.*** White robes and all. Except under the robes you can tell he's buff."

"He got abs?"

"You bet your ass."

Banyan always wished he had tight abs. "And the top with Tahiti on it? Required uniform?"

"Hell is in Tahiti. Under Mount Orohena to be exact. So, yea, the shirt is from there. Funny thing though, I thought maybe my suicide landed me there, you know like the Bible says."

"Thought the cops shot you."

"After I fired first. If that ain't suicide, I don't know what is. God told me he likes suicide—shows you mean business. It was some of the other stuff he wasn't crazy about."

"Isn't Tahiti a bit small for the entire population of Hell?"

"Follow any volcano down far enough, and you'll hit a hot spot on the ocean floor where Hell can spread like an oil spill. You know, seventy-five percent of the earth's surface and all."

"You know I don't believe you exist. You're just a symptom of my lapse into insanity."

"I get it. But let me tell you one thing, from a man who once lost his mind. You don't see imaginary stuff when you go nuts. You go nuts because you finally see ***real*** shit you ain't ever seen before."

Banyan nods. "You gonna be around 24/7?"

"Nah, I have to hit Tahiti and report in Mondays, Wednesdays, and Thursdays."

"Those are the days I teach."

"We all got a schedule to keep."

"I better shower. Caley will be pissed if I drop hair all over the place."

"My wife used to get pissed about that."

Banyan wonders if he should tell John that his wife is taking Banyan's English 100 class, or how she's the only student who's writing essays that don't resemble ones he's read a hundred times before. "My essay is about the time my high school marching band went to Japan." Please, God, make it stop. It isn't that Banyan's job is hard—he knows it isn't—picking ticks off a dog isn't especially hard either, but doing it for a hundred dogs every week takes its toll.

Banyan wonders if John can read his mind. However, John is just sitting there, staring at his short legs propped up on the mini shopping cart and munching on his banana, so Banyan assumes he does not possess ESP.

"Okay, well, I'm off," Banyan says.

"I'll be around."

Banyan passed on the free hair wash at Fantastic Sam's, so now he's in the shower, rinsing tiny hairs off his scalp. He gradually makes the shower colder and colder, like a drunk trying to sober himself. Caley opens the door. "We're back. My mom dropped us off."

Banyan turns off the shower and grabs a towel. "What if I told you our house might be haunted?"

"God, what did you do to your hair?"

"Oh, figured something different."

Caley sighs, exits the bathroom, and closes the door. It's like an announcement to him that, hey, I had Raimi all day; now it's your turn. Raimi pounds on the door. "Daddy. Daddy. Read book daddy."

On the bright side, maybe his student, Kai Krill, wife of the deceased, can tell him more about what kind of ghost he's dealing with. Banyan knows he will come off as a nut case if he tells her about it, but he figures she's nuts for taking his class in the first place, so he won't be alone. "Not right now, sweetie, daddy needs to do work. Want to watch Elmo?"

"Read book, please."

Though he rarely refuses, every time he fails to read to his kid upon request, he feels like a heel. However, he needs daddy time to sit on the toilet and figure out what he should do about the fact that his house is haunted. He turns on the television in the bedroom and plays the Sesame Street DVD as he remembers parental promises made during Caley's pregnancy, like not too much television for the kid, promises shattered by reality. That nine-month period was when he was most fond of his wife: the prenatal vitamins, the ease in which she gave up drinking, and the diet—for the first time since he'd known her, she actually craved seafood and vegetables. The first pictures of Raimi, who was the size of a grain of rice inside her mother's womb, the headphones on Caley's growing stomach each night before bed. She actually left dishes in the sink for more than a day and threw away coupons and receipts instead of binding them together with rubber bands and storing them in a labeled kitchen drawer. Those nine months of pregnancy were the only time period Banyan could remember when Caley spent more time with Raimi than he did. Not like now, when sometimes Banyan is overcome with guilt as they pass Raimi back and forth like they are playing a game of hot potato. Once Raimi started talking, she never stopped, and Caley practically beaned the potato at him.

The DVD will occupy Raimi for maybe ten minutes tops before she searches for Banyan. He considers telling Caley about the ghost of John Krill. She may buy it. Her casual interest in Jesus, and her more than casual interest in astrology and tabloids with unflattering pictures of drug-addled actresses splashed on the cover, almost convince Banyan that she'll believe him. Perhaps she won't give him her trademark sigh, a restrained exasperation that starts off airy but ends in a throaty grunt. But he'll probably get the sigh, and he wouldn't hold it against her. She'll take Raimi to her mother's house and demand that Banyan seek therapy. Though he has never been to therapy, he's often been tempted—the idea of confessing thoughts without shame has definite appeal.

Raimi bangs on the bathroom door and he wonders if a therapist would find a link between the ghost and the little girl on the other side of the door, the little girl who is a burden and whom he cannot imagine doing without. Deciding against therapy, he opens the door. Raimi is smiling, her two front teeth slanting outward from too much thumb-sucking. Banyan scoops her up and the love grips him.

He puts Raimi down and thinks of John's warning, his purpose, as Raimi hugs his leg. Why come back from the dead to protect a wall? He has a son. Wasn't the kid way more important? Then the truth hits him. If John is from hell, or Tahiti, or whatever, isn't the idea for Banyan to not give into what he wants? What he wants, or doesn't want, must be evil—he is a minion of Satan after all. Banyan picks Raimi back up and hugs her. As she kisses him on the cheek, the desire to demolish the perfect rows of concrete blocks that surround his house overwhelms him.

II. The Luapele Street Posse

1

A coworker of Banyan's calls Honolulu Community College the Pineapple School. The old Dole Cannery used to be a couple of blocks away, beneath a giant pineapple tower that held 100,000 gallons of water. The giant pineapple landmark was torn down, and Dole Cannery was replaced with a yellow shopping complex with a food court and movie theaters. Professor Nakashima still calls it the Pineapple School, probably because the students, many of whom are first- and second-generation Filipinos who are here trying to avoid employment in the new pineapple fields—hotels—as maids and janitors, still remind him of the heritage of Hawai'i. Nakashima is creating a sophomore literature course on the Harry Potter books, pitching it to the rest of the department, and Banyan, who has nothing against J.K. Rowling or half-blood princes, wonders about the utility of such a course. Then again, he is not sure what utility ***Beowulf*** and ***Everyman*** serve either, but it's not like anyone takes Brit Lit anymore, and since the new mantra of the school is enrollment, he supposes a course on why the Bloody Baron is the only ghost who can control Peeves the Poltergeist serves some purpose.

The meeting is adjourned, and Banyan has a class in fifteen minutes. It's the third week of classes, another grammar week for his students, and he remembers when he was fresh out of grad school and used to teach using peer groups and movies, trying to be innovative, only to learn that many of his students had the reading and writing skills of primary school kids. A year later, he changed his freshman comp classes to meat-and-potato courses—welcome to the world of dangling modifiers, thesis statements, and five paragraph essays on abortion, euthanasia, the death penalty, and whether or not marijuana should be legalized. Occasionally, a student will write an essay on whether black men are better at sex than all other races. Amusing the first time, not so much after. Banyan steps out to the hall and is tapped on the shoulder.

"You OK? You look beat."

Banyan turns around. It's Nakashima. "I'm fine. The move and all."

Nakashima, who has moles on his neck the size of rabbit pellets, mindlessly scratches at one. "Should get some sleep. You're backing me on my new course, right?"

"Sure, but only if you promise to teach it wearing a pointy wizard's hat."

Nakashima stands there, scratching a mole, not sure if Banyan is joking or not. "Of course, I'll back you," Banyan says. "Now, I need to get back to my office."

"Papers?" Nakashima asks.

"Always," says Banyan.

Banyan has newspaper articles on John Krill bookmarked on his computer. Half Samoan, half haole, once a first-team all-state pitcher for the Wai'anae Sea Riders, John graduated from the University of Hawai'i, got an engineering degree, and opened his own small contracting company. He married his high school sweetheart, Kai, and had a son named Josh. There was the usual shock from family and friends, the bewilderment as to how someone who was such a middleclass success story and had so much could do such a thing, but the news stories tapered off quickly, and no one even guessed at an answer despite the glaring fact that John had lost an infant child years before. Even Banyan, who cannot stomach thinking about a dead baby for too long, can't imagine being rattled by a dead child ten years after the fact. How can something be more painful after a decade of healing?

Banyan wants to write out a quiz for the ghost, ask him questions that only the true ghost of John Krill could answer, maybe questions about that first son, then check these answers with Kai, but there are two problems. He isn't sure how to go about answer-checking with Kai, and he isn't sure that he wants to discover that the ghost is a sure sign he is going nuts. He'd rather just believe ghosts and menehunes exist, but the fact that John Krill looked nothing like the menehune he sees makes believing a tough proposition. He leans forward to study the thumbnail of Krill's, now his house. The front door is almost imperceptible, while the photos of the wreckage—the bulldozer and Mililani Town Center—are big enough to see the makes and models of the flattened cars.

Kai knocks on Banyan's office door. Banyan scrambles to close the web page. "Come in," he says.

She hugs her books and sits in a chair. She stares at his couch, an old, tattered pink thing that has coffee stains on it. Banyan's embarrassed. "It's not what you think," he says.

She smiles. "Right."

"Colleague needed to get rid of it, but there's no way my wife would allow that thing in the house."

"Don't blame her," she says.

"Seriously, it's not like I'm some kind of creepy teacher."

He points to his computer's wallpaper. It's a picture of Raimi. "Look. I have a kid. And a wife. If that's not a turn-off, I don't know what is."

"She's cute."

Banyan looks at his computer and smiles. "She is, isn't she?"

Kai fiddles with a pen, spinning it like a propeller between her fingers. "Look. You must think I'm a nut taking your class, and I probably am kind of nutty. But I'm actually here at school to go to school. I was wondering if you wanted to get a beer or something, and we can talk about this."

Banyan glances at a stack of ungraded essays, catches the author name on the top page—Yao Ming Ng. He turns his head to Kai. No contest. "Sure," he says.

Kai stands to leave the office, looks once more at the couch, shakes her head, and leaves. "A student has never touched it. Seriously." And he is serious.

Banyan calls Caley, tells her he has a faculty senate meeting and will be home later than usual, listens to her sigh, then, after classes, he and Kai head to the bar in the strip mall across the street. It's about two-thirty, early for drinks, and Banyan admits to himself that he will be stuck in traffic for over an hour because of this detour.

They enter the bar, and the two Korean hostesses look disappointed that a man and woman have walked in together. ESPN is on the four televisions, a preview to a Thursday night college football game. They choose a booth close to the bar. The only other customer is a postal worker still in uniform. Kai orders a Budweiser, and Banyan does the same. They sit there silent, waiting for the waitress to come back. Banyan watches ESPN, vacant. He turns to look at the clock.

Kai grabs her beer and doesn't wipe the mouth of a bottle with a cocktail napkin before she drinks. Banyan's feels silly, but he's floored. He's lived with a woman who wipes everything for so long that it hasn't occurred to him that there are people out there who don't. He resists the urge to wipe his bottle and drinks. Still alive. Not sick. He drinks again. "I feel tough now," he says, "drinking from an unwiped beer bottle."

"So how's the house?"

Banyan thinks. "The wall. I gotta cut part of it off."

Kai nods. "Should tear the whole thing down."

"It's crossed my mind."

"So yea, don't worry about me. I'd die before living there again."

Banyan nods. He read her essay. "So where you at now?"

"Wai'anae."

"That's quite the commute."

She takes a swig. Banyan tries to think up a quiz question for the menehune John. "You have a son right? When's his birthday? I'm into astrology. I can predict his future."

He has a hard time keeping a straight face on that one. "March 23. What does that make him?"

Oh shit. Kai watches him struggle and laughs. "Some astrologer."

"I meant Chinese astrology. Not the bullshit haole one. The real one."

"Oh, the reeeeal one. Stop making up small talk. You're killing me. Let me do it."

Banyan can't speak for Kai, but he can't remember the last time he had a talk with another adult that did not involve when to try potty-training, the virtues of teaching Harry Potter, or conjunctive adverbs. Maybe he forgot how to do it. Kai talks fast, like someone trying to get words in while being pursued by a gunman, asking him the usual barrage of questions. Where did he grow up, where did he go to high school, did he always want to be a teacher, how long has he been teaching. Normally, this sort of verbal resumé exchange would bore Banyan, but the mixture of conversation and cold beer makes him feel like a regular guy instead of a guy who is plagued by a three-foot man haunting his house. A guy who seldom sleeps anymore, instead imagines himself as burly Paul Bunyan taking down the wall in a waking dream.

The bartender switches one of the televisions to CNN. Breaking news on the controversy of whether Pluto is a planet, something on the fifth anniversary of 9/11, and the national concern over an actress's sudden loss in body weight. The

CNN ticker at the bottom of the screen provides a ten-word account of today's Iraq death toll. The bartender turns the station back to the college ball game preview.

"It's weird how it doesn't feel like we're at war," Kai says.

"Bush would probably love hearing you say that," says Banyan.

"I should care. My son is a few years away from eighteen. But for some reason, I just can't muster up the outrage."

"A colleague of mine spams campus-wide anti-war email. I'm more outraged by the spam."

"By the way, I'm not crazy," says Kai. "I just saw your name in the registration booklet and couldn't resist. I don't have any plans to stalk you or anything crazy like that."

"I believe you." And Banyan does. He tries to slow the pacing of the words so that he can savor the adult conversation. For all he knows, it may be his last for another two to three years. "So what are you majoring in?" He's already looked it up, so he knows the answer.

"I was a legal secretary for a couple of years. Did some other stuff. So I'm thinking anything that's as far from the old as possible."

"Didn't like your old job? Overexposure to lawyers?"

She pauses. "People have it all wrong about lawyers. Not all lawyers are liars, cheats, and ambulance chasers. They really aren't. What bothers me is that they hate people."

"Misanthropes?"

"Misanthropes—yea, I like that word."

Kai is very pretty, but there is something in her face that keeps it from being beautiful. Banyan can't place it. Her eyes, nose, lips all look like they could be cut out of a glossy magazine, but there is something in the color of her face, a dull, pale hue, an ashy tint that makes him think of the phrase "close but no cigar." Another customer walks in, a big, scowling guy wearing a T-shirt a couple sizes too small; his hairy gut peeks out and hangs over his surf shorts. "You and your son okay now?" Banyan asks. "I know you got foreclosed on, and I'm starting to feel kind of like a jerk for buying the house, but are you guys okay?"

"We get by."

"I have a kid. A two-year-old daughter."

"It's amazing isn't it? The birth and all that."

"Greatest moment of my life, no kidding." And he is not kidding.

Kai wraps both hands around her beer. "My son is older now, just starting high school. I know it sounds clichéd, but enjoy them now, because all that attention they lavish on you goes away at a certain age."

"So I hear. I actually like the attention for the most part. There are tantrums here and there, and she doesn't listen to me at all, but that's all fine. The thing that gets me is the fear. It's like no one tells you having a kid is to live in constant fear for her life."

"Josh was born a month premature. He weighed three pounds. I know all about the fear. Just a couple of weeks ago, I come home from work and find him beat up with lumps on his head. Scared the hell out of me."

"Trouble at school?"

"Some bullies picking on him. But now this cop wants to be Josh's friend. I don't know how I feel about that because what kind of adult wants to be friends with a teenager? Molester? Know what I mean? On the other hand, Josh has no friends, so how can I object? This cop, we met him, well, we met him at the funeral. A couple of cops were there. It all seems too coincidental." She glances up at the TV. "When your life has gone bad, coincidence is a scary thing. It's too close to fate."

They order two more beers. One hostess takes their order while the other brings them a small, white plastic bowl filled with white, yellow, and pink deep-fried shrimp chips. Both hostesses look at least forty-five. Kalihi has bars like this, bars where over-aged hostesses come to eke out the twilight of their careers as buy-me-drinkee girls. "It's funny, but I'm thinking about it now, and I have no friends," Banyan says. "I used to have a lot. I suppose if I called some of them, said let's go have a couple of drinks, some would say sure, and we'd have some beers and talk about old times. But somewhere along the line, I lost them."

"Same here. Same with my husband. I think that's a small reason why he did what he did."

"He went crazy because he no longer drank with the boys?"

She pauses again and Banyan thinks, mental self-editing. He likes it.

"I'm no expert," she says, "but I think going crazy, I dunno, it's never just one thing. It's like a hundred little things going on at once, like trying to stack books, one on the other. The stack can only go so high before gravity takes over. Everyone gets obsessed about the title of the last book, the one that brought the pile down, but I dunno, maybe the other books in the stack are just as important."

Banyan pauses, thinking about the menehune back home, shocked that it's the first time the image popped up since he began talking to Kai. It's like the conversation is medicine. "So the title of one book was 'No friends?'"

"And another was 'Fear for My Child's Life: A Twenty-Four Seven Tale.'"

"And another was 'Money: I Don't Have Enough. Help Me Tony Robbins, You're My Only Hope.'"

Kai laughs at that one. "Okay, here's one. 'John Krill versus The Mililani Town Association: The MTA Strikes Back."

"'You Think You Have It Bad? There Are More Mines Than People In Afghanistan: Stop With The Self-Pity American Middleclass Scum.'"

He expects Kai to bring up the dead child, sooner or later, but instead she says, "'Kai, You Cheating Bitch: A True Story.'"

"I don't like that book," says Banyan.

Kai sips her beer. "It's a big book, like a portfolio filled with glossy pictures of ancient Incan art. Do you get along with your wife?"

He thinks about the folding of plastic shopping bags into perfect squares, like it's origami, the knee brace, and wine residue at the bottom of pink plastic cups. "Something's wrong with her knee," he says.

"What?"

"I asked once. Never said anything. In fact, I can't remember her complaining about physical pain once."

"Sounds tough," she says.

"I think it's more like she tolerates me. She is a helluva mom, though. If it wasn't for her, Raimi would probably be living on pizza, sleeping at two AM, and all her teeth would've rotted."

Kai's arms extend across the table. She reaches for Banyan's hands. "I don't have friends either. Professor Mott, let's be friends."

Her boldness throws Banyan off. "Sure. Call me Banyan, though."

"Named after a tree? My husband hated exotic names."

He pulls his hands away. "Did you know the Banyan tree can grow roots out of its branches? There must be some symbolism there, but it's completely lost on me. And I'm a lit guy."

"Don't feel bad. You're a community college lit guy."

Banyan feigns a shot to the heart. "Ouch."

"Let's do this every Monday," Kai says. "***Monday Night Football,*** we'll say. Going out and getting beers for ***Monday Night Football?*** What red-blooded American would deny us this constitutional right?"

"I'm not sure if I can. Though I suppose any Commie who would deny us could be reported to Homeland Security."

"Not letting a man watch ***Monday Night Football*** is practically terrorism."

"But football season doesn't last forever."

"Don't get ahead of yourself, Banyan," she smiles.

A hostess walks by the table, slows, glances at their drinks and bowl of shrimp chips, then walks on. She is wearing a cheetah-print long-sleeved top that squeezes her chubby arms like sausage casings;legs and varicose veins squeeze out from the bottom of a tight black skirt. "Depressing," says Kai.

They sip beers as melodramatic Korean music from the jukebox muffles out talk of Heisman hopefuls. When the hell was her kid's birthday again?

2

Back in the day, at Wai'anae High School, there was a story circulating about how on a Friday night, after a baseball game, John Krill and his girlfriend were approached by two men armed with butterfly knives, drunks upset over John's shut-out versus the Leilehua Mules. The story went something like this:

"Ho, you heard about Big John? Two guys pulled knife on him after the game, when they went bowling alley."

"Ho, what happened?"

"They started talking about what they was gonna do to his chick, and the fucka went nuts. Grab one guy's arm, swung him, and launched him through the window, then the other guy went stab um in the ribs. But was like John didn't even feel it. He threw one elbow in the guy's jaw and people inside heard one popping sound, the kind of sound that you know something hurt bad, loud, like he went bowl a one-pin strike. The kind of scary sound give you chicken skin."

"Ho, he okay?"

"Had cops, everything. John stay hospital now, but he gonna be okay."

Back in high school, Kai heard the story over and over that entire week, and was irked that her name was never mentioned. It was always "John's girlfriend," "Big John's chick," or "that kind of hot chick always with John." She understood that she was hardly the star of the story, which was a true story. The sound of that man's jaw snapping made her feel queasy every time she recalled it. She was just irritated that no one called her "Kai." "Kai, the girl who scored 1450 SATs and is probably going to a good college."

She hadn't been sure whether or not she loved John until she heard that man's jaw pop. Shaking and feeling some nausea, seeing John standing over the unconscious man, and asking if she was okay, Kai was so in love at that moment that she wanted to marry him and have his children right away. She never mentioned this to anyone, feeling stupid for being struck with love for such seemingly barbaric reasons—but after a while, she could rationalize it just fine. People supposedly fell in love over things like beauty, money, a sense of humor, or the way a guy looked driving by in his dropped mini-truck, elbow sticking out of the window, cigarette dangling from his lips—well, Kai was in love with someone strong and brave, the kind of guy who could stand there after he was stabbed and ask if she was the one who was okay. Despite her parents' efforts to keep her ignorant of fairy tales, he was the knight in shining armor that she'd heard about all her life.

The marriage and kids didn't come at that very moment. It took a year, and everyone forgot about the 700 verbal on her SATs as John went to college and she stayed home to take care of their first son, Xavier Teve Musashi Krill. When he was born, John cried and cried, sobbed, asked if she was okay, and she was, because the epidural had made her completely numb from the waist down. Even when the doctor cut her from vagina to anus, she didn't feel it. She loved John even more and was glad to stay home, put college on hold, to raise John's son.

Two years later, Kai was pregnant again. "You guys are dumb as hell," were her father's exact words. John was just starting his major at the University of Hawai'i School of Engineering, Kai was a waitress at Pizza Hut, and they lived with Kai's parents. After her father found out she was pregnant again, he took out the money he'd been saving for Kai, for college, gave John what he needed to finish school, and locked up the rest in a mutual fund for Xavier. Words like "misogynistic" and "marginalized" popped into her head, words she was hoping to use in a college classroom someday, but words that were pretty useless in the confines of Pizza Hut or her parents' house.

Kai's father had emigrated from the Philippines to Hawai'i when he was six; her mother was a local girl, third generation, who had just about every imaginable ethnicity in her blood. She had never worked. Kai's dad was adamant about her being a stay-at-home mom, even with just the one kid. Kai wondered how such a beautiful woman had wound up with a five-foot-three Filipino tyrant with glasses, a man who chain-smoked Kool 100s and was never able to shake his accent. Gladys would stay at home and make sure the house was well kept and that his daughter did her homework, read books, and did not go out with friends on weeknights; Kai would get good grades so she could go to college (to avoid her mother's fate?), and Ben, her father, would slave away at Outrigger East Hotel in Waikiki as a custodial manager, making sure he put away enough money for Kai's college, so much money, in fact, that if she wanted to go to someplace like Harvard, she could do so with only a little help from student loans.

She never made it to Cambridge, so her father mapped out John's future instead. Ben treated John like his own kid, which meant he shouted at him as if a violent reaction from John was never even a possibility. And John was the obedient son. He had absolutely no interest in engineering. He and Kai's father had picked the major out of a college catalogue, like it was a game of Pin the Tail on the Donkey, but John majored in it anyway, and he was always very appreciative of Ben for paying his tuition and giving his family a roof over its head. Kai sometimes fantasized about John throwing an elbow at her father's jaw, but after it became evident that would never happen, she got a job and tried to scrape together enough money so that once John graduated, they could move out before the graduation bubbly warmed.

Ernie Souza, a guy Kai worked with at Pizza Hut, had lost a sister in a head-on collision on Farrington Highway. A week later, his brother was swept out to sea while picking ʻopihi at Kaʻena Point, probably ʻopihi for his sister's wake. Then a month or so later, his mother died from a stroke. After his mom died, Kai never saw Ernie again, but she thought about him a lot, about how things like that are bound to happen. If normal Joe Blows thought about all the times they found themselves in a car with an intoxicated, speed-demon driver, all the times they had unprotected sex, all the times they'd swum too far out into the ocean at night, all the times they'd done something incredibly risky and stupid during their youth and had still come out unscathed, well, they'd have to conclude that some people were bound to take up the statistical slack. Sometimes they took up way more slack than they deserved.

First, Kai's father got lung cancer, and the hospice was full, and he made surly demands for the attention of everyone in the house at all hours, which often turned into an across-the-house screaming match between her parents at three AM:

"Gladys!"

And she'd yell back. Louder. "Aieee! What, I busy!"

"Gladys!"

"What!"

"Gladys!"

"Shut up, I busy!"

It could go on for a half hour, until even the neighbor would chime in with shut-ups of his own. But Kai could handle it. She was, however, unnerved by her mother's lack of patience, and then by her relief when the old man finally died. She could handle the death of a parent herself, but when her firstborn, Xavier was diagnosed with Acute Lymphocytic Leukemia when Kai was six months pregnant with Josh, the feeling was as powerful and indescribable as the emotions she'd had when he was born—only it was the polar opposite, squared. She'd slumped down to the floor, and then, she never got up, didn't even try, and she found herself hospitalized. She wanted to die. She began to resent her unborn second child for not allowing her to do so.

John had already lost both parents and had no siblings and was raised by a derelict uncle whom he described as kind only when drunk, which was often, fortunately. When Xavier got sick, John cared for his son with jaw-breaking will. He finished his last semester in school, helped out with Kai's father, and tried to care for her, too. He was like a circus freak, a man juggling baby elephants. He'd never been more brave, but Kai no longer saw a knight in shining armor, only a clown, a man doing the improbable with a painted smile, a man doomed to fail without grace. Between hating her father, mother, husband, unborn child, and herself, most of all, she couldn't muster up the energy to spend enough time with the only one she could love then—the dying child, who had only to say **Mommy** once, and she'd be floored. In all the years since Xavier's death, she and John had only a single conversation about this:

"We have to go on," he said. And she said, "Bring it up again, and I promise, I will kill myself."

He never questioned her seriousness, because everyone in that house knew that every night she sat in the closet on an unopened can of baby-blue paint, amidst baby shoes and high heels and photo albums, hugging a framed picture of her son. Months later, her second son, Josh, who couldn't crawl yet, pushed himself on his back across the floor and into the closet and looked up at Kai with accusatory eyes. She stopped sitting in the closet then, surprised to find herself in a brand-new house in Mililani Mauka, the down payment funded by Xavier's college fund, her husband gainfully employed as an engineer, and her son regularly motoring across the carpet, a spot rubbed bald on the back of his head. "I found you a job," John said. "A friend of mine, a law firm."

He'd been taking Josh to childcare for months, and never asked if she wanted to stay at home and care for a child again.

A couple of years later, when her mother died in the hospice her father never got into, she was so busy shocking herself with her own behavior that she felt only a faint twinge of grief, as if she'd learned of the demise of a distant relative, the bell-shaped aunt with short hair that you saw only at weddings and funerals. She did feel guilty, though. Guilty, because maybe the worst thing you could do to a parent, aside from screwing up your own life or dying on them, was to be indifferent about their existence or lack thereof. After the death of her son, she discovered that guilt was the only thing that made her act normal, made her pretend she was into family and motherhood and all that jazz, so she put herself in situations that guaranteed a rush of guilt. She'd come home with a fake smile on her face, scrub the toilets by hand, cook perfectly golden grilled-cheese sandwiches, and rock her husband's world in the bedroom.

Kai is under the tarp now, holding one of her few last pictures of Xavier, lantern light reflecting off the photo paper. She's guilting herself up for the next move. A sound interrupts her. It's the neighbor's tied-up dog trying to eat the tree. He is really attacking it, growling while trying to wrap his jaws around the trunk, but the girth is too much for the animal. The dog has been losing weight over the last month, even though it's fed regularly.

Kai considers the numbers. She has been banking enough to pay for rent, but her declared bankrupt status has been an insurmountable obstacle in the competitive world of finding a place to live. She peeks into the tent, gazing at her sleeping son who is sprawled out in his boxer shorts. Was a hot day. But it's cold now, so Kai puts a blanket on him. Josh's feet are ashen with sand, his hair sticky from the salty coastal air.

She never sees him anymore. She leaves him twenty bucks a day. He goes to school. She goes to school and work. She is not sure if she ever really saw him that much, having worked nights for most of his childhood. By the time she got home, he was sleeping. By the time she woke up, he'd be in school. That the sight of him homeless on the beach has not motivated her to take more extreme measures in the search for a residence is only slightly less upsetting than the fact that when she dies, Josh will feel the same indifference she felt when her parents died.

She lets go of the creased picture of Xavier Teve Musashi Krill, and the wind rolls it away, beyond the lantern light.

3

The thing about making something out of wood is that when you saw, you have to have the perfect combination of caution and confidence. Most of the caution comes in at the measuring and drawing of lines, and the confidence comes in when you cut the wood. If you are too hesitant, your lines are jagged, each pause marked with an ugly groove. If you move at a consistent speed along that pencil line until the end is reached, you come out with a clean, straight cut. It's as if human hands hate wariness—cutting wood, hammering nails, or breaking bricks with karate chops can all result in not-so-hot outcomes.

Josh works on a coffee table for his mom, a first piece of furniture to christen the new house when they finally get one. The circular tabletop was easy enough to construct—it's the bowed legs that has Josh blowing through so much wood that Dan now calls it the thousand-dollar coffee table. "I wanna glue some kind of picture on the top, then like put lacquer over it," says Josh.

Dan bends a thin piece of sheet metal over his knee. "That's doable. Maybe a globe, since the table is round and all? Like an old map from back in the day?"

"Hmm, maybe. Or maybe like an old picture? Can you like take an old picture and make it bigger and cut out a circle?"

"Dude, they can make dinosaurs in the movies with computers and all. I'm sure it's doable." Dan puts the bent piece of metal on the ground. They are in a room that was once the back patio, but is now enclosed, filled with tools and machinery, all used to manipulate wood or metal. Wood shavings and pieces of failed bowed legs litter the concrete floor. Dan grabs a mallet and picks up the warped sheet of metal. "Don't know if I'm ready for plate mail. What kind of picture you thinking of? A buddy of mine in the Department has an awesome computer set-up."

"I dunno, maybe something having to do with my dad, or my brother."

"You got a brother?"

"He died when I was a baby."

Dan stops hammering the metal. "Goddamn Josh, your life story is about as uplifting as a Greek tragedy. How'd he die?"

"I dunno, really. Some disease. My parents never really talked about it."

"If that's the case, maybe making a thousand-dollar coffee table with a big goddamned picture of him on the top isn't such a hot idea."

"Yea, they didn't really put pictures of him around," Josh says. "Except my dad had a picture of him tattooed on his shoulder."

Josh puts the table top on a pair of sawhorses and sands the edges. Dan opens a mini-refrigerator and takes out a strawberry soda. "What does your mom like?"

"I dunno. She used to like that show ***Law and Order.*** She reads books sometimes, especially now that she's going to school. She thought Pierce Brosnan was hot. She never had a hobby or anything like that."

Dan takes a swig of soda. "You see, that's just sad," he says. "Everyone had a hobby when they were kids. Had something they really dug doing. Could be as useless as collecting stamps, but adults, you know, old people, man, they drop their hobbies too much. Keeps a guy sane."

Josh smiles. "You're old."

"Haha, screw you, dude. I ain't that old. Well, even if I am, I got me a hobby. Doing stuff like this, it keeps me from going out there vigilante-style and cracking some skulls. Other cops, the ones not doing the whole wife and kid thing, they just drink beer or lift weights. Goddamn gorillas. See, stuff like this, it makes you use your hands and your mind." Dan points to his temple, but his finger is out there, as if his brain extends beyond the confines of his skull. "So your mom don't like anything, huh?"

"Books, I guess."

"Reading ain't no hobby. Not a man's one at least."

"Yea, I guess."

"Shit, speaking of beer, I'm supposed to go to this karaoke room in about an hour. Friend of mine got promoted, so we're having a little party. Your mom working?"

"Yea."

Dan crushes the empty can and throws it on the floor. "Wanna come? There's food at least. Can feed you and drop you off at the beach, or hell, you can crash here again if you like. We won't stay long. Can meet some of the rest of the gang."

"Yea, sounds better than sitting around watching the fishing pole all night, waiting for the bell to ring," says Josh. "Is fishing but catching no fish a hobby?"

"Yea, but you just suck at it."

"Wise ass. Don't make me lay you out," says Josh.

Dan laughs. They dance around the room, sparring with light slaps. Wood dust kicks up off the floor, and Josh wonders, if he were to light a match and throw it down, would the entire floor catch on fire?

A three-hundred-pound cop sings Juice Newton's "Queen of Hearts." A group of five plays Texas Hold'em in the far right corner. The others are standing around, some grazing poke, boiled peanuts, and beef jerky while drinking Heinekens, smiling and laughing at the three-hundred-pound cop. There are no women in the room, and fourteen-year-old Josh, his three thin chin hairs hanging on for dear life, is the only non-cop.

The diversity in the room surprises Josh. The three-hundred-pounder is obviously Hawaiian and a weightlifter, and there are a couple of others, leaner, but with biceps also stretching their T-shirt sleeves. There are a few thin Caucasian guys who look more like officer managers than police officers, and a Filipino who must weigh less than his mom. Of them all, Dan is the only one who looks like a blue uniformed cop you might see in a movie—haole, short hair, lean jaw, prominent chin—only short. It's the first time Josh notices Dan's smallness, the way he sticks his chest out like a walking bird, his handsomeness defused by furled-brow defiance. Josh likes the look of these guys, and law enforcement is looking like a nifty future job to Josh. It's the first time he's seriously considered an occupation since his childhood dream of becoming Thor, God of Thunder.

Dan and Josh are sitting at the table across from a middle-aged Chinese cop who has a helmet of slick, pure black, side-combed hair—a Buddha with a toupee. He's been staring at Josh all night, looking back and forth between Josh and Dan. He's still doing it as he tells them about how last weekend he took his son fishing for the first time.

"I told him come fishing or clean yard, so we go out in the boat. Thirty minutes later, the kid all sick, throwing up. He tell me, 'Dad, we go back in. I like clean yard.'"

Dan has the look of someone politely tolerating a story he has heard before, a face Josh recognizes all too well, considering that he's a kid, kids being the most common victims of repeat-story offenders. But Dan's face wakes up when one of the weightlifter cops pulls up a chair and sits across from them, hands folded behind his head, further stretching the sleeves of his Honolulu Police Department tee shirt. He's not as big as the three-hundred pounder, but looks like a decade long disciple of the Atkins diet. "Jesus, Cap, you telling the fishing story again?" he says.

"Watch when you guys get kids. All you guys gonna do is talk about them, because not like you partying, talking about chicks, anymore. You either talk about kids or the beef stew you ate last night. Which is more interesting?"

"Josh, see this guy over here." Dan points at Mr. Atkins, who seems to be flexing his biceps like a fish spreading its gills to intimidate the rest of the aquarium. "He breeds cats. Now you look at him, big tough guy. Played football for St. Louis." He raises his voice. "Kaniau, what kind of cats do you breed, the smashed-faced ones?"

"Blue Point Persians."

"Show the kid some pictures," says Dan. "I know you have some in your wallet. Goddamn classic."

"What? I sell them for like eight hundred bucks. Better than you, you crazy medieval bastard. What kind of nut makes chain mail armor and shit like that? When you bring chicks home, they must take one look at your shit, and walk out the door."

"Fair enough," says Dan. "I'm just trying to show the kid something. It's all about hobbies, Josh. No matter how crazy the hobby seems, it's all about not being bored. Kaniau breeds little smashed-faced puff balls; I make armor and weaponry out of wood and metal; Cap over there tortures his kids with seasick fishing trips."

Cap digs a peanut out of its shell. "Yup, all the kids we bust, most of them bored, so what they do. Go smoke ice. Steal shit. Nothing more dangerous that a bunch of bored kids sitting around brainstorming what they can do for kicks."

Josh points to the three-hundred-pounder, who is bent over now, feeding the karaoke machine a dollar bill. "Is his hobby karaoke?" Josh asks.

"Karaoke isn't a hobby unless you sing good," Dan says. "For the rest of us, it's either comedy to avoid real conversation or an excuse to scream at the world."

Josh points a thumb at Dan. "Man, I've been listening to this all day. Is he always so full of shit or what?"

Cap, Kaniau, and Dan look at Josh, then bust out laughing.

"He doesn't drink either," says Kaniau. "Needs to keep a clear head to give us pearls of wisdom. When did you stop drinking, Dan?" It's clear he assumes that every adult drank at some point.

Dan looks at Josh, serious. "When I saw that goddamn bulldozer in Mililani," he says. "Transferred to Wai'anae."

Cap shoots Dan a stern look. "You need help," he says.

"No, I need to piss," says Dan.

Dan gets up and leaves the room. Cap studies Josh. "What?" Josh finally asks.

Cap looks at Kaniau, who shrugs. "How'd you meet Dan?" Cap asks.

"I dunno. I got jumped and he saw me walking down the road."

Cap looks at Kaniau again as if he's trying to get permission to say something. "Was probably patrolling, keeping a look out for the kid."

Kaniau stares at Cap, slams his hand on the table, gets up and leaves. "He didn't tell you who he is?" Cap asks Josh.

"What?"

"That's not right."

"What?"

"Your dad had a gun."

Josh looks at Cap, confused. "That's what I heard."

"He was gonna kill somebody."

Josh thinks about that. "I doubt it."

"He hit a cop, remember?"

"Yea, tear gas or something."

"I was there."

Josh shivers. "He shot you?"

Cap looks at the door. "No. But in a situation like that, you shoot back."

Josh follows Cap's eyes. Dan is standing there looking back. The three-hundred-pounder launches into John Lennon's "Imagine." His face twists as he effeminately tiptoes around the room, bellowing the words. Josh gets up, shoves Dan out of the way, and runs out of the bar.

A strung-out woman is in the street shrieking, while a man stands on the edge of the curb, heels dug in, his slippered toes hanging off the edge. He extends his arm like a gaff, searching for a fish underwater. Cars slow and maneuver around the woman. Josh can't help but to stop and watch.

"How you cheated on me?!" she yells. "I didn't do anything to you!"

"Shut up, already! Go home!" the man says.

"I didn't do anything to you!"

She yells that last line at least a half a dozen times in between threats of throwing herself into traffic. Hysterical rage—Josh is surprised by the repetition of words. It's obvious the woman does not hear herself, or see herself, for that matter. Josh isn't sure how infidelity should be handled, and he has pondered adultery more times than any teenaged boy should, but standing in traffic? Packing your bags and not looking back—maybe that's the way to go.

Dan is on the move—surf shorts and a tee shirt—nothing to indicate that he's a cop. He side-eyes Josh and marches right to the woman and picks her up. Soon, the woman is over his shoulder screaming, her fat face ugly with fury, spit spraying out of her mouth, but it's not until Dan gets her on the sidewalk, on her own feet, that she attacks him. She is bigger than Dan and punches like a man. The skinny, slippered man, who has disturbingly long toenails marbled white and olive, is now on Dan as well. How this guy manages extra-marital affairs is beyond Josh.

Dan's body bursts forward. Josh is struck by the speed of the violence. A bucking horse is what Dan reminds Josh of now, and soon the man is pinned on the ground taking repeated hammer fists to the face as the woman throws bombs on top of Dan's head. The spectacle is like a deranged totem pole. A couple of other cops come out of the bar and restrain the woman. Dan continues to rain down the blows. It eventually takes two more cops to get Dan off the now unconscious man. Dan looks at Josh, eyes welling with tears. Josh is about to run away, but Cap grabs his arm. "Need a statement," he says.

The cuffed woman sulks in the back of a squad car, the man sitting on the bumper of an ambulance. Josh is telling Cap what he saw. "He should've worked over the girl, if you can call her that," says Cap. "Fuckin' ice." Crystal meth—ice—Josh knows by now that it's the supposed cause of every social ill in the state. They thought his father was on ice when he rolled over Mililani, and days later, news reporters made it a point to tell viewers that John Krill in fact did not have traces of ice in his system. They'd presented this fact with a slightly interrogative tone, as if it were a miracle.

Dan is standing by a squad car, talking to Kaniau. Cap points to him. "He's a good man. The best. You know he got stabbed more times than anyone in Honolulu Police Department history?"

Josh wasn't aware that records of such things were kept, but he's struck by one thing about off-duty cops. They all seem trying hard to be funny. "Your dad had a gun," Cap says, as if it's supposed to mean something. "He shot a cop."

Josh points at Dan. "He killed ..."

"Once your dad pulled the trigger, he was dead anyway."

Josh looks down and nods. "If it was me," Cap says, "all due respect, I wouldn't feel the least bit guilty. But you see that guy there? Ask yourself why he transferred to Wai'anae."

"Yeah, right," says Josh.

"He was gonna quit the department, asked for a transfer instead."

"Why?"

Cap lights a cigarette and blows out smoke. "Fuck if I know."

Dan and Josh are on their way back to the Leeward coast. They pass Waikele, the outlet superstores. Later, the freeway narrows to Farrington Highway, and they pass Ko 'Olina, the resort lights like stars converging to form lines. Through the entire trip, the only thing Dan says is, "It's a helluva thing being a cop." He hands Josh a cell phone. Josh gives it back to him. Dan shoves the phone against Josh's chest like he's trying to bury it in his spine, so Josh pockets the phone.

Dan stops the car at the camp. Josh opens the door, trying to hurry out. Dan grabs his arm. "Wait," he says. "Use the phone if you need anything. Anything."

Dan pulls down the neck of his shirt and points to a round blossom of scar tissue under his collar bone. "A few inches down, and I would've been dead."

Josh steps out of the car runs to the beach. He trips in sand. He gets up and looks over his shoulder as Dan pulls out of the parking lot and drives away.

4

They call themselves the Luapele Street Posse. Hardly gun-totting justice vigilantes of the Old West, this posse resides in a series of two-story middle-class homes in a cul de sac where get-togethers are evoked by early evening, post-work bicycle-riding, childrens' birthdays, hobbies, and the celebratory successes of their kids. Not all join in—there is the professional surfer who is never home, and the parents of the neighborhood ice addict, the only one whom no one ever sees, but the rest are gathered this evening to watch the Carballo girl sing on TV—she's a contestant in some glorified nationally-televised karaoke contest where the viewers at home vote for the winner. Banyan remembers reading that ten times more phone votes are submitted per week from Hawai'i than the total votes for the latest gubernatorial race.

They are all at the Carballo home, the one directly across the street from Banyan's, the home with the monster maroon SUV in the driveway. The neighbors are seated either on the sectional or the rug over the laminated bamboo-colored flooring, the women with glasses of pinot in their hands, and the men with beers, Guinness. Children run in and out of the room in a group, Raimi, the youngest, trailing behind. While the adults discuss singing, Little League, and fantasy football, Banyan thinks of Kai and wonders how she and her husband fit in with this bunch, how such high dysfunction could have possibly functioned in what Banyan can only describe as a suburban platonic orgy. Caley is sipping her wine, chatting with The Heap wife—an art dealer for a gallery in Waikīkī that exclusively sells cartoonish paintings of underwater sea life, full of dolphins, whales, and colorful reef fish, but apparently lacking sharks and pollution. Wearing two knee braces now, Caley seems to be in hog heaven.

The posse quiets when the Carballo girl is about to sing. She's a pretty little thing, high-school-aged, stuffed in a full-body leather get-up and wearing what has become a trademark hibiscus above her right ear. Improbably, she is going to sing the AC/DC song "Shook Me All Night Long." Banyan cringes as tears well in the Carballo father's eyes. "That's my baby," he says.

The Heap husband, a firefighter and an obvious steroid-monger, puts one of his meaty hands on Carballo's shoulder; Carballo is rubbing his good luck charm with his fingertips, a three-inch decorative mother-of-pearl Hawaiian fish hook that hangs from a gold chain necklace. "Too bad you couldn't go," he says.

"It's okay. Her mother and sister are there."

By the time it's 9:30, the Luapele Street Posse women are in their houses putting the kids to bed. The men are still at the Carballo house, in the garage, admiring Bart Carballo's Harley Davidson, which is shining especially brightly under what Banyan can only remark as the most intense fluorescent lights he has ever seen. "One of you guys need to get one," says Bart, who is older than the rest. "Since my oldest went to college on the mainland, and with John gone, I haven't had a riding partner."

Jesse Suzuki, the navy man who fixes nuclear submarines at Pearl Harbor says, "My wife would die before letting me get one. How is Bart Jr. doing in college anyway? Good thing he went to Afghanistan and didn't get stuck in Iraq. I hope they don't call him back."

"He was in Bosnia, too," says Bart. "But yea, you figure me, my dad, my grandfather all went to war. Korea, Vietnam, me the good Iraq War, and Bart Jr. Afghanistan. The government should leave us alone already and get some of you dicks to participate."

"Don't look at me," says Roy Heap. The neighbors call him Ster-Roy. "Two kids, preschool, a mortgage, and truck payments. War is for kids."

Banyan says, "I must be getting old, because when I look at that motorcycle all I see is Raimi growing up fatherless."

They laugh. "So how is it living in that house?" Ster-Roy asks. "Any ghost sightings yet?"

Banyan ponders this, assumes none of the others see John Krill standing on his wall in the middle of the night. "Yea, but it's more of a menehune sighting. He's really short, has a beer belly and a goatee, and wears a tank top from Tahiti. Hell of a nice guy."

Bart Carballo laughs. "John? That's not John. No beer belly or facial hair on that guy. And he never wore tank tops. Damn half-haole half-Samoan walked around this street looking like King Kamehameha would on the cover of a romance novel. Really good-looking kid. Good-looking wife. Good son. Quiet, but nice as hell. It's the kind of family you'd see on a billboard advertising new houses built by Castle and Cooke. Still can't believe it."

"Hear about Kai?" Ster-Roy says. "I had a call, some dumb-ass almost drowned trying to give his dog a burial at sea. Saw the kid there. Had to hide behind the truck because I didn't know what to say. Think Kai and the kid are living at the beach."

"Fuck, man," says Bart. "I told them they could stay with us as long as they want. Jesse, didn't you offer them your apartment in town for super-cheap rent?"

Jesse has his hand on wires behind the Harley's carburetor, his small, chubby hand like a child's, stuffed, reaching for something under a couch. He looks like a giant toddler with a Boy Scout's haircut, except his once black hair is graying prematurely. "I did," he says. "She never took me up on it."

"She still working at Zippy's?" Bart asks.

"Hell if I know, I'm afraid to go eat there," says Ster-Roy. "If she does, think about the kid. From private school to Wai'anae High? Her working nights? They probably never see each other. She should've at least let the kid stay with one of you guys. Should see the trash that goes to Wai'anae. And the dumb-ass homeless who live on the beach? Poor kid."

Banyan is tempted to say that he sees Kai every week and has read three essays by her now—one a personal experience essay on how her mom taught her to swim, another a compare and contrast essay on Mililani and Wai'anae, and the third an instructional manual on how to drive a man insane, where she wrote that prying the truth from a liar was like trying to open a fire hydrant one-handed. He also hangs out with her every Monday night as well. They bet on Monday Night Football games, and despite his protest, loser pays the entire tab. He's been getting his ass kicked anyway, and the way she brags about winning, her absolute glee, he can't feel sorry for her. He loves seeing her like that. Her last win prompted her to jump on the table and do the Macarena, which dated her, but the fact that he loved it so much dated him even more. All this time, and he didn't even know she was possibly homeless.

Two men enter the garage. "You guys are up late," one says. It's the gay couple who live next to Banyan. The Japanese one is a veterinarian, the haole a mortgage banker. Banyan didn't even know they were gay until Caley told him. The haole is crazy about his garden and last week offered Banyan just about any kind of plant from it. The ti leaves, ginger, and bougainvilleas in his backyard tell him John and Kai must've been good friends with their neighbors.

"We were just talking about John and Kai," Bart says.

A swell of pity rolls over Banyan. He announces his departure, shaking hands before crossing the dark, but peach-lighted empty street. And as he is getting ready for bed, Banyan finds it hard to believe that everyone in the Luapele Street Posse is as bright and nice as they seem.

John Krill was probably one of these guys, bright and nice, and Banyan supposed that what everyone missed was what bubbled deep beneath the surface, like a volcano venting smoke underwater, like the sleepy snores of a dragon on the bottom of the ocean, and that all these bright and nice neighbors had the same geological or mythical phenomena going on in their own lives, but with the way they hid it, you'd need some kind of high-tech submarine to find it.

Caley is asleep in Raimi's room. As Banyan moves Raimi to make room on the big bed in the master bedroom, his thoughts oscillate between two things: I need to help Kai, and what the fuck is up with that little teenaged Filipino Carballo girl trying to sing AC/DC?

Just as he begins to doze off, he sees the shadow of John Krill leaning against the doorway, wearing a fedora and smoking a cigarette. It's the first time the menehune has entered the house since Banyan started spending Monday nights having a few drinks with Kai. He sees John a few nights a week, marching on the top of the wall like a protester, but other than that, he's kept his distance. Banyan gets up and walks up to John. "Kitchen," Banyan says. "Don't smoke by my kid for Christ's sake."

Banyan walks down the stairs and heads to the kitchen. It's dark, everything hazy but visible. He pulls out a chair and sits. John stands quietly in front of him, hat tipped, hiding his eyes. "What can I do to get rid of you?" Banyan asks.

"You don't look so good, sweetheart."

It's true. He's hardly been getting any sleep—living in a haunted house tends to have that effect—and more and more people are noticing. Caley made a doctor's appointment for him that he skipped, and one of his students told him he looked like a vampire. Vampires being all-around cool, he was more flattered than worried. "Your fault," says Banyan. "So let me ask again, how do I get rid of you?"

John shrugs. "Running around with my wife ain't helping."

The phrase "running around" is a bit strong for Banyan. They aren't sleeping together. But Banyan isn't surprised that John knows he and Kai have become friends. I mean, if you can't look up from Hell and see what you're missing out on, it doesn't seem like it could be that bad a place. "It's kept you out of the house," says Banyan. "Heard she's homeless? Just found out tonight."

"Good for that bitch."

"And your son?"

John takes off his fedora and puts it on the table. He sticks out his tongue and presses the ember of his lit cigarette on the tip. He stares at Banyan as the ember sizzles and dims. "Stay away from my kid, or I'm taking yours."

"What the hell are you doing here anyway?" Banyan asks. "You got a kid, and all you can do is harass me? You must've been a shitty father."

"Look who's talking."

"What's your kid's birthday?"

John doesn't answer. Banyan closes his eyes tightly. He opens and looks. John's still there. Banyan does this several times, but John doesn't budge.

Frustrated, Banyan sits and pounds his fist once on the table. The hammering motion gives him an idea. He knows exactly how to get rid of John. "Don't you do it," John says.

Banyan heads to the garage and pulls out his sledgehammer. He opens the garage door and marches to the wall. He spits in his hands, raises the hammer, and swings with everything he's got. Half a cinder block explodes and shattered pieces hit the sidewalk. He swings again. The hammer head punctures the wall, and Banyan has to jiggle the handle to get the hammer out. The work feels good, mischievous in a way, like he's a kid throwing rocks through the windows of a haunted house.

He swings again and again until his palms blister and bleed, but he doesn't mind. It shows he's doing man's work. As he lifts the hammer again, someone is screaming behind him. He spins around and is relieved to see it's Caley, not John. "What the hell are you doing!?" she yells.

"The little fucker is gone, isn't he?"

Caley, frightened, takes a step back. It's the first time Caley has ever looked at him and become scared. It makes him feel good.

The lights are on at the Carballo house. His neighbors across the street stand in their open garages, curious, but not nosy enough to step on their driveways. He tosses the hammer on the lawn and heads inside. "Let's get some sleep," he says.

"I'll sleep with Raimi tonight. You sleep in her room."

Exhausted, Banyan does not argue. He crawls into Raimi's empty twin, pulls the pink sheets over his head, and feels a momentary chill about sleeping alone in bed in a haunted house. Downstairs, the refrigerator thumps as it shuts off. He forces himself to stay up, waiting for any signs of John. He pulls the sheet off his head, stares at a framed picture of him and Raimi at the zoo and falls asleep.

5

In a small, isolated river valley in Uzbekistan, a tuber called the golden sansam thrives near a village of people who sometimes live to be 120 years old. After the Iron Curtain fell, Western explorers and scientists discovered this village and were stunned to find great-grandfathers and great-grandmothers riding bicycles to the cotton fields, golden sansam sandwiches packed for lunch. Apparently, Alexander the Great explored this place and fed his horse these tubers. The horse lived to be sixty-seven years old.

That's what the pamphlet, filled with charts and testimonials, says anyway. It shows how scientists took ten years to work on distilling the essence of the golden sansam into a wonder juice that blocks and absorbs free radicals, how the company, Golden Sansam Inc., issues the Twelve Week Challenge—anyone who takes an ounce of Sansam per day for twelve weeks and does not feel remarkably better, well, they don't get their money back or anything, but take it for twelve weeks, and they're guaranteed to see health improvements like reductions in joint pain and stiffness, blood pressure and sugar, and heart rate.

Kai listens to the pitch in a small banquet hall in the Pagoda Hotel. The lights are dimmed and a DVD plays on the projector, a man on stage stirring up a crowd with images of the good life: European sports cars, homes with curved staircases and marble floors, and speed boats skipping across the ocean. It bores Kai, so she stares at the stainless-steel water pitcher on the table in front of her; the sweat on the pitcher glistens from the light on screen. The young guy the next chair over nudges her. "Man, I could drop out of college and sell this stuff."

The man on screen explains how there are red, blue, and yellow people, talking about how to sell to each type. He is perspiring, really worked up, but his shirt and shiny polyester suit remain unspotted by sweat. In the following scene he is dressed like a caricature of a farmer—denim overalls, straw hat, corncob pipe, a red bandana tied around his neck—and Kai is wondering what she is doing here.

The juice, packaged in a 750 ML wine bottle with the word "Sansam" printed in ersatz calligraphy on the label, is sold in a five-hundred-dollar kit that includes three bottles of juice, a glossy pamphlet, and a copy of the DVD they just watched. A man on stage dressed in an aloha shirt and cheap, oversized slacks, scribbles math on a whiteboard, explaining that if you pitch the kit, which they call "For Your Eyes Only: The Confidential," to a hundred people and ten agree to pick it up, you make $250. If those ten people do the same you get a $1,700 per month residual. If the thing goes one level further, well, that's $16,000 a month. When Kai raises her hand and asks if this is a pyramid scheme, the man throws the most polite hissy fit she's ever seen. He pulls up his slacks and says, arms flailing, "Miss, a pyramid scheme has no product. This has a product, and a damn good one, as you can see by the testimonials. This is multi-level marketing. One of our top guys is an NFL Hall of Famer, and he swears by it."

Before she can ask why the illustration for the marketing is in fact shaped like a pyramid, he pulls up his pants again and continues. "What's a corporation shaped like? You got the CEO on the top, then vice-presidents, then managers, then assistant managers, then employees. Everything is shaped like a pyramid. What are the chances of the employee becoming CEO one day? Well, with 'The Confidential,' you can become your own CEO. The people you get, well, they can become your vice presidents and managers.

"When you buy something from the supermarket, how many hands have touched that product? You got the farmer, the distributor, the store itself, etc. The product is marked up every step of the way. With Sansam there is no middleman." He winks. "You're getting your product straight from the source."

She wants to point out that the top guy already occupies the CEO chair, and the first sellers are already the VPs, and there is no way they can climb above those people who, unlike a real business, will only retire when the company tanks, but he moves on to another question. It's the college kid. "So, like, that guy driving around in his Maserati. Is that for real?"

The man smiles. "I just had dinner with him last week in Phoenix. You better believe it's for real, only he brought a Hummer to the five-diamond restaurant that night."

Kai finds this entire scene depressing, especially because she's considering picking up a $500 case. Hope, that deceptive bitch, is whispering in her ear: What if it's all true?

Fortunately, she is sidetracked by the time—she is supposed to meet Banyan at their bar to do what has replaced Monday Night Football as their favorite pastime: seeing who can locate and sing the cheesiest pop song on karaoke—loser pays for the karaoke room. They had to institute the "no Air Supply, Journey, Lionel Richie, Celine Dion, or late Stevie Wonder" rule to spice things up. Banyan slew her with "Muskrat Love" the week before, especially since he sang it with such horrible gusto. Tonight, she comes armed with "Yummy Yummy Yummy (I got love in my tummy)." She is fairly confident this will be the all-time best.

They meet every Monday at the Karaoke Room in Pearl City. They bring their own wine and share a private room with a sofa, a TV, a binder filled with song titles, and a machine that eats dollar bills. After feeding the machine money, a person can punch in a series of letters and numbers and put just about any conceivable pop song up on the screen. Each song has a corresponding music video, and Kai is awed by the fact that there are people out there who direct these videos, people who, she imagines, carry business cards with the title, "Karaoke Film Director." It actually strikes her as a sort of cool job, at least vastly superior to being a waitress at Zippy's.

Banyan has beaten her there—probably let his last class out early again—and when she arrives he is working on opening a bottle of Merlot and having a hard time removing the foil wrapping from the twist-off cork. At first she was disappointed in his extreme haircut, but now she finds it cute, like a boy trying desperately to look like a man.

"Thank God, my hero," he says. "Can you help me with this? My hands are busted up."

It's one thing that always strikes Kai as nice about Banyan—unlike other men she has known, he unabashedly asks for help. She takes the bottle from him and catches a glimpse of the scabs and blisters on his palms. "You must be the jerk-off world champion."

"Fifteen rounds. It was like the Thrilla in Manila."

"What really happened?"

Banyan puts a dollar into the machine. "Let's get started."

Banyan starts off the competition with Jefferson Starship's "We Built This City." His voice is plain, like that of the boy band member who is constantly in the background. When the notes get high, his sound gets soft. She believes him to be tone-deaf to boot, but the strain in his face and neck, the earnestness of it, gives the rendition undeniable comedic effect. They sometimes debate over who is the worse singer, as they are both fairly awful, but he is so bad that she sometimes lets her voice crack just so she can keep up with him. She applauds. "Great choice. A bit obvious, but yea, that song is bad. 'Macaroni plays La Bamba'—my God."

"I'm personally partial to 'Who rides the wrecking ball into our guitars.'"

She is often struck by how the two of them think so alike. Think the same things are funny, always looking for something that's funny, as if they both consider humor, the absurdity of things, all that tethers them to sanity. She is surprised she's never met anyone like him before, and wishes she had done so much earlier in her life. "Okay," she says, "take a seat, amateur."

They sing other songs, like Eddie Murphy's "Party All The Time," but she wins hands down with "Yummy, Yummy,

Yummy." Banyan had never heard it before, but afterward, he concedes that it is so bad that they might as well find another Monday night hobby. The two bottles of cheap Merlot are empty, and they leave. Banyan pays for the karaoke room.

She has this image of him as a teenager—the skinny, gangly kid who was never without a skateboard but was the worst skateboarder among his friends. He was the quiet one that the rest picked on; I was only discovered in college that, despite his narrow shoulders and sunken chest, his face was so pretty, long eyelashes framing big eyes like a Japanese cartoon, that girls were never going to be a problem again. The pierced nose struck her as a sort of cry for help, or maybe a purposeful disfigurement to keep the junior college girls off him, but if anything, the white gold stud made you look at his face, and he had you after that, or at least he had her.

He is quiet tonight, skittish, not really paying attention to her for the first time since they started their Monday night outings. Normally, as the evening winds down, Banyan talks about his daughter, Raimi, with an ear-to ear-smile, thanks her for a good time, and heads home. He hasn't mentioned the little girl once tonight, so she's worried.

They lean against the wall in the parking lot as the sun fades to dark blue and slow-moving cars switch on headlights. Banyan squints at the traffic, like he's looking at the faces of drivers passing by. "I'm a horrible mother," Kai says.

Banyan looks at her. "It's hard, isn't it?"

"At least you see yours."

"That's not what I'm talking about, Kai."

He always calls her Kai, not "babe" or "baby," like every other man close to her, even her father. "What then?"

"For one thing, this whole Luapele Street Posse thing. I don't fit in. My wife loves it, though. My kid, too. Shouldn't I love it?"

"Ah, the Luapele Street Posse. Be careful with them. They aren't all they're cracked up to be."

"They seem pretty nice."

"Want the dirt?"

"Sure."

A group of eight, all in their early twenties, stream into the karaoke bar with coolers and grocery bags filled with chips and pretzels. The last one to enter, a potbellied girl who might or might not be pregnant, waddles in carrying a twenty-pound bag of ice in each hand. The insides of her elbows are dotted red, heat rash, maybe. "Let's just say Bart is not so nice to his wife. As for Jesse, his favorite pastime is hitting massage parlors, which he likes to call 'getting a soapy,' and Ster-Roy, well, even I slept with him. So many secrets. The unbelievable thing is everyone knows everyone else's secret, except for the person the secret will hurt—the wife, the husband. It's an intelligence network more competent than the CIA."

"Jeez, and the gay couple?"

"George and Kelly? They aren't really part of the Posse, and I used to think it was because they were gay, but after a while I figured that it was because they were the most normal. It's like their lack of dysfunction embarrassed everyone else. Unless you count rabid pot-smoking as dysfunction, which I don't. They are the only ones I miss."

Banyan nods. He starts to say something, changes his mind and leans against the wall and sighs. Kai, nervous, moves closer to him. Their arms touch and Kai shivers as they stand side-by-side.

"Need me to make the first move?" says Kai.

Banyan frowns. "What are you talking about?"

His response scares her, and as he stares back out into traffic, he seems oblivious to what he just said. She's noticed the gradual paling of the skin, the weight loss, the darkening of the circles under his eyes, and has taken them as signs that he was, without a doubt, losing sleep because he was a married man in love with her. The idea that this might not be the case has her scrambling.

"Is it because I'm a homeless woman? That'd gross me out."

Banyan, quiet, doesn't seem to hear her.

"No one will rent to me," she says. "The best I can do is some rat trap with a community restroom occupied by degenerates hitting the pipe."

She grabs his face. "Are you listening to me?"

"I'm crazy," he says. The way he's looking at her, she knows he means it.

"Welcome to the club."

She pulls his face down to hers and kisses a shaky Banyan; she's shaky too. She presses against him hard, trying to suppress the quivering. They break the lip lock, and he leans into her so that she's practically holding him up. He catches his balance and looks down at her. She touches his nose with her finger. "You should lose the nose ring."

"I should."

"I'm trembling," she says.

He smiles. "I'm trembling with desire."

"I long for you. Your kiss makes my heart pound a mile a minute, as my knees weaken from my heart's secret, forbidden desire."

"God, Kai," he says, "you crack me up." He wraps his arms around her and squeezes tightly. His strength surprises her. They kiss again. He pulls back, his eyes red and welling with tears, probably thinking about his wife and kid. She tries to get his attention. "Break out, Banyan," she says.

"With a sledge hammer."

"Ride the wrecking ball into guitars."

They leave Kai's car and drive off, and she is already brainstorming excuses for Banyan's Monday night tardiness, since he doesn't look up to doing it himself. Hope is whispering in Kai's ear, and the voice is so sweet that it conjures images of a modest home, not in Mililani Mauka, not anywhere in Hawai'i that she knows, with a teenaged boy and his tiny step-sister holding hands, laughing, and running through an oscillating sprinkler in the front yard. She and Banyan are sitting on a porch bench humming "Yummy, Yummy, Yummy." Their goofy smiles are almost grotesque.

6

Way back when, before Hawai'i was colonized, the Hawaiian people had no surnames. It wasn't until 1860 that King Kamehameha IV put the Act to Regulate Names into law—the Hawaiian people were to use their father's name as a surname and adopt Western first names. This law stood in Hawai'i until 1967.

But Josh didn't know any of this. He found it odd that this homeless woman who was frying a big pāpio in an iron wok said she had no last name, despite the fact that he hadn't asked for one, and to just call her Aunty Ku'uipo. Her kids, Kamealoha, fifteen, Mehealani, nine, and Makana, seven, supposedly didn't have last names either. However, Josh knew Kamealoha from World Civ Class, and when attendance was taken, he answered to Michael Opio-Santos—hyphenated names basically meaning that a kid doesn't have a real daddy. So Josh isn't quite sure what this woman is up to. Even though Josh told her his name, the woman simply refers to him as "boy."

"Eh, boy. I seen you around. Where your madda?"

"School today, then work."

"What, she no cook for you?"

"She gives me money."

Aunty Ku'uipo hoists the fish up by the tail with oversized chopsticks, and diced onions and lup cheong—sweet Chinese sausage—spill out of the wok. She scrapes spilled filling and oil onto the fish. Then she turns off the propane tank. She's a big woman with broad, swimmer's shoulders, and her body is resistant to fat except at the abdomen. Josh wonders how it is that her three kids are impossibly thin—skinnier than he is, even. Kamealoha, or Michael, as Josh calls him, is shirtless, and his body reminds Josh of something different entirely—a bantam weight on the pre-card in a pay-per-view boxing match about to get his ass kicked. Even the dog seems to be losing weight, its collar almost loose enough for it to make a grand escape.

"Ah, Mom, onion?" Michael says.

"Eh, you guys need vegetables, too."

The five of them sit at a fold-out table and eat the fish with rice. Surprisingly, it's only the second meal Josh has had on the beach. The first was when he brought his McDonalds Value Meal back to the tent, paranoid that someone was going to steal his stuff. Once blowing sand contaminated his Big Mac and fries, he said, screw the stuff, and had eaten indoors at fast food joints ever since. "Eh, so what kind mother leaves her son out here to fend for himself?"

"Ah, Mom," Michael says.

"She really doesn't like it here," Josh says. "So she is trying to get money together to rent a place." Kai grew up in Hawai'i and never learned to swim; her hatred for the beach, even as a vacation spot, was obvious.

At school, Michael was a homeless social outcast like Josh, only with shabbier clothes, but it was his profound ignorance that drew Josh to him. First off, Michael thought the octane of gas indicated the year it was made. And second, because of the old American map pinned up on the wall in World Civ class, he thought Hawai'i and Alaska were right next to each other. Their classmates were relentless with their insults, but Josh was thinking: a kid who doesn't know these things and is obviously not retarded must have his head filled with other, more mysterious things. Josh wanted to find out what they were. Besides, he bet that there were other kids in the class who thought Alaska was right next to Hawai'i too, and were relieved when it was Michael and not them who revealed the truth to the rest of the class.

"She can at least make food before she takes off, boy," says Aunty Ku'uipo.

"She never cooked," Josh says, "even when we lived in a house. My dad did. She cleaned, though. Cleaned a lot. But I guess there's nothing to clean here." He looks at Aunty Ku'uipo's hair, a bundle of stickiness that seems to have been subdued with rubber bands and garden shears. She also has a thing for socks. Socks with rainbows, socks with bunny faces at the toes, and socks with hot air balloons hang from the tree. She is wearing Stars and Stripes socks under her slippers, but they are old, dirt-stained, and have holes at the heels. Looking at the socks, Josh is shocked at how good the fish is, but is afraid to ask for seconds.

"It don't seem right," she says, as even her daughter and younger son look embarrassed by her outspokenness, but in a defeated way, like they know better than to try to stop her. They are picking onions out of the fish with their re-used plastic picnic forks. Ku'uipo—Josh has seen enough gold Hawaiian bracelets to know it means "sweetheart" in Hawaiian—he has no idea how some man had the stomach to impregnate this woman, not once, but three times. He's known all his life that his mother has parental shortcomings—doesn't mean he wants it pointed out by some stranger he suspects has failings of her own.

After dinner, Aunty Ku'uipo mixes the remaining rice, oil, and fish, bones, head and all, and gives it to their dog, the skinny one that's tied up close to Josh and Kai's tent and spends all its time barking, snapping at laundry, or eating the tree it's tethered to. Now, ignoring its meal, it's digging a hole. This is the first dog Josh has seen ignore table food.

Josh and Michael straddle their bikes, Michael's is a strange mixture of parts, like the product of a junkyard. Before they take off, Aunty Ku'uipo says, "Eh boy. Anytime you like eat dinner here, just come. No worry, Aunty Ku'uipo feed you."

Josh's tires sink into the sand, making it difficult to peddle up the sloping beach, the tires at times spinning in place. But he manages okay, unlike Michael, who trails behind him, a silhouette against the shore break, where waves are crashing on rocks, imperceptibly chipping them away.

It's almost dark when the two boys pass the Wai'anae District Court, which is near a Samoan and Tongan take-out. The court is the only storefront in the yellow-bordered strip mall without iron bars over the windows and doors. They stop at a liquor store, flint, hard alcohol, dice, and crack seed behind the counter, and Josh buys some lemon peel.

The boys continue on, dried lemon peel between cheek and gum. Michael wants to show him something. They stop at the homeless shelter, sitting on their bikes, front tires pressed against the chain-link fence. When Josh peers through the open front door, the big tent building inside strikes him as office-looking. Dozens of partitions under a skeletal roof-lit fluorescent. People are on the move behind the partitions, but Josh only hears them, hears a chaos of conversation and clanging. It's almost like an internment camp, a low security prison, or halfway house. "Neat, huh," Michael says. "Got keys and everything."

"How come you don't live here?"

"My mom says too many rules. My dad lives here, though. I want you to meet him."

They wait around several minutes, flexing the fence with their tires, trying to get a better look inside, until the father shows up on a dirt bike. Darkness hasn't completely set in. "Eh, Santos," he says. "Ready to go?"

The man, so skinny his laugh-lines sag like a bulldog's, has a biker look about him—handlebar mustache, gray ponytail, leather vest, wind-worn face—except the bike is a dirt bike, another junkyard special. He throws a rope to Michael, who clamps it to the frame of his bike. "Try keep up, boy," the elder Santos winks at Josh.

They are off toward Farrington Highway, and even though the small motorcycle tows the bike behind it slowly, the rope slackens then jerks tight a few times along the way, almost pulling the bicycle out from under shirtless Michael. They don't stop until they're at a beach park restroom, the light of evening gone.

They are in the men's room now, Michael holding a flashlight, all three of them uncomfortably sharing a stall, piss all over the toilet seat. Michael's dad loads up a glass pipe with crystal meth, and Michael's elbow hits the stall door by accident. The light shines down on his father's forearms. The thin, veiny skin is spotted with circular scars. "Eh, Santos, watch the light," he says.

Josh once saw a documentary on drug addicts on TV, and was mystified by the phenomena of collapsed veins described as kinks in a water hose. But he doesn't even question whether or not he will take a hit, his first, and he isn't sure why. He doesn't feel peer pressure or anything, but it seems silly to be standing in a bathroom stall, in a puddle of piss and broken glass vials, and not be smoking ice. Neither father nor son gives him any hint as to whether he should stay or leave, except for when Michael first tugged him into the stall. Maybe he is curious, though he's not sure, and doesn't really care anyway. They pass the pipe to him and he mimics their motions. He only takes a couple of hits and holds in his cough, feeling the peer pressure only after the puffs, trying hard to hold his smoke. He leaves the stall before the other two.

A half-hour later, Josh and Michael sit cross-legged in Josh's tent with the lantern. Michael teaches him how to tie leader, lead weight, swivel, and hook onto a fishing line. The only effect from the drug that Josh feels is an unending swell of optimism, not the philosophical kind that tells him everything in his life will turn out fine, but a more immediate optimism, like the incoming second, the one following the present second, will be hunky-dory. They are at it full-speed, tying leader line, looping the finished product together with a twisty, one after the other until they run out of line. Even though the Krills bought the fishing pole, tackle box, bell, and sand spike a week after they came to the beach, more for trying to fit in than anything else, Josh had never managed to catch anything but a few eels. He knows he will catch fish now, maybe pāpio like they ate earlier in the evening, or maybe even an ʻulua—pāpio ten pounds and over, the big kind you see on the cover of a skin-diver magazine.

The two boys are setting up the poles now, and Josh is surprised that even though he is just sitting here, staring at the bell attached to the fishing pole, he is not bored at all. He feels as if he has super-powered perceptions, like he can hear a newly created grain of sand drop and hit the ocean floor after a wave crashes into the rocks. Well, that's a bit extreme, he thinks, but he swears he hears the flex in the graphite pole every time the undertow pulls on the line. He studies the skinny dog tied to the tree, and tries to diagnose its rapid weight loss, despite an utter lack of knowledge in veterinary medicine. "Hey Michael," he says, "why is the dog getting so skinny?"

"We took it to the vet," Michael says. "It ate rocks. Big ones it dug up. All stuck in his stomach. It'll cost three thousand bucks for surgery. Stupid ass dog."

"Wow, is it sore?"

"Nah, but we should put it to sleep. No hope. Eh, I heard Sandy Pacheco thinks you're cute."

Sandy is both taller and heavier than Josh, and he's pretty sure she could take him in a fight. "Nah."

"Should rush. What, maybe she give you one blow job after school. Heard she blew Kaipo Stevens."

"Mean. Now I really wanna check her out," Josh says, sarcastically.

"What, you one fag or something?"

"No."

"Prove it."

Josh has no doubt that he'd prove it in a second if there was a hot girl like Cindy Chang, a girl in his Algebra class, offering, but he thinks about his dad, and how that guy was destroyed by sex. It wasn't just sex, but what sex produced: Xavier Teve Musashi Krill. That brother he never knew, tattooed on his father's shoulder, the one who died on all of them. He remembers his father coming home drunk every year on Xavier's birthday, going up to Josh's room and laying it all on him—how Xavier had grace, the most graceful kid he ever saw, how he went out hard, almost never complained, how Kai didn't know that the death was just as hard on him. He told Josh that the reason he didn't crawl into a ball and want to die like Kai did was because he actually watched the kid go and was goddamn inspired. Xavier's strength, his grace ... John had to live up to it. It nearly killed him to see his son go like that, but he had to show Xavier, who was no doubt up in Heaven watching, he could be graceful, too. Adults repeating stories to kids—try hearing that one once a year from six on. No, the last thing Josh wants is to impregnate some girl, even Cindy Chang, and risk going through all that shit. He looks at the dog, so feeble it can barely stand. No thanks.

Josh is about to crack that he'll prove he's not a fag with Michael's mother, but the thought makes him throw up a little in his mouth.

Kai doesn't arrive at the beach until a few hours later, and joins Josh by the sand spike. Michael is long gone, school tomorrow, and Josh wonders how he manages sleep, feeling like this. His mother puts a hand on his shoulder. "How's it going, kiddo?"

Josh's heart, which was beating fast, is beating even faster now. "Mom," he says. "We gotta get out of here."

"I know," she says. "I'm working on it."

"I mean, not your way, though," he says. "The fast way."

He looks up at her and can tell that she's hurt, but he also sees that her sense of urgency is not like his. She goes back to the camp, and he knows that she is washing up with baby wipes like she does every night. He doesn't want to do it, but he pulls out the cell phone Dan gave him earlier in the week and calls him. "Dan," he says. "Please come and talk to my mom. I can't stay here anymore."

"Okay, kid," Dan says and hangs up.

Listening to the waves, pondering that on this coastline, there isn't really a shallow end, just a steep drop from shore to ocean, Josh thinks about the Santos family, about Michael, AKA Kamealoha, and is sure about one thing: Michael's destiny is set. It's like that big old rock out there that the shore break is pounding. The only way that rock doesn't eventually become sand is if you remove the whole damn thing and put it someplace else. Josh isn't sure what would be more difficult, getting the rock or the entire Santos family further inshore. Also, four damn hours, and not one nibble on his line. Josh knows what he knew the day they came here. He doesn't belong. And it's not because he is better; it's because he's already been ground down by waves, different ones, and he isn't being ground down here, just sinking like a rock carelessly tossed to the bottom of the sea.

III. Suicide at Pōka'ī Bay

1

The Luapele Street Tool Exchange—it goes beyond ladders, ratchet sets, paint brushes, and drill bits. The Carballos, automotive and motorcycle specialists, have an air compressor, a motorcycle tire-changer, and a three-ton floor jack. The Heaps, home improvement fanatics, have a carpet power-stretcher, a router table, and just about every kind of sealant or adhesive imaginable. However, it's the Suzukis who have the exotic stuff, and among these tools is Jesse Suzuki's diamond-bladed concrete chainsaw. Banyan realizes that John Krill was probably a major contributor to the tool exchange and feels bad that his meager offering is a sledge hammer and an electric screwdriver—not even a contribution really, since the other three families already have both.

While the women and the kids are at Hawaiian Waters Adventure Park, riding the various water slides and eating over-priced cheeseburgers, Banyan imagines Caley stuck at Keiki Kove, the toddler pool, with Raimi. She's nearing three, and Banyan is grateful that his daughter shows signs of over-cautiousness, fear of anything that involves her feet not touching ground. She is like him in that regard, or at least how he is now, and Banyan knows that he and Caley should have switched places. Keiki Kove is more his speed, and Caley would have loved to see the chainsaw carve through the concrete wall. In fact, she would have probably trusted her sense of straightness more than Jesse's, wanting to saw away in her two knee braces, while ignoring that Jesse had actually used the thing before.

However, after the other night, when he woke up the neighborhood, pummeling the wall with the hammer like a madman, Caley announced she was taking a week's vacation. Then she demanded Raimi sleep with her in the living room every night. Banyan couldn't take Raimi to the water park because Caley no longer trusted him to be alone with her. When he got home late after spending the evening with Kai, Caley was even more concerned. She probably imagined him driving around aimlessly, stalking cinder block walls surrounding other houses in Mililani Mauka. Imagine what the neighbors will think? He could hear it coming from her. She wouldn't imagine him cheating on her, not in a million years, which makes him feel like an even bigger heel. So when she suggested that he ask the posse to help him take down the wall, even though he felt it in his bones that it was meant to be his job alone, personal business between him and John Krill, he consented.

He thinks about Caley as he watches Jesse, a short, stocky, sumo-like Japanese man, prep the chainsaw. Banyan had met Caley at a bar— sadly, it's how the majority of the people he knows met their future spouses—and he'd been struck at how this overly thin, fastidious, freckle-faced girl could consume so much alcohol. It was a birthday celebration, and all night she and her much louder friends were taking shots, and there she was, maybe a dozen shots in, still with complete control over the tempo of her voice. Banyan, not much of a drinker, was piss-drunk by the time he started talking to her, though his head was clear enough to notice that she was still in control of herself, still in balance, unlike her two friends, one of whom was dancing on the bar, too close to the edge, while the other stumbled to the bathroom to retch out tequila. When the dancer on the bar finally lost her balance, Banyan leapt out of the way while Caley moved in to catch her friend. This girl was more man than he'd ever be, and for some reason, it had turned him on.

Seven years later, and it's not so much of a turn-on. He has long suspected obsessive-compulsive disorder, even before the whole "red-cutting-board-for beef, green-cutting-board-for-vegetables, yellow-cutting-board-for-chicken" rule; and at first it seemed like another bonus, considering how chronically disorganized Banyan was. But after a while he noticed that desire for order left desire for little else. It prevented her being intimate with anything beyond a nightly bottle of wine. He'd lied to Kai when he told her Caley was a terrific mother. Yes, if he were Raimi's single parent, she would live on pizza and have rotten teeth and be as spoiled as hell, but he did not think Caley was a good mother at all. Caley always looked for chores to tend to in order to avoid dealing with Raimi. Her idea of interaction involved discipline more than anything else, and she treated Raimi like a stain on the carpet, rubbed hard until the spot matches the rest of the surface. He could see that by the time Raimi was ten, she'd probably hate her mother.

Jesse, who's partial to wearing Honolulu Fire Department tank tops and caps despite not being a fireman, cranks up the concrete chainsaw. Ster-Roy watches in boyish anticipation. Banyan thinks about Raimi, and doesn't understand why his wife doesn't get it. He'd never hurt his kid, and Raimi's the reason why he needs to get rid of John Krill. He's trying to protect her. You didn't need to be a rocket scientist to figure out ghosts, whether from Tartarus or Tahiti, didn't come over to your house to chill out and make friends. They wanted to take you down with them.

"Holy shit, that's cool," says Ster-Roy. All four men wearing clear plastic goggles.

Jesse pulls the chainsaw out of the wall. "Wanna give it a try, Mott?"

"No way. Remember, I'm on labor duty. I'm just throwing the rocks into the truck. I've never even used a regular chainsaw, much less a hydraulic-powered concrete one."

"Suit yourself. You look all had-it anyway. Roy, Bart?"

Bart ignores Jesse, who stares at his house across the street. Ster-Roy takes the chainsaw from him. "I'm all over this, boss."

"Be careful now," Jesse says. "Remember, go slow."

"Dude, I've cut people out of compacted cars. I can handle this."

And sure enough, he can. Ster-Roy is really moving now, the chainsaw like a lightweight toy in contrast to his bulging, veiny arms. His line is confident and straight, and he sees why Kai carried on with this guy. Look up the word "man" in a picture dictionary, and you'd see something like Roy Heap, an energetic bulge with five percent body fat and an eagerness to get a job, any job, done just right. He reminds Banyan of a St. Bernard, cunning and strong, digging through the remains of a Swiss avalanche. His wife would be a lucky woman, if it weren't for all the bar fights and cheating.

The job, which Banyan imagined would take several weekends of labor, is done that afternoon. His back is killing him, thanks to the hours he spent tossing all the discarded concrete into the rented dump truck, so he's glad to be sitting in a lawn chair on Bart Carballo's driveway, sipping a Guinness, and watching the neighborhood kids ride their bicycles in figure eights to and from the end of the cul de sac. He likes drinking more than he ever has. One of the bonuses, besides the buzz, is that alcohol goes a long way in explaining the tiredness and redness in his eyes.

When he and Kai stayed at the hotel room till two in the morning the other night, and he got home at three, he managed to sleep for six hours straight. He found it odd, the fact that he slept so well the night he cheated on his wife. After Raimi woke him up that morning by stomping on his balls, he got up and made Caley's favorite breakfast, canned chili over scrambled eggs. It certainly didn't clear his conscience, but regret was dulled by six solid hours of sleep and late morning indigestion. The guilt did something he didn't expect either—he went the entire day not thinking about the menehune John Krill.

Bart's sitting next to him. He's been quiet all afternoon, content to toss concrete into the truck. Roy's wife, Jocelyn, the pretty but overweight art dealer, is teaching Raimi how to ride her pink tricycle and having much more success than Banyan ever has. His daughter passes him on her way to the end of the cul de sac. "Look daddy! Look daddy! I'm doing it!"

"Good job sweetie!" She has yet to master the turn, but the tricycle is moving now, and Jocelyn has to work herself into a slow jog to keep up. Meanwhile, Jesse, his wife, and Caley drink wine and grill steaks in Bart's backyard. It strikes Banyan as neat, the way these people silently delegate responsibility. The Suzukis cook, the Heaps watch the kids, and the Carballo man sits on a lawn chair like a Hawaiian sugar plantation luna—boss—close enough to the grillers and babysitters to assign jobs as they come up. Soon they will need to bring out the folding tables and chairs for dinner. Banyan wonders what the Krills' function was. He thinks about John and how Banyan is probably a very sad replacement. As if reading his mind, Bart, fiddling with his Hawaiian fish hook charm, says, "John would be out there with the kids, amazing them with bicycle stunt work. He was an athletic son-of-a-bitch, not like that muscle-bound fool out there."

Roy tries to pop a wheelie on his mountain bike, but pulls way too hard and then is flat on his back on the sidewalk. "He okay?" Banyan asks.

"Only thing Roy was better than John at was being indestructible. Nothing bothers that guy, even physical pain. Should hear some of his fireman stories, the kind of gruesome shit he sees and charges right into."

"And Kai?" Banyan asks, careful with his tone, purposely casual, so he doesn't betray anything.

"Either talking about plants with the two homos, or in her house watching ***Law and Order*** re-runs." Bart pauses. "Sorry man, a little harsh. With my wife and two daughters away, it's got me a little grouchy. I like those guys. But Kai, man, I'm thinking she's the one, not the dumb Mililani Town Association, that drove John over the edge. Did you see how fast the wall-cutting went? John could've probably cranked it out faster than the four of us combined."

Banyan stares at his open palm, the loose skin of old blisters torn off from hauling concrete. It itches, so he scratches, but is unable to stop the itch. "Can't believe the MTA took the wall thing so seriously," Banyan says.

"They don't," says Bart. "Someone on this street had to have complained and reported him."

Banyan opens and closes his fist, trying to work the itch away. "Wow, who?"

"Not sure. I was at first thinking Ster-Roy over there, just to get under John's skin for being just as manly as him, or maybe for other reasons." Bart smiles, his teeth showing light-brown with age. "But like I said, nothing bothers that guy, so I doubt it. And the gay duo across the street—too nice. And me, Jesse, hell, we messed around helping John put up that damn wall."

A dropped Honda Civic speeds up the cul de sac. It has some kind of tailpipe attachment, which makes the car sound like a giant lawn mower. The kids quickly get off the street and onto the sidewalk. Banyan stands up. Jocelyn has Raimi safely off the street in no time. "Don't worry," Bart says. "She got her."

Ster-Roy stares through the tint as the car slows and passes. He then approaches Banyan and Bart and grabs a beer from Bart's cooler. "That fuckin' kid," he says. "One day he and I will have a chat."

"Can't talk to a tweaker," says Bart.

"Oh, I'm not gonna be talking," says Roy.

"Go out there and practice your wheelies more," Bart says, smiling.

"No shit, I need to work on that." Ster-Roy puts the beer back in the cooler and is back on the bike. A few seconds later, he's lying on the pavement again. "He's some piece of work," Bart says. "He was close with Kai, but after the John thing, he avoided her big-time."

Kai never did talk much about her affairs (for obvious, shameful reasons), but one night, while they playfully arm-wrestled in a pizza joint, she said that only two could be defined as actual relationships, and claimed further, while he had her forearm a quarter away from the table, that she had only slept with maybe nine men in her entire life. She added defensively, what other twenty-first century woman under forty could claim that? Like a lot of men, Banyan had spent too much time pondering numbers, in terms of a woman's former sexual partners, and he immediately understood the significance of the number nine—one below double digits. Low double digits wasn't too bad, unless oral sex wasn't counted, a pleasure he missed dearly in marriage, but an almost unthinkable act of depravity if performed on someone who was not himself. And now he's really working the itch in his palm, his nails leaving white streaks, while he says without thinking, "Oh shit. You think maybe Kai called the town association?"

Bart stands up and heads toward the garage. "Let's get those tables and chairs set up, okay?"

Banyan follows and Bart, his back still to Banyan, says, "Good choice on losing the nose ring. We were beginning to think you were some sort of queer."

Banyan is not aware of any link between pierced noses and homosexuality. The only reason he'd done it was to play guinea pig for his sister, who was branching out from hair-coloring skills into body piercing. The nose just struck him as the least painful option—eyebrow, chin, tongue, nipple, yikes, no way. And afterward, the only reason he'd kept it was that it irritated Caley and Raimi adored it. "Kai really called the MTA, didn't she?" Banyan says.

Bart lifts the fold-out table and extends the legs with his feet. "You talk like you know her," he says. "And yea, her calling the MTA? The thought has crossed my mind."

This isn't what the move to Mililani Mauka was supposed to be about. Banyan was not supposed to come out here and get haunted by a ghost, start up an affair with the ghost's widow, and develop an obsession with a cinder block wall. If anything, the escape to new-house higher ground should have made it impossible for these very things to happen. In Mililani, diabolical wives are not supposed to report on their husbands to the MTA in an attempt to drive them mad. This is where you're supposed to come and live in a world where the only thing that can hurt people is the occasional exploding outdoor propane-powered gas grill.

Banyan grabs a fold-out chair and sits. "What kind of bitch does that?"

Bart pulls up a chair beside him. "The worst part is the son. He loved his old man like you wouldn't believe."

Banyan feels a rush of shame. How could he have been carrying on with this woman and not even think about her poor kid?

During dinner, Raimi sits on Banyan's lap, picking what her next bit of food will be. The other kids have no problems eating their vegetables, and Banyan is envious, because Raimi wants only the steak. "Honey, you need to eat the corn, too."

"I want meats."

That's about as far as conflict goes between the two of them. On the rare occasions that he does get mad, she obeys him, no questions asked. Banyan puts a piece of steak in her mouth, wondering if John Krill spoiled his son as much as Banyan spoils Raimi.

Caley is across the table from them, no food in front of her, going at it with the wine. The other wives seem to be trying to keep pace, and Banyan knows hangovers are in the cards. She reaches across the table and snatches Raimi from Banyan's lap. In a rare display of physical affection, she nuzzles and kisses Raimi's neck. "I want Daddy, I want Daddy," Raimi says.

Caley begins tickling her until she's laughing so hard that daddy seems to be no more than a faint memory in his child's sharp but yet-to-be-developed mind.

Banyan nods in and out of sleep, his brain lighting up like a bug zapper every time consciousness is about to slip away. He spends several hours like this, waiting till three AM, just a late night hour picked at random to sneak out of the house. Most of this time he thinks about Kai: her leading him to the hotel room as if he were a blind man, him sitting on the hotel bed, feeling like he was back in college where there were no sighing wives who fold plastic shopping bags into perfect squares, no two-year-olds demanding he hold up a Dora the Explorer figurine and say "hi" a thousand times, no mortgages he couldn't really afford, no bad five paragraph anti-cloning essays that use sci-fi movies as credible references, no more concrete walls, and no more menehunes. He was back in a time when getting laid didn't make him feel like a little kid getting his crack whore mom to play Candyland with him. When Kai undressed in front of him, all he saw was her. The relief from everything else almost made him weep.

And after it was done, and Kai dozed off next to him, he sat up in bed and rubbed his bare chest and thought about the fact that this was the first time he'd cheated on anyone his entire life. He wasn't sure if that was supposed to make him feel good or bad. Bad, probably, but it was hard to feel bad completely considering most of the people he knew cheated at one time or another. People still managed to love them.

But now, sitting in his own bed, he's thinking about this kid, this teenage kid camping on the beach, probably dodging feral tweakers, longing to be in the bedroom down the hall, life wrecked because his father rolled over Mililani with a bulldozer. He wants to pick that kid up off the beach, bring Kai too, have them stay at the house, their house, and the five of them can live as if they're in some batty 60s commune. But he suspects that's against MTA regulations, not to mention Caley regulations, which he must admit are justifiable. Then there's the sixth man, the ghost of John Krill. But he has plans for that guy. Banyan gets out of bed at three to execute them.

Caley, out cold from two bottles of wine, sleeps on the sofa like a guard dog. Raimi, on a blanket spread out on the floor beneath her mother, sucks her thumb rapidly as Banyan approaches. He bends down and lightly touches his daughter's forehead. It's another habit of his, randomly checking her for fevers even if she doesn't look sick. The thumbsucking eases, and he touches her arm with a fingertip, gets up, then unlocks the sliding glass door and slips out.

It's cold out and Banyan regrets walking over the dewy grass barefoot and wearing only boxers. He hugs himself and rubs his arms as he surveys the now shorter wall. He walks right up to it and touches the jagged texture on the top. He waits for John. He looked it up on the Internet—to get rid of a ghost, you simply ask it politely to leave (this one made him frown skeptically), or let it know it's dead and tell it to head for the light, where it'll be happier (John already knew he was dead, no dice), or three, use your imagination to conjure the image of a loved one to guide the ghost back to the light (that was the ticket—imagine Xavier Krill and have the boy take his dad home). After he read other pages that advised he talk to the ghost firmly, but without anger, and tell it to leave, he had to glance up at the URL to make sure he wasn't reading about dog obedience training. Out of everything he read, the Xavier thing seemed to be his best shot.

Banyan presses his hand against the wall and closes his eyes. He's not quite sure what the boy looks like, but he imagines a beautiful boy in his father's hands being twirled around in waist-high ocean waters, the boy's feet like rudders cutting through the surface. The boy laughs and laughs then floats out of his father's hands, cradled by gentle winds. As he hovers over his father, he reaches down and says, "Take my hand, dad, and come with me." The father reaches up and squeezes his son's hand, and it is the son now twirling his father around and around as the two sail for heaven.

"All tapped out on holy water? Should've at least painted your door red before trying this."

John Krill steps next to Banyan, shirtless as well. He's tall now, like the real John Krill, taller than Banyan, handsome, and terrifying, a menehune no more. "You feed me," he says.

Defeated, Banyan opens his eyes. "I know."

Banyan turns to face him, and knows right away he's no match for this John Krill. It's not the size that intimidates Banyan, it's the density. John's skin is so stretched by the muscle, blood, and bone beneath that there is a translucent quality to it, like plastic when it's strained near its breaking point. Banyan wonders if this makes the skin weaker, like maybe he can punch right though it. "You'll lose," says John.

Banyan throws a punch anyway. John does not move, and when Banyan's fist hits John's jaw, the pain sets off a scream in Banyan. John laughs. Banyan swings again and again, but John's face is unmovable, and each hit is delivered with less force than the last. John laughs until Banyan is on his knees, his good hand, trembling, holding him up against John's rock thigh.

"You thought you could kick my ass?" says John. "This is the first time I'm looking at you and thinking you just might be crazy."

Banyan struggles to his feet. Just as he pulls his hand back to swing again, an arm wraps around his shoulder and pulls him back. He falls on his back, the dew on the grass cooling his hot body down, and he expects to look up and see Kai. Instead, it's Caley, and finally, mouth gaping and eyes wide, she looks like she's just seen a ghost.

2

Years ago, when Josh was seven, he asked his mother why she never learned how to swim. The three of them were at the dinner table—a rare occasion. John pushed for family meals, but had never succeeded in getting Kai to cooperate. Kai thought, Josh didn't know the half of it. She had a hard time putting her face directly under the stream of a shower.

"I don't get it," seven-year-old Josh said. "Can you ride a bike at least?"

She couldn't do that either. Just learning to drive had taken monumental effort, and she hadn't gotten her license until she was twenty-three. It was after Xavier died, when it didn't seem to matter as much if she plowed under the wheels of a semi. "Your grandmother tried to teach me, but it didn't work out. You're lucky, Josh. Where your father and I grew up, we learned to swim in the ocean, not in a swimming pool with a swim teacher."

Kai was four when her mother decided that it was time for her daughter to learn to swim. Her mother always did that—in her mind, it was as if anything could be taught on a random, single afternoon—and was sorely disappointed when she found it not to be true, at least with Kai.

The two of them were at Pōka'ī Bay Beach Park, before the rampant homeless problem, before people used sunblock or water wings ... in Wai'anae at least. It was before seatbelt laws, and Kai sat in her mother's lap on the drive to the beach. Four steps into an ocean with no real shallow end, Kai's mother was armpit deep in the water, holding Kai's face above the surface.

She turned Kai on her stomach, one hand under her chest, the other on her pelvis, and told Kai to kick. The kicks were pretty pathetic: a slow, knee-bent splashing that Kai could not quicken even as she felt her mother's body teetering from the current. "No, that's not how you kick. You kick from your hips and don't bend your legs. Better, now use your arms to hold your head above water."

Kai swung her arms like she was trying to get smoke out of her face. Her movements must have looked good enough, because her mother let go, and Kai did the panicked seizure-stroke right to the bottom of the ocean. It's one of Kai's earliest memories, her feet kicking wildly, hands digging up sand, and she was coughing under water. She couldn't have been down there more than a few seconds, but she'd probably looked like a little girl trying to dig to the opposite side of the earth, just for a breath of air.

When her mother pulled her up, she coughed out water, screamed, then coughed out more than water, all over her mother's face. The tighter her mother held her, the more she screamed and tried to get away, as if her mother was there trying to drown her, as if she'd be better off seizure-stroking to the bottom again. When they got to the shore, her mother, who rarely swore, said, "Fuck this," and they drove back home, with Kai this time in the passenger seat, wrapped in a towel, consciously knowing something for the first time in her life: I am never going to try to learn to swim ever again.

After she told Josh this story, his father winked at him and said, "She had it easy. My uncle just threw me in the water and said, 'Swim boy!'"

This infuriated Kai, as if for years John had been trying to one-up her in front of their son. He cooked better than she did, he taught Josh more than she did, he made more money, his life had always been harder than hers, but he faced it with a lot more courage. Worst of all, he loved their son more than she did, and at that point, her fist gripping her fork, she knew it was all true, and she believed that it was important to John that their son be reminded of it every day of his life, as if Josh didn't know all this anyway, ever since he'd motored into the closet on his back, willing his mother from grief to reality. She can't remember which extra-marital affair soon followed, but it must have been one of the rare, satisfying ones.

Thirty-one years after the failed swimming lesson, Kai is at Pōkaʻī Beach Park once again, contemplating the police sweep that is coming for them next week. Police are handing out eviction notices and scouting for the next camp location to bust. It was the cop, Dan, who notified her. The smallness of him had surprised her—hands and shoes no bigger than hers—as did his good looks. He wasn't masculine like her late husband or girlish like Banyan, but handsome, like the hardened baby face you might find in an old group shot of American GIs fighting in a forgotten war. Or maybe it was just that his hair was perfect—straight, but thick, the sheen of a light gel or mousse flipping all but a few loose, clumped-together strands from one side of his head to the other. The way he held his arms away from his torso and dared people with his puffed-out chest made him look like a man with something to prove—the worst kind of man for a woman to deal with. Dan grabbed Josh's face and looked at his eyes. After he released Josh's face, he said, "Stay here while I talk to your mom."

When he asked her to sit in his car with him, in the backseat, she was thinking she might be under arrest. It was only then that he introduced himself. "Dan Kruetz," he said, shaking her hand.

"Hi. Kai. What's all this about, Officer?"

"How long have you guys been living out here?"

Kai was sure he knew the answer to this. They were past arrest and into interrogation. She says, "Several months."

"No way you can stay on the beach anymore."

She opened the door and got out. He followed her through the same door. "Hold it," he said. "Don't bullshit me with a dramatic exit. If you could've stopped that first kid from folding, you would've, right? Well, this kid is gonna fold too, unless you get your head out of your ass."

Kai stopped but did not turn around. She looked up as if consulting the stars. "People won't rent to me." No one seemed to believe her on this. "What do you want from me?"

"I want you to live with me until you find someone who will rent to you."

"I don't even know you."

"You don't even know the goddamn people who live within ten-yards of your camp either, but that didn't stop you. Besides, we're closing down this park next week. Next time you might be unlucky and camp right next to a friggin' child-beating crackhead."

"What's with the charity? You trying to fuck my son or something?"

"What the fuck?"

"Well?"

Dan gathers himself. "I was there when your husband..."

"And?"

"I shot him."

Kai sat in the sand. "They never released the name..."

"Yea, they try not to do that."

"Well, what?"

"He fired. I shot back. Simple as that."

Kai believed him. Shockingly, some things were as simple as that. "Why feel guilty then?"

"I didn't sign up for this shit."

"What do you mean?" Kai thought, ah the complicated part.

Dan sat by her. "Criminals, you know? He wasn't, like, a criminal. Just a guy with a family who'd had it. I didn't sign up for that shit."

"More my fault than yours," she said.

"Figured."

Kai turned and faced him. "But now," he said. "There's this goddamn poor kid. No father. Life fucked. I dunno ..."

She stood up and dusted herself off and walked, hoping that the little cop would not follow her. On the way back to the tent, she spied a fiberglass truck camper under a tent. She focused on the strangeness of it while Dan's car started up and rolled off.

So here she is now, at Pōka'ī Beach Park, trying to stay near the lighted parking lot. She peers up the beach at a tent corner held down by a broken mobility scooter, the rusted basket still attached to the handlebars above the two front tires. She looks farther out at the line of fishing poles. No bells are ringing here. There is a commotion on the other side of the parking lot, and she makes her way there with the rest of a slow-gathering crowd, people converging like scouting ants to a soiled spot left on a kitchen counter. It's past midnight and a man sits in the front seat of a rust-bucket Chevy screaming threats of suicide, a noose around his neck and tied to the steering wheel. An old woman, his mother maybe, pleads. "Don't do it. I love you!"

"Get the fuck outta here or I going kill myself!" he screams back.

This conversation goes back and forth for a good five minutes before the firefighters show. The words don't change, and Kai wonders if the object is to see who can say their line the loudest. Kai recognizes one of the figures descending from the truck. It's Roy Heap. She moves behind a big man, switching glances between an approaching Roy and a concealed, camera-like view of the suicidal man through the crook of an observer's elbow. Roy is the first one at the driver's side. The suicidal man begins to jerk his head back against the seat repeatedly, eyes squinting, cheeks puffy and red, a man holding his breath while his skull silently crashes against the stuffed vinyl. "Listen, numb nuts," says Roy. "You can't hang yourself from a fucking steering wheel."

As cop cars arrive, Kai slips away from the crowd. She shakes the dirt and sand out of her shoes before she enters the car. She heads back to her camp. The storefront lights of the strip malls are off, but she can read the signs—Rent-A-Center, Cash/Checking. When she gets back to the camp, Josh is still awake, sitting on damp sand with the lantern at his side, disassembling the fishing rod. Something smells awful. Kai walks up to Josh and sees the bait—chopped-up eel clumped in a blue plastic bag. As she looks from the bag to a crouching Josh, she also sees a baby shark, its entire body powdered with sand. The skin, which probably looks sleek underwater, is tough and grainy. "I finally caught something that's not an eel," says Josh.

Kai nods. "Talked to Dan."

Josh picks up the baby shark and stands. It twists in his grip. Kai jumps. Josh whips it into the water. He sits back down. "Dad was the bad guy, wasn't he?"

Kai's still shocked that Josh was able to pick up the shark so casually. "What do you mean?"

"Like in the movies. The bad guy."

Kai thinks about that. "No I'm the bad guy. It's always been me."

Josh nods. No disagreement. "I don't care. I just can't stay here no more."

Kai stands, half-expecting the baby shark to crawl right out of the water and nip at her toes. She dusts herself off. "Start packing what you want to take. We're leaving. You can call Dan in the morning."

Josh smiles. Months earlier, they came with clothes packed in two suitcases and a duffel bag, a couple of backpacks, Josh's bike, the tent and canopy, a case of Costco baby wipes, and three coolers—one empty, one for water, and one filled with bath and body products. The only thing they've acquired since then is the fishing gear that Kai bought for Josh.

It starts to rain. They are leaving with less, moving only the luggage full of clothes, one cooler, and Josh's bike to the car. Kai wipes water off her face and points her flashlight down as raindrops dimple the sand. "Leave the rest," she says. "Do you have paper and a pen?"

Holding the flashlight in her mouth, she sits in the tent and writes a note: "First come, first serve." Outside, she skewers the paper with the sand spike. The ink starts to bleed. They pass the starving dog, its fur damp, and rain reactivates the smell of flea and tick shampoo. Kai is shocked that the owners wash the mutt, and is tempted to pet it. But the dog leaps for her, stretching its rope, and snaps at the air between them. It does this repeatedly as they get farther and farther up the beach, barking and snapping, and it strikes Kai as one of the fundamental differences between humans and animals—facing futility, man gives up far quicker than beast.

In the car, Josh asks where they are going. "We are going to stay at Ko 'Olina, the resort, for a couple of days." She is excited about splurging on an unnecessary spa treatment, a haircut, and a bath—my God, a bath. She is sick of locking the door of the employee restroom at Zippy's, throwing a foot in the sink and shaving her legs. She remembers that the speed with which she could do this used to frighten John when he'd look over in their bathroom while brushing his teeth. He should see her now, armpits and legs done faster than an order of Zippy's fries.

"Isn't it too late to check into a hotel?" Josh asks.

"A hotel is like any other place open twenty-four hours, pleasantly surprised about making money at a godforsaken time."

Windows down, they travel up the Wai'anae Coast, stop at a 7-Eleven to pick up odds and ends to sustain their day-and-a-half of resort paradise—chips, a sixpack of diet soda, some chewing gum, and peppered beef jerky. A couple of men pay for Double Big Gulps in front of her, big guys, obviously weight-lifters, with perpetually furled brows and intimidating facial hair. One has on a black tee shirt with a picture of a rottweiler and a monster truck on the back. The shirt says, "Driven by Instinct." It confirms for Kai a truth about present day Wai'anae: overall, the home dwellers are a lot more scary-looking than the homeless.

As they drive up the coast, Kai searches for the lights of the resort, and thinks about Banyan. She can hardly expect him to have his marriage wrapped up in a day-and-a-half, but she clenches her jaw and fantasizes anyway. She turns to Josh. "You sure about this?" she says.

"Yea." He yawns. "He didn't really think about me, did he?"

"Who? Dad?"

"Yea."

Kai doesn't know what to say. Josh falls asleep.

They pass newly constructed townhouses, mostly timeshares, she suspects, and there are three to-dos at the top of her list: bath, exfoliation, and serious eyebrow plucking. Her hair will be cut and highlighted tomorrow, and she might even fork over for a collagen facial, ti leaf body wrap, French manicure, and an aromatherapy massage. She will be a new woman, like the model on a brochure, all for

Banyan. She can't blow her entire checking account, though, because there is no way she is living with that cop without paying rent. They enter the parking structure. Josh sleeps while Kai dreams.

3

Somewhere around the age of nine or ten, most people learn the art of hobby specialization. Before this, everything else, like curiosity about hot rods or rare gems, is just passing interest. Like many boys, Josh's first specialization was comic books. Every Sunday, his father would take him to the comic book store and help Josh blow his allowance. Josh had a thing for ***The Avengers,*** and Thor: because of Thor, he read Norse mythology. Then because of Captain America, he read about World War II. Other characters appeared, like Quicksilver and the Scarlet Witch, which led him to discover the X-Men and Wolverine; because of Wolverine he read about the actual animal, Gulo gulo, member of the Mustelidae, member of the weasel family, an animal which, despite its small size, can kill moose and chase off bears. His father at his side, sharing his hobby, remarked, "Always remember that. Size matters, but if you're hell-bent enough, you can make it less of an issue."

His second hobby, taken up a couple of years later and also closely chaperoned by his father, was aquarium fish. This one led Josh to study the cichlid family, its members territorial and often vicious. How much would size matter here? They set up an eighty-gallon fish tank in the garage, and the alpha of the tank was a foot-long Tiger Oscar cichlid his father named El Toro; Josh referred to him as Fat Bastard. The challenge for Josh was to find a different type of cichlid, a smaller one that could stand up to the big Oscar and dethrone him. The Jack Dempsey, the Convict, the Auratus, the Red Devil, and the tilapia from the river (a desperate, last-ditch effort), all failed miserably. Maybe his father was trying to teach him something about manhood with those fish, but all Josh came away with was a refusal to eat Filet O' Fish sandwiches because they were made from tilapia—a fish he associated with aquariums and the polluted streams of Hawai'i.

His last hobby was real-time strategy computer games, games with titles like ***Warcraft, Starcraft, Age of Empires,*** and ***Command and Conquer.*** His father set up a LAN in the empty bedroom and tried to keep up. But Josh discovered that you could play against other people on the Internet, and soon became so good, he could decimate his father's forces in a matter of minutes, though his favorite method was letting his father's forces grow while Josh secretly built his larger army, then he'd sweep in with a frontal assault so massive that artillery defenses were aflame before his father could click on Surrender. His father stopped playing with him after that. Josh felt bad, but it was the first time he was hands-down better at something. If he'd known what his father would do several months later, he would've let him win every game. It was a regret Josh felt deeply—more than his regret at not being able to tell his dad that he loved him (masculine reasons; chicks wouldn't understand), which he did, more than anyone else he knew.

He doubts Kai even suspects that he knows what he knows, but all those nights coming home late, once catching his father going through her purse and credit-card statements, Josh knew what was up, but she'd been at it so long that he figured his father didn't care anymore. And then Kai started spending all that time with Uncle Ster-Roy, and the letter about the wall came from the MTA, and John was the one coming home late. Josh anticipated a step-mom and a divorce, happy knowing that of course he would live with his father. If only his father had allowed him to share the hobby of turning a bulldozer into a tank, Josh knows he could've talked John out of it. But it was John's private hobby, one he kept in a warehouse after he secretly closed down his small contracting business.

Josh is reminded of all of this as he looks at Dan's fridge in wonder—it's the first he's seen in years that doesn't have pictures of children on the door, held up by magnets. There aren't even magnetic alphabets and numbers. There is, however, a familiar calendar, which reads:

Josh: Monday through Friday, school 7:30 a.m. to 2:45 p.m., except Wednesday, 1:15 p.m. Kai: school Monday and Wednesday, 10:00 a.m. to 2:15 p.m., work 4:00 p.m. to 11:00 p.m. Tuesday to Saturday. Dan: Monday through Friday, work: 8:00 a.m. to 4:00 p.m.

Dan made the calendar, explaining to Kai that it's just so he knows when someone is available to take Josh to and from school, but to Josh it looks too much like the calendar his father kept, an occasional source of arguments between his parents, when Kai would arrive home late from her job as a front desk clerk at the Hilton Hawaiian Village. Feigning offense at the questioning, his mother would claim a late check-in or traffic. Good one, Mom, Josh would think, nothing like that midnight traffic. Now, after ten years at that hotel, she was a waitress at Zippy's in Pearl City. Josh had no idea why.

The calendar for November, a sheet of paper held up by an ice-cream scooper magnet, takes Josh back to another memory of his father, Thanksgiving and the Turducken—a chicken wrapped in a duck then wrapped in a turkey. His father spent hours deboning that thing, only to find it didn't really taste better than the usual roasted turkey.

It's Saturday November 4 now, and "Medieval duel" is written in the date's box. After Josh's mother leaves for work, Dan wants to take armor and weapons down to the beach and have a "contest of courage." That's what he called it after ceremoniously slapping Josh's face with a rubber dishwashing glove. Dan's excited that the royal guard burgonet helms he ordered from eBay have arrived. At first, he wanted only to study them for replication, but now he wants to test them out, and he can't think of a better place to do so than Ulehawa Beach Park—one of the two the cops cleaned out the week before.

Kai announces that she is leaving a couple of hours early to avoid traffic. Traffic seems to be a twenty-four-hour-a-day phenomenon for Kai, and Josh suspects that if anyone is a traffic expert, it's a cop, and he wants Dan to call her on it. But Dan just shrugs and says, "Have a good day," winking at Josh, who has decided to look for the beef jerky in the refrigerator. Peppered beef jerky is a staple of Kai's, often replacing entire meals, and since they moved in, the only sign outside of her bedroom that she even lives here are that all her foods are in the fridge, even if they don't need to be—the jerky, the Korean pears, and the spicy dried ika, a kind of squid that Josh remembers dipping into a mixture of mayonnaise and soy sauce while watching ***Law and Order*** in his parents' bedroom. His memories of these bed-picnic TV sessions are sometimes fonder than those about the comic books, aquariums, and real-time strategy games. His mother always did have a thing for spicy, gut-eroding food, and the two of them would silently compete to see who could take more of it before heading off to the kitchen for a refill of milk.

But now she seems to want all of her preserved foods cold. Josh sympathizes, as they haven't had access to a refrigerator in months, and Dan's is a big two-door stainless-steel job that shines with the promise of only the best yuppie food.

After Kai is gone, Dan sneaks up behind Josh and taps him on the shoulder. When Josh turns around, Dan drops a chain-mail gauntlet at his feet. "You, Sir Knight, are a cad," he says. "I demand satisfaction."

"God, you're mental," says Josh. "And you're so going down."

"Help me load the car."

When they get to Ulehawa Beach Park, the homeless encampments are gone. Instead, there are a few weekend campers. One canopy has cellophane birthday balloons tied to it. A group of kids play flag football on the sand. There's also a volleyball net, a bouncer shaped like a castle, and an outrigger canoe setting out to sea. Out toward the horizon, a white, thousand-foot cruise ship meanders in the deep.

Dan leaves the police light flashing on the roof of his car as they arm themselves. The chain mail sags heavily on Josh. The helmet, which has air holes, much like a jar containing a lizard, blocks peripheral vision. In fact, Josh can barely see what's in front of him. He's glad in a way—he doesn't have to see the strange looks that must be aimed their way. Once they get a few yards up the beach, Dan says, "On guard, you cur!"

Josh takes a few steps back. He is wearing tennis shoes, and there's a terrible pressure on his knees, back, and shoulders. He grips the daito, a solid, wooden katana, as Dan charges him with a flail made of wood and a baseball. Each time he is hit with the baseball, he almost falls over. When Josh kicks Dan in the chest, it's Josh who falls over. He expects Dan to rain the baseball on him, but Dan holds back, laughing at the spectacle of Josh deadlifting himself onto to his feet. Josh is mad now.

"Sir Knight," Dan says. "I shall snatch your fiefdom from your impotent hand." Josh swings the sword. Dan is really laughing it up as he absorbs blow after blow. One hit dents Dan's helm, and Dan steps back, twirling the flail. Josh loses it.

Josh takes off his helmet and charges Dan. His next hit lands on Dan's slightly exposed collar bone and snaps it. Dan drops to his knees, suddenly still. Panting, Josh wonders, did I kill him? He bends down and removes Dan's helmet. His jaw is clenched and tears drip from the side of his eyes. The broken bone tents but does not break the skin. Dan smiles. "Jesus, kid. You better go fetch the apothecary."

A small crowd gathers. A child asks his mother, "What are the funny men doing?"

Josh is crying a little. "I'm sorry," he says.

A man grabs Dan by the arm, trying to pull him up. Another dials 911 on his cell phone. "Off with you peasants!" Dan shouts as he rises to his feet. One shoulder sags as he walks. The crowd steps back. They are obviously dealing with a crazy man.

"Josh, can you drive?" Dan says.

"No."

"Well, it seems like a good time to learn."

It takes them a while to get Dan into the car. As they drive to the emergency room, the car jerking down Farrington Highway, the police light still flashing, Josh is afraid of the traffic zipping past him in the opposite direction. They pass a roadside memorial, flowers surrounding a portrait of a dead teenage boy, remnants of a head-on collision. Josh clenches his jaw, even more aware of the danger of oncoming traffic, and he forces himself to apply more force to the gas pedal as he holds in sobs.

"Dude," Dan says. "Don't feel bad. I'm goddamn proud of you. Never feel bad about putting someone down who is giving you shit."

"I was so mad," says Josh, eyes glued to the road.

"Remember when I told you a man can't become a real man until he makes something out of wood? Well, that's just step one, the step that teaches you confidence and control. Step two is learning to not take shit from anyone. You get your ass kicked, you get your ass kicked, but this world, it shits on you something fierce, and a real man shits on it right back. But never be a sore loser. Stay in control. Start over. Fuck, my shoulder is killing me."

Josh considers this. “My dad made stuff.”

“I never really met your father, but I’m thinking he just took shit for too long. You let it build and that’s what happens. Never let it build. You see a shit storm coming, don’t take cover. The longer you hide from it alone, the scarier it gets. Go out there and meet it like a man.”

Josh’s driving smoothes out as they near the hospital. He wonders how his family would’ve turned out if his father had met whatever problems he was having head on at the beginning. Instead, he’d spoiled them all. He’d spoiled Josh’s mother, letting her do whatever she wanted. Their cars, their furniture, their little family vacations were all picked by Kai. The flowers she planted in the back, despite John’s allergy to pollen. He’d tolerated all her late nights at work. Kai even went to Vegas by herself once or twice. Even when John cooked, it was always food that Kai and Josh agreed upon as tasty—spicy beef curry, deep-fried drumettes, lasagna, and chili with shredded beef, no beans. Always too much, often skipped for beef jerky, and it was John who ended up taking the leftover food to work for lunch, despite the fact he didn’t really like any of these dishes. Even the Turducken was Josh’s idea, something he caught while channel surfing.

Aside from baseball, specifically the San Francisco Giants, Josh cannot think of one thing that his father took deep interest in. Standing at the counter, filling out forms for Dan, it dawns on him that just by filling out this medical form he’s learned more about this strange, kind, hot-tempered, wanna-be knight cop than he ever knew about his father.

Maybe the more time you spent with a person, the less you knew about them. They were ever-present shadows that melded into yours, and you tricked yourself into thinking they are just like you. Then the shadow jumps and materializes, flesh and bone, and the change is paralyzing because it destroys the dark notion of what you think is true.

On the other hand, it might just be about self-centeredness. How can you see anything if all you do is look inward? The answer is simple. You can't.

4

Banyan lies on a hospital bed wondering how people can sleep on their backs. Every time he tries, it feels as if his lungs cannot fully expand, like someone small is sitting on his chest. However, there's no sign of John Krill. He examines the cast on his right hand. Metal rods had to be inserted after he pulverized bones against the concrete wall. Caley told him it was the wall he was hitting, and he must admit, it makes more sense than him hitting a ghost with a rock jaw, but he still can't help but doubt reality. He ***saw*** John Krill. Even if he was really hitting the wall, couldn't it have been some phantom's trick? Well played, John, well played.

Caley hovers above him, shining a pen light in his eyes. She checks his eyes, ears, then blood pressure with unnerving professionalism.

"Where's Raimi?" Banyan asks.

"With my mother."

"When can I get out of here?"

"How did your talk with Dr. Sorensen go?"

Pretty well, he thinks. I lied my ass off and he seemed to buy it. He never mentioned John Krill to the shrink, just the wall, how the wall loomed over his mind and prevented him from getting sleep. When the doctor looked at him skeptically, like that's not near enough to make a man walk up to a wall in the middle of the night and shatter his hand on it, he had to give the doctor something else as well—his one night of cheating and how the guilt was overwhelming. The doctor perked up hearing this one. So he told the doctor about his fears, afraid of his wife, afraid that the other woman will find out he's off-kilter and not want to see him again, but mostly afraid that this whole mess will jeopardize his role in Raimi's life. Dr. Sorensen asked, "You're an English professor, right?"

"Yea."

"And you can't see the symbolism in breaking down a wall, creating a passage for escape?"

"Well, I teach mostly comp."

The doctor looked at him, not sure if Banyan was being serious or cracking a joke. Banyan, of course, saw the symbolism, But that wasn't it. The idea was that as he broke down the wall, John Krill would grow and grow, the translucent skin stretching as the wall shrunk, and once enough of the wall was gone, Krill would pop like a balloon. He knew how crazy it sounded, but that was what he was thinking.

He didn't really lie, he thinks, both his obsession with the wall and his infidelity were true. He just left out some juicy details, like how even now, as he closes his eyes after the intrusion of the pen light, the bacterial sparkles organize themselves into portraits of Kai, Josh, and Raimi, and shine in his vision like constellations.

Banyan returns to the present to answer Caley's question. "Doctor-patient confidentiality." he says, opening his eyes and winking at Caley.

"You're not funny," she says, then lets out her guttural sigh. "Why do you always think you're funny?"

He owes her a moment of seriousness. "It's the house. I was fine until we moved into that house. Maybe we should move." He wishes there was a way to give the house back to Kai and her son, minus the ghost, who would probably not be too kind to his widow.

"How? It would actually cost us money to sell the house and move. We don't have that kind of money."

"Well that's that then. Get me out of this goddamn hospital."

Caley sighs again.

"And stop fucking sighing. I hate that."

He gives her his best steely look and wonders what she's thinking. Does she want to have him committed? Does she plan to take Raimi away from him?

Caley turns to fold a blanket. She's wearing denim jean shorts and a loose blouse over a black camisole. It occurs to Banyan that she doesn't look comfortable unless she's wearing nurses' scrubs. He feels like picking a fight watching her fold the blanket, feels like if they divorced, he'd actually be doing her a favor. "Bet you got more than you bargained for, marrying me," he says.

Caley picks up another blanket to fold. "You mean I got less than I bargained for," she says, smiling.

"Look who's trying to be funny now."

Banyan flexes his right hand, winces, then conjures more pain to egg him on. "Is this working for you? Because it's not working for me."

Caley lets the words hang there while she folds. After she's done folding, she scans the room, probably looking for another chore. She spots a flowerless crystal vase filled with mildew and stagnant water. "Lazy. Probably from the last patient. Don't see why they didn't throw this out." She takes the vase to the bathroom and closes the door. Banyan hears water stream from the faucet. After a minute or so, she emerges with a clean vase. "Did you hear what I said?" Banyan asks.

She holds the vase up against the light. "Stop talking. Dr. Sorensen will prescribe you some medication, and we'll get out of here and pick up Raimi."

Caley picks up a tissue and dries the vase. As Banyan watches her carefully blot off tiny drops of water, he imagines another year with this woman. Another five. Ten years. Twenty. After that, it's pretty unimaginable. He's known it all along. He was never in love with his wife. Sure, there were times when he did love her, like when she refused epidural and gave birth to Raimi, and was on her feet within the hour and spirited her daughter out of the plastic basin filled nursery, but even that was more admiration than love. He did always admire her.

But he never looked at her with the desire to embrace her hard, squeeze her until his heart popped.

He thinks of John and Kai Krill, sadness turned to madness, the stuff serial affairs and Komatsu bulldozers were made of. Years of planting hate in a tiny Mililani Mauka garden—he didn't want to do the same with Caley. Banyan flexes his hand, now at the point of tears. "I cheated on you," he says.

A vase flies straight towards Banyan's face. After it hits his forehead, there's definitely someone sitting on his chest, for real this time, and as two knee braces clamp around his ribs, he's having a hard time breathing because bony hands are wrapped around his neck, squeezing as his heart races. He tries to twist out of her hold, but her knees dig in harder. He grabs a wrist with his still-functional left hand, and yanks, but one hand remains, fingernails digging into his throat. He's dizzy now and can't fight off both hands. Her face inches toward his, as she throws her weight to her arms. He swings his cast and cleaves the flesh on her cheekbone. She's off him now, holding her cheek, screaming at him. He jumps out of bed, raises the cast above his head like it's a caveman's club, takes deep breaths in between coughs, and waits for her next move.

5

When Xavier Teve Musashi Krill was born with jaundice, Dr. Chock told the Krills to stuff the newborn with as much fluid as possible. Since he wasn't too fond of breast milk, they invested in an assortment of aids—a breast pump, formula, and a contraption that embarrassed Kai, a bottle necklace with two thin tubes attached to it. She taped the ends of the tubes to her nipples and fed Xavier that way. The idea was that it would get Xavier used to the breast. But Xavier wasn't a fan, and Kai felt humiliated. It didn't help that whenever John saw this get-up, he burst into laughter. When Xavier turned three months old, he was put on formula permanently. Sometimes Kai imagined that this is why he became sick.

She'd seen women, in tabloids and real life, who dropped the pregnancy weight in three months, but Kai's body resisted, mostly because she justified her post-pregnancy gluttony by believing that she was giving her child as many nutrients as possible. After the switch to formula, she tried to control her diet, but instead of flattening, her stomach remained a loose roll of stretch-marked skin that sagged over her pants. The more weight she dropped, the more her breasts and stomach sagged, and it seemed to her that filling the sag up with fat made her look a lot better. She became an ardent fan of television shows on plastic surgery makeovers. When she mentioned plastic surgery to both her mother and husband, they were all for it, despite the cost, which made her feel even worse.

John was in college, and Kai never thought about how her husband, who'd only gotten as far as algebra in high school, must be struggling to catch up in math, all the way up to Calculus II. Instead, images of keggers, sex-hungry co-eds, and John reading poetry and playing an acoustic guitar to girls under the shade of a palm tree plagued her, despite the fact that John didn't like poetry or know how to play a guitar. It was at about this time that they had their first conversation on infidelity. She was bathing Xavier in a little blue plastic tub while John was lying in bed, trying to make sense of the numbers and letters in a math textbook. "Let's make an agreement," she said. "If you ever decide to cheat on me, have the decency to tell me and leave me first."

He looked up from his book. "You better do the same, because if I ever catch you cheating on me, I'll cut off your goddamn head."

Somehow that made Kai feel good, loved. "If you ever cheat on me, I'll cut off you-know-what."

"If you ever cheat on me, you better tell me right away. Then maybe I won't go nuts. But if I find out ten to twenty years later, find out I've wasted all my time on this looking like an asshole, I swear to fucking God, Kai, I will kill you."

His conviction comforted her. Her suspicions of his infidelity lapsed from obsession to fleeting moments of suspicion, usually following arguments concerning dirty dishes left on the night stand, or his saving cans for recycling but leaving them unrinsed all over the kitchen counter. But back then she never would have imagined that it would be her who would break the pact and that any conversation on the ideal way to handle potential cheating was couples kidding themselves. Who in their right mind would admit to an affair? She began to take her dishes to the sink after she was done eating, but then thought better of it. A cured bad habit could raise suspicion.

After Xavier's death and the move to Mililani, she began a series of affairs, starting with John's lawyer friend, her boss. The affairs eroded her respect for men in general. First off, most men were uglier naked than clothed. And second, sex excited them far too much—it was like throwing steaks to starving dogs. That first one, Rudy Kealoha, was short, fat, and ogre-ish, the physical opposite of John, and Kai wondered how he found suits that fit him. Despite his looks, the guy was confident and had a head full of trivia that he would blurt out any time the opportunity arose. Kai would say something like, "Hey, did you hear that Howard Cosell died?"

Then Rudy would say something like, "Did you know his real name was Howard Cohen but he changed it to Cosell when he was in college?"

"Hear about the earthquake in Japan?" Kai would ask.

Then Rudy would say something like, "That's nothing. A quake hit Japan in 1923 and took out over 100,000 people."

She liked the guy, though, and thought it was cute to watch all that confident bluster wash away during sexual intimacy. The state of his body made her feel much better about hers—thin now from the emotional wreckage of a dead son, though the loose skin was still there. But when he, who had a wife and child, began suggesting divorce and remarriage for the both of them, just because of the sex, Kai quit her job. The following weeks she feared every phone call and knock at the door, and she distracted her fear with the furious cleaning of her home. The image of her head on a pike in the front yard was not an easy one to shake. It was then that she finally consented to driving lessons from John, figuring that spending more time together would mend their marital problems.

She wondered if it was a ploy of John's to have baby Josh in the backseat during these lessons, to force her to be more careful. It seemed inappropriate since any one of the neighbors would have watched Josh during these lessons; just about the entire cul de sac worshiped John. She was hardly a natural driver, and every time she made a mistake, braked too hard, or began veering too close to the curb, John would say, "Jesus Christ, you trying to kill the kid?"

Josh, despite all the front seat antics, fell asleep on each outing, but the sound of rapid thumb-sucking would start up each time John yelled at Kai. He was a worse teacher than she was as a student, and the majority of the lessons would end with her tears. She wondered if he knew about the affair and was getting back at her. "You need to toughen up," he'd say. Maybe it was his mantra throughout the college-and-dying-child ordeal. What poor teachers the super-strong make.

The first thing Kai did after she got her license was look for a new job. By this time, she'd fallen in love with driving and wanted a job far from Mililani. Without a college degree or much work experience, the best she could do was the front desk at the Hilton in Waikīkī. Even this would have been out of her reach if not for the four years of Japanese she had taken in high school. They started her out as part-time and on-call, always the worst late-night and graveyard shifts. At first she hated the job. She was always tired and dealt too often with surly, sunburned tourists who'd spent too much time at the Tapa Bar. She resented John again, this time for being the one who had the college degree. It should have been her. She had higher academic aptitude. She'd taken calculus in high school.

But it was better than being at home. Her lack of cooking skills was one of John's favorite topics, so he took over that responsibility. Her inability to teach Josh how to do basic stuff, like put on his own shirt or use the potty made her feel like a failure as a mother. "You just have to be patient and consistent," John would say. She expected Josh to learn things over the course of a single afternoon.

Her home life consisted of lectures from her husband and incessant chatter from her son. She began boycotting John's gourmet fare; her dinners consisted of beef jerky, dried ika, or fresh vegetables dipped in any kind of hot sauce.

The period in which Josh discovered his own voice was the most difficult for Kai as a mother. God, the kid could talk, his favorite word of all time "why." It was exhausting. So despite being barked at by cantankerous old men, in English and Japanese and other languages she had a hard time identifying, she preferred work to home, preferred the gossip mill of her co-workers and the sometimes sweet tourist who would comment on how beautiful she was.

Working at a hotel is a dream occupation for those hell-bent on cheating. Twenty-four hour access to alcohol and private rooms, not much can beat it. The front desk gave her access to just about every tourist in the twenty-two acre resort, or at least those staying in the Tapa Tower. The flirtatious visitors, often there with their wives, were easy pickings. There was the Russian artist, the dentist from Pittsburg who satisfied her curiosity about balding white-haired men and sex, the Korean pop star, and the Pro Bowl running back who was the only one that made Kai feel ashamed of her body. Some were regulars who came to the Hilton a few times a year, and unlike her ex-boss, Rudy Kealoha, none were looking for permanent attachment. She was part of their vacation package, and sometimes, she would slip away from work early to go up to their rooms, which was of course a big no-no, and be back at home maybe a half an hour to an hour late, which was hardly enough time for John to suspect an affair.

This went on for ten years. Kai's guilt fueled her; her house was often the cleanest on Luapele Street. She took over washing the cars and doing the yard, which she filled with ti leaves, bougainvillea, dangling orchids, and a rock garden with a pond filled with koi, and decorated with a statue of a little boy pissing water in the pond. Josh emulated the statue once or twice, which were the only times Kai wanted to give him a serious spanking, pissing on her fish like that, but he was twelve the last time he did it, far beyond the age of slaps to his bottom. Kai and the neighbors, George and Kelly, the ones who taught her about flowers, and learned about plants from their dorm closet pot-growing endeavors, often traded secrets on fertilizer and fish foods that brought out the orange in koi.

All this time, she knew John suspected something was going on. He seethed each time she came home late, which was most of the time, though most of the time it wasn't because she had been sleeping with someone, just dawdling after work. Whenever he started an accusation, she postured like a cornered crab, lashing out defensively with vocal claws. By year three he didn't even greet her when she arrived home, just looked up from whatever he was doing, then down again. By year five, he didn't acknowledge her return at all. They had slept in different bedrooms when Josh was a baby, John with Josh in the boy's room, Kai in the master bedroom, the idea being that John was trying to acclimate his son to his own room, but she suspected it was because John refused to let illness go undetected with this son. By the time Josh was fine on his own, John had bought a queen and put it in the spare room. She never did say anything about that. They didn't say much to each other at all. Oddly enough, their sex life never completely stalled out. Her guilt fueled more than her cleaning; every now and then she'd visit him in the middle of the night, spend a sweaty, aggressive half hour there, ask if he was okay, then return to her room.

He had suspicions, often manifested in sloppy detective work. The medicine cabinet searched. Her purse searched. Imaginary missing condoms. Opened credit card bill envelopes. Car mileage recorded and checked off. Hacked e-mail. She'd had the wisdom to get rid of her cell phone long ago, and her lovers—what an odd, embarrassing word—called the hotel if they wanted to find her. The hotel's detective was more competent. She'd been caught going up to the room of the Korean pop star, a skinny kid with unusually clear skin, skin she was convinced was the product of a spicy Korean diet. She was fired on the spot.

She never knew if John had hired a private detective, or if he just figured that a strong suspicion, even if you lack evidence, means it's probably true. His feelings were ultimately confirmed by the bulldozer. What she did not see coming was arriving at home early after being fired and seeing her son sitting at the kitchen counter, with her pay sheets spread out, calculating her hours and writing them in a notebook. She snatched up her time sheets and walked upstairs, saying, "I quit that job." She was out of breath when she reached the top. It was a couple of days later that she caught Josh pissing in her koi pond.

Not having much in the way of employment recommendations, the best she could do was Zippy's—a Hawai'i franchise that was a crossbreed of coffee shop and burger joint, a sort of Hawaiian Bob's Big Boy with take-out. She was a waitress, once again part-time, on-call, with the worst shifts. After the scare with her son, she was done with the cheating. Considering the look of her co-workers at Zippy's, mostly forty-year-old grandmothers or greasy short-order cooks, she was confident she could stick with it. And she did for a year. Then the newest member of the Luapele Street Posse moved to the neighborhood—a bodybuilder firefighter named Roy Heap, his wife, and their two daughters.

At first it was the daughters that caught Kai's eye—adorable little things, three and two, with pierced ears and elaborately braided hair. After years of avoiding the posse, Kai found herself drawn to the nightly talk stories by the sight of the little girls. Their hyperactivity was cute instead of irritating. She watched them interact with their parents—the mother, a slightly overweight woman who wore Wonder Bras and tight slacks with vertical stripes, one of those women who had problems dropping baby weight, struck Kai as downright mean to her daughters, apparently taking great joy in a brutal re-braiding whenever the elaborate package of hair loosened. Kai assumed it was the mother who'd decided to get their ears pierced at such an early age.

The father, Roy, was the pushover, the one who would pull gummy bears from his pocket when their mother wasn't looking. The massive bulk of his body was clumsy—except for when he scooped up those girls, one in each arm, as if he were picking up socks off the ground. Kai half-expected him to pluck the girls up with his toes and catch them midair. The younger one stroked the back of his neck, while the older one took great joy in punching his cheeks or counting the acne scars on his face. The punches were feminine and cute, and Kai pondered whether she liked it because she was somehow taught all little girls are adorable or whether there was something buried deep in all people that simply made it so. It was as if adult males, and even most adult females, including Kai, could not resist.

There were exceptions, of course, like Mrs. Heap, and Kai's own parents. Her mother and father treated her more like a boy than a little girl—they were irritated when she was hyper. They trusted her to walk to school on her own from the age of five. She was allowed to get dirty, was arm-twisted into organized sports despite lack of talent, and instead of chores like cooking, laundry, and vacuuming, she mowed the lawn, washed and polished the car, and even painted the house once. She never got around to having her ears pierced, and could not remember ever having her hair braided. Fairy tales were forbidden. Her mother told her that they all taught some ridiculous lesson about how if you have a fucked-up single-parent childhood, it'll make you a better person. It dawned on Kai that when she got pregnant as a teen, the shock to her parents must have been doubly painful. This was not supposed to happen, considering how they raised her. It was the only time she sensed that her parents would have preferred a son.

Watching the little girls brought about questions. Was the loss of her child so hard to bear because, as a son, he was meant to redeem her, his gender a counter to her mistakes? Did her initial love for John stem from a secret desire to be a girly-girl, something her parents refused to let her be, a damsel in distress? Did she carry on with affairs because her attitudes concerning sex were like a man's—the more casual, the better? What would she have been like if she were raised like the Heap girls, disciplined by a strict mother, but disciplined in a pink fairy tale girly-girl environment? Just when you think you have yourself all figured out, two little girls move to the neighborhood with their pink tutus and plastic tiaras and force you to re-evaluate all over again. This was about the time John started building the wall around the house. He used to share comic books and aquariums with his son, but he didn't share his son's computer-game hobby.

With her husband and son gone days, with Roy's wife gone days as well, with her evening shifts and Roy's two to three day a week, twenty-four-hour work schedule, Kai had easy access to the Heap house, to the little girls, and later to Roy himself, who as a firefighter, was home on most days. When they took the relationship further and became work-out partners, Roy her new trainer, she came no closer to answering the questions brought up by his two little girls. But the questions faded like barbeque smoke while her body tightened from exercise and a singular thought tightened in her mind: I want this family instead of my own. I want a happy-go-lucky over-testosteroned husband, this man who looked like a product of Photoshop—a nerdy, pimply face superimposed on a body-builder. I want two little girls I can dress up like dolls. When Roy taught her the fundamentals of free weights, splitting up days into body parts, explaining the heart rate that needs to be sustained to optimally burn fat, she could not help noting the contrast between Roy and her husband—Roy's workouts often ended in exhausted laughter and Vietnamese French bread sandwiches instead of driving-lesson tears.

She knows now that she should have for once followed the cheating pact she'd made with John so long before, confessed before consummation, and asked for a divorce. But dishonesty has its own unstoppable momentum, like a swell-turned wave. She tried to goad John into action, divorce action, by calling the MTA, reporting an illegal structure surrounding the Krill home. And when John was the one who uncharacteristically began coming home late, beer on his breath, Kai just hoped that he would not ride the dishonest momentum for long, but would have the strength to fess up and admit an affair. After all, he was the strong one. She had no idea what he was secretly building, no idea that he'd laid off all his employees and shut down his small contracting business, and no idea he spent his nights welding sheets of steel to a bulldozer.

That morning—the morning it all blew up—the sound of the big trailer approaching the cul de sac woke her, but she figured it was the garbage man. Then she heard the bulldozer wake, its guts coughing up smoke from pistons firing, so she got out of bed and looked out the window. She watched it back off the rig trailer. She watched it rumble down Luapele Street. It paused in front of the Heap house, made a turn toward it, but then turned back toward the street and straightened out. It lurched, almost jumping, then headed downhill, fueled by a momentum of a different type. Kai turned on the television and waited.

After it was all over, Kai and Roy reached a silent understanding, and never spoke to each other again.

6

The only evidence of Dan's family can be found in framed pictures in his bedroom. Like the two other bedrooms and two baths, the space is small. His California king is pushed into a corner, and there isn't room for anything else but a night table, an electric fan, and a standing halogen lamp. The pictures of his family are arranged by generation, one generation to a wall. The first wall has a few grainy black-and-whites, one of a Chinese girl who must be Josh's age standing in front of a small 19th-century steam locomotive, holding a baby bundled in blankets. The other two pictures are almost identical—a Portuguese man's saggy, sun-beaten face, wearing long-sleeved white shirt and pants, sugar canes twice his height behind him. On the next wall, the next generation, the pictures are more numerous—a Hawaiian with boxing gloves crouching; the same man in full military dress; a worn, colored photo of a couple standing in front of a '57 Chevy; a hapa woman crouched in front of a water hose, cleaning mullet. The remaining two walls are pictures Josh has seen all his life—events like graduations, birthdays, ocean outings, and vacations to famous American landmarks—Disneyland, the Statue of Liberty, Wrigley Field. Baby Dan perched on his haole father's freckled shoulders. In general, the old ones are far more interesting, but there's one newer picture of a younger Dan in a tuxedo, standing beside a woman in bridal whites that interests Josh as much as the ancient black-and-whites. Josh puts the tray of scrambled eggs, bacon, and papaya down in front of Dan.

"You were married?" he says.

"Yup," Dan says, scooping up scrambled eggs to his mouth left-handed.

"What happened?"

"Here's an interesting fact you can Google. Cops have a higher divorce rate than any other job."

"Why?"

Dan gets most of the spoonful of egg in his mouth, but several bits drop onto his sling-wrapped arm. "Beats me," he says, chewing. "What's not to love?"

"Where is she now?" Josh asks.

Dan puts his spoon down and swallows. "Someplace where she will never be found."

Long pause. "Damn, Krill, you're so gullible. She's in San Jose married to some computer guy, last I heard. Tell your mom good eggs, by the way."

"I cooked those, jerk. And the bacon. She cut the papaya in half."

"Good, leave the cutting to her. You're a goddamn menace to society."

"I said I was sorry!"

Dan gives up on the eggs and eats the bacon. "There he goes again, gullible Krill."

"So what happened with the wife?" Josh asks.

"What can I say? Wasn't happy, took off. I deal with lunatics all the time, guys who lose it because their girlfriends or wives leave them. When it happened to me, I dunno, I just couldn't muster lunacy. Remember that screaming couple outside the karaoke bar? That's like the twentieth time I've seen that conversation. Pretty sick of it."

Josh picks up the tray. "I'm pretty sick of all of it," he says.

"He's probably a better guy than me anyway, the computer guy in San Jose," says Dan.

"Is my mom being nice to you while I'm at school?"

"She's been great. I feel bad. Told her she didn't need to do anything, but she's like a sneak thief with my laundry and dishes."

Josh stares at the grainy black-and-white of the Chinese girl. She looks nothing like Dan, whose Chinese blood has been diluted by three generations of Portuguese, Hawaiian, and haole fathers. The girl looks more like Cindy Chang, the pretty girl in Josh's Algebra class. Although it'd be hard to imagine the girl on the wall getting busted for leaving her cell phone on in class.

"I don't like leaving the two of you alone," Josh says.

"Jesus, you're like an old woman. Speaking of school, you better get your ass there pronto. Do me a favor and smuggle the papaya to school with you."

Dan only finished the bacon. "Alright," Josh says.

"Hey Krill. You're a goddamn prince." Dan points to the pictures on the wall. "Keep it up, and one day, you too will make the Wall of Fame."

Josh takes the plate to the kitchen, wraps the papaya in plastic, and sticks it in his back pack. He walks to his mother's room. The door is open, and Kai is crouched over her coffee table, working on a crossword. The design he'd settled on for the top of the table was of two koi intertwined. It was difficult to tell if the pair of fish were embracing, fighting, or trying to untangle themselves from one another. "Time to go, Mom."

On the drive to school, they pass wooden signs advertising 'ahi and laulau for sale. Josh glances past his mother to take in the beach. He thinks about the picture of the Chinese girl and wonders how she ended up here. Maybe she was the daughter of an immigrant shipped here to work as a maid. Maybe a mail-order bride boated over, summarily rejected by a Chinese laborer because her earlobes were too small, then forced to marry that grubby-looking Portuguese guy who worked the dirt of the plantation in long sleeves. He wondered what she'd thought of the beach, the ocean, as her ship docked, as people spat foreign words at her, people who dismissed her as stupid for not understanding English. He marveled at how much harder her life must have been than his, his mother's, Dan's, his father's, and even the people living out under tents on the Wai'anae Coast.

He looks over at his mother, frets over the sudden change in her—sullen and ghost-like her first week in Dan's house, she's now doing laundry, dishes, the crossword, and cutting papayas in half. She even talks to people on the phone, mostly to someone named Banyan. He has never known her to have friends, and is glad that she seems to have one, but there's something about the hushed tone of these conversations, coded, that makes him nervous.

They get to the high school, a series of dark cream and blue-trimmed buildings, some of which are mobile homes turned classrooms. The field lights tower over the landscape. Josh thinks of Cindy Chang, her cell phone going off in Algebra class, giggling, embarrassed. She's one of the pretty, popular ones, who tries her best to become invisible as she passes the big Hawaiian girls on her way to her locker. Cindy Chang, mail-order bride, yea right.

As he exits the car and gives his mother a vacant goodbye, he realizes that even though Kai's life has not been as hard as the life endured by Dan's Chinese ancestor, it's his mother, not Cindy Chang, who resembles the girl in the picture. They have the same fearful look, as if catastrophe possibly lurks around every corner. His mom looks like a scared kid. Maybe they are alike. Xavier Teve Musashi Krill was a mighty hardship, and here she is living with the cop from Nānākuli (who shot her husband no less—not that she cares—nor does he anymore), a guy he's not even sure she likes.

On the way to homeroom, Josh bumps into Michael Opio-Santos, AKA Kamealoha. The skinny guy has his arm around a girl who looks twelve. "Hey, Josh, haven't seen you since the popo busted up the camp. My mom asks about you."

"She goes to school here?" Josh asks, pointing to the girl.

"This is my girlfriend, Gina," Michael says. "She's supposed to be some kind of genius so she skipped two grades."

Gina rolls her eyes. Then the two start making out, tongue and all. Jesus Christ, Josh thinks.

Marching to homeroom, Josh thinks about people suffering in this world, leaving behind only a few kids and some grainy photos to testify that they were here at all. His chest burns—peppered beef jerky indigestion, he suspects. Why the hell can't people see that 19th-century Chinese girl in front of the train, and make themselves happy? He sits on a bench and takes the papaya out of his backpack. The morning bell rings as he is scraping at the flesh of the fruit with a plastic spoon, hoping that the chunks of sweetness will soothe his heartburn.

7

Banyan, dressed in jeans and a hospital gown, walks barefoot from Queen's Hospital to Kalani's Used Cars. As he enters the graveled lot, cast on one arm, stitched scar on his forehead, and bruises around his neck, he's amused that this may be the first time in American history that a used car salesman will not give a prospective buyer the time of day. However, the salesman, a Korean in short sleeves and tie, is quite nice. There's just enough money in his checking account for Banyan to buy a Chevy S-10 beater. The Korean man, whose name is Dong Jin, not Kalani, sells him the pick-up and sends Banyan on his way. Before Banyan leaves, he asks, "Who's Kalani?"

Dong Jin shrugs. "Just sound catchy eh?"

Banyan peels out in the used car gravel pit and heads for the freeway.

There's a lot on Banyan's mind as he drives towards Honolulu Community College. First off, there's Raimi. He hasn't seen her in a few days; this is the longest he's been away from her. Seeing her would be first on his to-do list if Caley hadn't filed a temporary restraining order against him an hour after she tried to kill him.

Then there's Kai and her son. It's time to get them off the beach. He has no idea where he'll take them, or if they'll even want to leave. He has to ask for sick leave, he has to find a place to stay, he has to go to Longs and pick up his medication ... he's missing something, he just can't place it. He pushes in the clutch and shifts to fourth, cast slipping off the gear stick, and remembers. He needs to buy slippers.

It's Monday, but past mid-semester (both professors and students slacking at this point), so the lot isn't full. After he parks and gets out, the security guard pulls up in a golf cart. "Can I help you?" the guard asks, but it sounds more like an accusation than a question.

"It's me. Banyan Mott."

The guard looks at Banyan skeptically before he recognizes him. "Oh," he says.

"Sorry, parking permit is in the other car."

Before the guard responds, Banyan is heading to Building 7, fifth floor. His Eng 100 class, the one Kai is taking, started five minutes ago.

When he gets to the classroom, the students look at him as if he's the first interesting thing they've seen all semester. Nakashima, who's been covering for him, grabs Banyan by the arm, pulls him out to the hall, and shuts the door. The excited whispers from the classroom flood through the crevices along the doorframe. "Ho, he went nuts I think," says a male student.

"Looks like knowing grammar got him far in life," a female student says. The class laughs. Banyan has to admit, it's a good one.

"What's been going on with you?" Nakashima asks, anxiously scratching at the pellet moles on his neck. Banyan is afraid that a pellet will dislodge and blood will spurt from his colleague's neck.

"Been in the hospital. Gonna take sick leave. Hey, Kai Krill show up for class? I didn't see her in there."

"Hold on. Let me grab my grade book. It's inside."

Banyan grabs Nakashima's arm. "Nah, you'd know her. Thirty-ish, sits in the front row, smart. Pretty as hell, too."

Nakashima frowns. "Oh God."

"Yea, I know," Banyan says.

"We just had a mandatory sexual harassment workshop, too. I guess we have you to thank for that."

"Stop being silly. She isn't in there, right?"

"Nope, no one fitting that description has been in this class since I took it over. Banyan, you should slow down. I don't know if tenure will cover this."

"Keep cracking jokes."

Nakashima shrugs. "Who's joking?"

Banyan leaves Nakashima and heads back to the stairwell. "You sure you're OK?" Nakashima says as Banyan walks the hall. "Maybe you should put in for sabbatical."

Sabbatical. A sabbatical from life in general would hit the spot right about now.

An hour later, Banyan drives along the Wai'anae Coast, stopping at each beach park. He's not really looking at the people, just looking for Kai's Sentra. However, he can't help but see them, homeless in worn-out clothes hanging laundry, filling water bottles, cooking, napping, playing—basically going on about the business of life. One guy naps in a small, zipped up tent, his ankles and feet sticking out of the doorway. It looks as if someone dropped a house on him. At the next beach park, a woman gently pulls at a pan handle buried by coolers, stuffed animals, sofa pillows, and Costco toilet paper. Just as she gets the pan out, everything avalanches at her feet. At another park, a shirtless boy and a poi dog dig a hole in the sand and watch it fill with water. The boy moves up shore a few feet and digs again while the dog yanks on the leash and drags the boy to the shore break.

As Banyan gets closer to Pōka'ī Bay, he spots a strip mall. He stops by Longs Drugs and picks up a package of white V-neck tee shirts and slippers. He also submits his Vicodin subscription, the pain in his hand rudely reminding him to do so. As he sips on a soda and waits for his meds, it comes to him. Josh goes to Wai'anae High. All he has to do is go there and wait for the kid to get out of school. When he gets back to the pick up, pops a pill, and struggles to get a tee shirt on, he remembers why he wanted to keep the hospital gown.

Wai'anae High School has the reputation of being one of the toughest schools in the state—not academically tough—tough like chuck steak gristle is tough. As the students stream out of their classrooms, Banyan can see why. Some of the guys strut through campus with eighteen-inch biceps, tattoos, and more facial hair than Banyan could grow in a year. The girls, several taller than he is, gossip out front, gold bracelets clanging as they cup their hands by their mouths, whispering secrets to each other. Jesus, they look twenty-five, he muses. He's sure there's a future sumo or MMA champ in there. A future Fulbright scholar? Probably not.

Most of the boys wear baggy denim or board shorts. Some wear beanies or caps. Several strum ukuleles, others carry limp, almost empty back packs. The girls, the big ones in tee shirts and jeans, the skinny ones in hoodies or halters, walk in packs like the boys, chattering, pointing, and laughing. It's the sheer volume, the collective roar of the students that jars Banyan out of his drugged stupor.

The smaller kids skitter through the afterschool crowd, walking around twenty inch rimmed cars blasting hip hop or Hawaiian music—dubs and sounds—Banyan wonders how these kids scrape together enough cash for twelve-inch sub woofers and shiny rims. Some of the younger ones head for the bus stop, others group up with their friends in semi-circles, talking, howling, and swearing while they punch each others' arms. Just as Banyan rifles his memory and coughs up the image of the wallet-sized picture Kai showed him a couple times, he spots Josh talking to a pretty Chinese girl. He's tall and thin, and has a slight paunch, probably from too much fast food. He has a serious, slightly anxious look too old for his years. Throw twenty pounds and a pair of crow's feet on him, he'd look older than Banyan. Josh turns his head to and fro, like he expects life to creep up on him and smack him on the back of the head. Banyan gets out of the pick-up and approaches. He walks around two boys sparring with Muay Thai knees and elbows.

Just as he gets to Josh, a uniformed cop in an arm sling steps in front of him. He's much shorter than Banyan, and he's smiling, but he doesn't look like he's got making friends

in mind. He puts his palm on Banyan's chest and gently pushes. "Who the fuck are you?" he says, still smiling.

"Oh, I'm Professor Mott," says Banyan. He hates calling himself a professor or doctor, but figures this is a good time to use the title.

Josh looks at Banyan. The Chinese girl, sensing trouble, walks off. If she actually had school books, Banyan imagines she'd be hugging them right now. Josh shrugs and looks at the cop. "I don't know him. He doesn't look like a professor either. He looks like a psycho."

Banyan puts his hands up like he's being arrested. "Call me Banyan. I'm a friend of your mother's."

By now a curious crowd is forming around the three of them, chattering pidgin in whispers. Josh and the cop look at each other, and seem to recognize the name. "I wanted to help out," Banyan says.

Josh furls his brow. "I don't even know you."

"I bought your house." Banyan doesn't know what else to say.

"You what?"

"In Mililani. I bought it."

Some of the kids whisper, "Kick his ass." They feel the heat coming off the cop. Banyan's a bit disturbed by the lack of charity considering he's standing there in a cast, but supposes that since the cop has an arm in a sling, it's supposed to be a fair fight. However, Banyan gets the feeling that all of them are sure he's the one who will catch a beating. "This was a mistake," says Banyan. "I'll talk to your mom."

That sets the kid off. Now Josh is the one throwing out heat as he charges Banyan. The cop wraps an arm around Josh's waist and pulls him back. Banyan takes a few backward steps, and slips off the curb, almost falling. This brings laughter from the crowd. Josh is screaming now, spit flying from his mouth. "You stay the fuck away from my mom!"

The crowd cheers. The cop, his hand gripping the back of Josh's neck, whispers in Josh's ear, which settles him down. Josh walks off to the cop's car, gets in, and watches from behind the windshield. The cop turns and faces Banyan, still smiling. He sticks out his hand. "Dan."

It's his right hand, the one that's attached to the slinged arm that's slightly extended, so Banyan has to twist his left to shake. He wonders why the cop wants to shake with his bad arm.

"I got this now," Dan says.

Banyan shrugs. "OK. Was just trying to help."

Dan glares at the crowd, stares at each kid until they walk away. The crowd disperses in murmurs. He turns back to face Banyan. "The kid is with me now," he says. "Her too."

Banyan turns and takes a couple of steps toward his pick up. He stops, then faces Dan, who's still standing there grinning. "What'd you tell him, to calm him down like that?"

Dan stands there thinking, like he's wondering if he should let Banyan in on the secret. His grin disappears, his face deadpan. "I told him, don't worry. If I ever see this guy around you or your mother, I'll fucking kill him."

"Oh."

Banyan heads for the S-10, thinking back to August, the beginning of the school year, when his biggest problem was a tiny, pot-bellied man in a "Kiss me, I'm Tahitian" tank top hanging around the house. Boy, does he long for those days.

8

Two months into algebra, and it was Cindy Chang who turned her cell phone off, put it in her Coach bag, and talked to Josh. Kneeling on her chair, she leaned over, exposing her black-bra'd cleavage under her loose halter. "Hey, are you that kid, you know, your dad?" She asked before class started, while the teacher, Miss Wang, a math major from Taiwan whom Josh could barely understand, handed out Xeroxes of the week's chapter.

"Yea."

"Wow. It's like you're a celebrity."

It spread after that. He expected the worst, wisecracks that his dad was nuts, further discovery that he had been homeless, and maybe a punch or two in the face for being such a freak. But it didn't go down like that. After lunch on that same day, a two-year senior, Kaika Bustamante, put his bare, tattooed arm around Josh as he walked out of the cafeteria. "Your dad was the fucking man," he told Josh. "That's how I wanna go out, hard like that."

Kaika slapped Josh on the back, then the two separated. But others saw. Being touched by Kaika Bustamante and living to tell the tale, that gave you some sway at Wai'anae High. Everyone knew that nineteen-year-old Kaika was one of the up-and-coming drug dealers on the Leeward Coast. He drove a tricked out Escalade to prove it.

The big boy with the Samoan fro who kicked Josh in the face and stole his bike back in August saw Kaika Bustamante give Josh his props. His name was Al Lolotai, named after the first Samoan to play in the NFL. His friends and family called him "Lolo," which meant "idiot" in Hawaiian. Lolo approached Josh after school, afro pick firmly planted in head. He apologized for stealing Josh's bike and agreed with Kaika Bustamante's sentiments. Josh's dad was the man, and he should be proud.

So as Cindy Chang sits across from him, downloading ring tones into her cell phone, he's wondering if his dad's suicide got him a date at McDonald's. He was invisible for two months, the only other kid he talked to was Michael, and now Cindy Chang is asking him if he likes McDonald's or Jack-in-the-Box fries better. She puts down her phone, and answers before he can. "McDonalds fries are the bomb," she says, sticking three in her mouth.

He wishes they were at the movies, so he wouldn't have to look at her face. The eye shadow and lipstick make him feel like he's out of his league; her brutal prettiness forcing his head down after each glimpse. She removes a lacquered chopstick from her hair, re-bundles her highlighted tresses, and inserts the chopstick, her armpits bare and unwrinkled. She picks up her phone again. "So what was with that weird-looking guy with the broken arm and the cop today after school?"

"The guy is stalking my mom or something. The cop is my mom's boyfriend. We live with him." The boyfriend bit is a lie, but he doesn't know how else to explain it.

Cindy, playing Tetris on her phone, says, "I know what you mean. Guys are stalking my mom all the time."

The tempo of the Tetris music quickens. Josh pictures the shapes raining from the top of the screen, Cindy flipping and spinning them, trying desperately to make horizontal lines of blocks without gaps. "So why did your dad lose it?" she asks, without looking up.

Though the question is personal, Cindy asks it with the same casual tone as she used when comparing McDonald's and Jack-in-the-Box fries. He's glad she's so distracted by the game, so she can't see him staring at her. Amazingly, she only has one piercing in each ear as far as he can tell, (unlike most of the other girls at Wai'anae, who seem to cram as many holes in their earlobes as possible), but when she flicks her tongue while rapidly pushing buttons, she exposes a barbell piercing. Josh is thoroughly impressed. He gets up off his side of the booth and slides in next to Cindy. Nervous, he points to the cell phone display. The blocks are really falling now. Cindy inches closer to him, so he can see the screen better. "I don't know how to explain it," he says, "but it's because his life looked like that."

Cindy gets it and seems pretty impressed with the analogy. "I forgot, you went private school," she says.

After McDonald's, and browsing videos at Blockbuster, Josh and Cindy end up at her house. The living room has more framed pictures than Josh has ever seen in one room—pictures of Cindy as a baby line the top of an old electronic organ missing several white keys, frames in formation cover the long cabinet, even the flat-screen television is framed with stickers from a photo booth, most of these pictures of Cindy with friends. Kim Taylor Reece prints hang from the walls—black-and-whites of female hula dancers in kahiko poses, topless except for strategically placed maile leis. Both Cindy's mother and grandmother work at Ko 'Olina, the mother a banquet waitress, the grandmother a security guard. They work nights, so Josh and Cindy have the house to themselves. Cindy drops her purse on the sofa, turns on the TV, and heads to her room to change. Josh sits and zones out on ***Biker Build Off.*** A Japanese guy named Chica builds a blue chopper that looks made for a super hero. Cindy walks in front of him in sweats and a sleeveless T-shirt, heading to the kitchen. When she returns, she sits on the sofa and hands Josh a martini glass. "It's an appletini," she says.

"When does your mom get home?" Josh asks.

Cindy shrugs. "A few hours."

They sit there as Cindy flips through TV stations. Nervous, Josh downs his appletini. Cindy decides on a channel. "This is my favorite show," she says. It's ***Sex and the City.***

As far as Josh can tell, Cindy's favorite show is about these four old ladies who drink and screw and complain about men, a lot. It makes him sad because they're older than his mom, and he starts thinking that this is how his mom wants to live, maybe how she always wanted to live. Instead, she got knocked up in high school, had a kid who died, and ended up in Mililani Mauka. He thinks of the other mothers on Luapele St., how they always struck Josh as way more normal than Kai, and how he wished that she was more like them—they all seemed to go to bed at nine or ten while Kai was often up till three AM watching TV, they all cooked dinner after getting home from work, usually some variation of boneless, skinless chicken breast, and they were all up, packing their kids into their SUVs, when Josh headed to school. Kai would on occasion still be sleeping when Josh got back home in the afternoon.

"I want to live in New York someday," says Cindy, wiping make up off her face with cotton balls and baby oil.

The man who showed up at school today, Banyan. The way Josh acted. He felt like a fraud, a boy trying to act like a man and wonders if he'd have even been able to lose his temper like that if Dan hadn't around to catch his back.

One of the old ladies gets naked and mounts some haole guy. The nudity makes Josh uncomfortable. He thinks of health class the other day, how the teacher told the class that almost twenty-percent of Americans have herpes. He figures all these old ladies in this TV show must've been spreading that shit for years, especially the naked one, who is now really moaning it up.

Cindy puts her hand on Josh's thigh, and he reacts by nearly jumping out of his skin. She leans in to kiss him, and as her lips press against his, he forgets all about his mother and the TV show. They kiss in sips, sitting side by side, until Cindy announces it's time for him to go. Her mother will be home soon. As he leaves the house, she stands in the doorway, adorable in her sweats, winks and says, "I'll show you more tomorrow after school."

Exuberant, Josh decides to jog back to Dan's. As he jogs and shadowboxes up Farrington Highway, the smell of baby oil still fresh, he knows that he'd marry Cindy Chang in a second. Was this what his dad was feeling when he first kissed Kai?

Was it what drove Banyan to show up at his school, all busted up with a broken arm? He understands these guys a bit better now. A feeling like this—you can't let it go.

The next day at school, Josh finds out Cindy isn't feeling the same thing. She's walking the halls holding hands—with Lolo of all people. Devastated, Josh skips his last class and goes to the beach. He runs across sand, takes off his shirt, and jumps in the water. He turns on his back and backstrokes away from the beach. He alternates between front and back strokes, sputtering out salt water. He looks like a swimming rotisserie chicken still on the spit.

As he swims back to shore, two things occur to him. First, Cindy is a goddamn bitch for doing what she did to him. Second, if it's true that twenty percent of Americans has herpes, chances are his mother, with all her cheating, has it, too. Hell for all he knows, Cindy could have it. And maybe he's a lousy kisser. Of course, it'd be unfair to judge his kissing based on that one night. It's the first time he kissed anyone.

He wishes he had never gone to Cindy's house, but hopes that if he sticks it out, maybe helps her with algebra, Cindy will forget about Lolo as quickly as she has forgotten about him. Josh dreams that she is his girlfriend, pictures of the two of them added to her living room, maybe those photo booth stickers that line the frame of the TV, Josh and Cindy smiling cheek-to-cheek, framed by red hearts, blue stars, and donuts glazed pink.

What would his father do in this situation? Probably wait like a sap until Cindy loved him back. What would Dan do? Whack her over the head, and carry her back to the castle? No, Dan told Josh about his wife and how he'd just let her take off and hook up with some computer tech guy in San Jose.

Josh sits on wet sand and buries his feet. It's the thinking that's driving him crazy. Even though he and his mother lived on the beach for months, it's the first time he's swum in ages, so he has a stark farmer's tan. The sun beats on his back, and he feels sunburn setting in. He presses his fingers against his red shoulders then lifts them. White fingerprints fade. He puts his shirt back on and walks up the beach, thinking about Cindy. He wishes he had Lolo's afro pick so he could stab it through his skull and pierce the feelings part of his brain.

9

Banyan and Bart walk into the Carballo house, one of the biggest on Luapele Street, a yellow two-story with four bedrooms and three baths. Bart's body sags as he climbs the stairs. His hand grips the wall, which has stickers of glow-in-the-dark moons and suns and framed illustrated birth certificates of his three children, as if being born were some sort of personal achievement.

"You sure it's OK if I stay here?" Banyan asks.

"Yea, take Lianne's room."

Banyan walks in the soon-to-be superstar's bedroom. Posters of surfers and rock stars cover the pink walls. The telephone, also pink, is smashed to bits on the bed stand. Bart's been down lately, as it seems the chances of his wife and kids coming home from California are getting slim, which may explain the phone. Banyan pops a Vicodin, lies down on his back and closes his eyes. He reaches to his side, his hand searching for Raimi, who of course is not there. He stands and looks out the window. He can see his house perfectly from here. The Volvo pulls up to the driveway. Caley, and what looks like a Buddhist monk, get out of the car.

Banyan is tempted to head across the street to see what's going on. But after a few minutes, he gets it. The monk walks the perimeter of the concrete wall, fanning each section with a handful of ti leaves. Then he removes a bottle from what looks like a holster, and walks the perimeter again, this time dripping liquid along the wall. He thinks Caley made a good decision, calling upon the representatives of the supernatural. The only problem is, Banyan doubts John Krill is a Buddhist. Besides, ever since Banyan pulverized the bones in his hand, there's been zero sign of John. Banyan doubts that it's because he showed the ghost some sand. It's probably because, supernatural phantom or not, Krill's just as scared as Banyan is of dealing with the only adult left in that house: Caley Mott.

When Caley and the monk leave in the Volvo, Banyan turns on the computer in Lianne Carballo's room to check his e-mail. Besides the usual spam from campus and porn sites, Kai has e-mailed him several times. He opens and reads. She doesn't know what's been going on with him the past few days, but she describes her week as exciting. She re-tells Banyan about getting off the beach and living with a cop with a broken collar bone (she already told him about it on the phone). She also discovered simple, fleeting bliss, standing out in the rain with arms and tongue extended, suggesting that Banyan give it a whirl. The letters are never pleading or desperate for reply, just status reports with a vivid description or two, how the cop's fractured bone is mending into a lump the size of a golf ball, or how the cop is armed to the teeth with medieval weaponry, or how the cop calls her son either "Krill" or "Prince," how he calls her "Big Krill," sometimes making her feel like a marine invertebrate or the sixth man on an NBA basketball team. The letters never speak of contentedness or sadness, never give specifics of the nature of Kai's relationship with the cop.

Banyan replies. He tells her about breaking his hand and ending up in the emergency room, then about how he confessed to Caley about the affair, which almost got him killed. He talks about the restraining order, and how much he misses his daughter, and how much he misses Kai. He also describes the run-in he had with Josh and the cop—Dan—and how he hopes the kid isn't still upset. He wants to meet.

After he finishes writing the e-mail, Banyan looks out the window. The Volvo pulls up. This time Caley has a priest blessing the wall, and oddly enough, the guy is using ti leaves and a bottle of liquid, just like the monk.

Kai's reply comes in. She definitely wants to meet him. He picks downtown.

Downtown Honolulu is a far cry from what it was a decade ago, a sort of mini-parallel to Rudy Giuliani and his clean-up of New York City. Banyan suspects that there must be similar clean-ups going on all over the country, local governments sweeping out the undesirables, the criminalized homeless, the con men, the drug dealers, the prostitutes. Banyan, who once attended a teacher's conference in Portland, Oregon, is reminded of that city now. Downtown Honolulu is a Portland-under-construction, a mixture of trendy restaurants, bars, and art galleries. One of these seems to deal exclusively in chandeliers and other light fixtures, another in geometric orange sculptures. They are even making lofts on the second stories of hundred-year-old buildings. But some of the seediness is still there. Old men with cigarettes and shabby clothes stand outside the run-down bars that serve canned beer. Women with bodies defeated by drugs, age, and childbirth loiter on street corners. Storefronts deal in pornography and Chinese herbs.

Banyan is meeting Kai at Indigo's—a trendy restaurant/bar that serves about twenty different types of martinis, most based on some kind of fruit. Banyan orders a bloody martini, which as far as he can tell is just a Bloody Mary in a martini glass. The bartender, a lean, muscled haole woman who obviously spends a lot of time at the gym, probably fighting off age, takes orders from bankers, attorneys, wannabe real estate moguls, and university professors. The younger crowd comes later, a mix of every race imaginable, the only singles' scene Banyan is aware of where a woman of sixty, hair dyed red like Lucille Ball, can sip a martini one table away from a group of athletic-looking affluent young men who probably spend most of their free time mountain bike riding or canoe paddling.

When Kai arrives, she has the look of a relic, a woman ten years out of how clubs used to be—ones for local, ethnic people like Oceans, and the ones for haoles—Caucasians, like Hard Rock Café. The attire is just as expensive, but more earthy and casual now, but Kai is wearing a shiny pink halter top, tight black bell-bottomed slacks, and high heels. Her hair used to be dried out, flat, dulled by exposure to beach air and short-order-cook grease. Now, cut, highlighted and pulled back in a chignon, it looks sleek and stylish. She is even wearing make-up. She is, in fact, stunning, and Banyan takes back his initial judgment of her, that she was pretty but not beautiful. It wasn't the dull, ashy skin that threw him off, it was the hair. Banyan, like most men, never takes hair into consideration when judging a woman's looks, unless of course it's an obvious mess, but now he sees for the first time why women are so obsessed and spend so much money on their manes. Kai takes a seat across from him.

"Jeez, you look fantastic," Banyan says.

She smiles. "And you look like a train wreck."

Her foot brushes against his under the table.

"What are you up to, Banyan?" she says. "Is our new game teasing rich alcoholics and making fun of young girls' husband-hunting expeditions?" She picks up the martini menu. "Wow. The martini has come a long way."

He feels self-conscious now, like a man who should not be sitting with this woman, but taking her order instead. "I don't know. It's sort of hard to make fun of this place and these people. I overheard one guy talking about how Dr. Melfi is actually Tony Soprano's consigliere."

"Never watched that show," she says, looking at the menu.

A waiter, who reminds Banyan of himself ten years ago, takes their order. Banyan is going to get another bloody martini, while Kai orders a nasty-sounding concoction, with strawberry and pineapple juice in it. "Well, this is no fun," she says. "Why did we meet here?"

Because, despite the fact that it's not true, he wants to put his problems on the side for a bit and feel like they're dating like normal people. "Look at these people," he says. "This would have been me if I'd bought a condo in town instead of a house in Mililani; these are the people I would like to be when I'm in my fifties and the kid is long gone at some prestigious college. I envy them."

"I see haoles and wannabe haoles. People who like the notion of being members of health clubs and environmentally sound. People who indulge in foreign beers, find chicken-fighting to be monumentally cruel, and spend their free-time designing self-promoting blogs."

She gets him going. "People who believe second-hand smoke is as lethal as nuclear waste," he says.

"People who are afraid the whole island will blow up if fireworks are lit every New Year's Eve, but some of them own handguns and assault rifles," says Kai.

"People who recycle cans and bottles and drop them off at the depository with eight-cylinder SUVs."

"People who volunteer for animal shelters, but buy handbags produced by little Chinese girls working sixty-hour weeks."

"People who complain about traffic, but drive to work alone."

"People with hobbies like photography, painting, travel, and sailing. People who think that their lives so interesting, they should write a book."

This one shames Banyan a bit. He's always wanted to write a book. Two girls at the next table are chatting about a burlesque show they're going to see later. Apparently, burlesque shows are chic now, sort of like home stripper poles for exercise. Tramp stamps, ginko biloba pills, stripper poles, tongue rings for better fellatio, and sex caught on tape on college campuses. He hopes this is not the world Raimi will inhabit, but certainly sees it as preferable to a GED, a teen pregnancy, and a series of failed fast-food jobs to cover the expenses of a drug habit. "So what's going on with you and the cop?" Banyan asks.

She pauses, thinks. "Crazy."

"What?"

"He shot my husband." Kai puts a hand over her mouth, laughing.

"What?"

She's laughing hard now, tears building. "It's not funny," she barely manages to get out.

Banyan nods as she gulps her martini. She rubs her face. What a nutcase, Banyan thinks. Just like me.

"He's good for my son," she says.

"I could be good for your son," says Banyan.

She seems to mull this one over. The two girls who were talking about the burlesque show are greeted by two men in striped dress shirts with big collars. The taller of the two tosses his wallet and keys on the table as if he's marking his spot.

"He's a bit weird," says Kai. "He makes armor during his free time. The kind you'd see at a Renaissance Fair. A couple of days ago, he and Josh were messing around in their get-ups and Josh broke the guy's collarbone. Poor kid felt so bad. Me too."

"You told me," says Banyan, "in e-mail."

The waiter comes back and Kai extends two fingers, silently ordering another round. Banyan isn't finished with his yet, so the waiter tells her she can't order two until the other drink is finished. She grabs Banyan's drink and gulps it down. She extends her two fingers again. The waiter shoots Banyan a sympathetic smile. The girls at the next table over are arguing with the two striped shirt guys about whether strippers make more money than airline pilots. Apparently, one of the striped shirt guys is a pilot for Hawaiian Air and is proud that he makes over ninety grand a year.

"So the wife gave you the boot, huh?" ask Kai.

"Yea," Banyan says. He feels the liquid build up in his eyes, and tries to keep his lids open, hoping that the air will dry tears. He feigns exhaustion and rubs his eyes, but they well again. He tilts his head back, using gravity to prevent the pools from overflowing. Kai pulls her chair over beside him and hugs him. He brings his head back down and the pools spill. Kai's eyes well, too. "You asshole," she says, "you're making me cry now."

They sit there like that embracing, tears wetting their cheeks. Banyan closes his eyes hard and the bacterial sparks form constellation portraits of all the people he's sorry to. Caley, Josh, Kai, John, both the menehune and actual version, and Raimi, most of all. He squeezes Kai. "How did I fuck things up so bad?"

Kai pulls away and laughs. "You're talking to a pro at fucking things up, and I don't even know."

"Don't you leave me for that cop," he says.

Banyan pulls himself together and gulps down his bloody martini. The waiter approaches, looks at the two of them, and decides to return later. The striped shirt guys side-eye Banyan with disappointed looks. Banyan feels like a child. "Stay with me," he says.

Kai nods.

As Banyan and Kai head out of downtown towards Waikīkī, he thinks maybe adults are not so different from children and only wear disguises of size, language, and body hair over their tiny brains and hearts.

10

When Banyan tells Kai about being haunted by John Krill, she almost believes it—well, a part of it. The menehune bits and pieces—the tank top and sweats, the fedora and smoking, Hell being in Tahiti—all of that strikes her as bullshit, but the small, dark figure patrolling the wall at night, the man with skin being stretched to its breaking point, fooling Banyan into shattering his own hand, that *felt* like John. Besides, who was she to say that menehunes or ghosts do not exist? Did she believe in them? No. But did she fear them? Absolutely. She remembers her mother telling her to not sleep with her feet facing the door, or the menehunes will come get her. She didn't believe in menehunes, but after that she also never slept with her feet facing the door.

As she and Banyan sit cross-legged in bed, she imagines the history of his marriage. Meeting Caley when he was at that age where after a hundred trips to the club too many, he was thinking that he needed to start taking life more seriously. Perhaps a three year relationship with no ring, too long for the woman, not long enough for the man. Then the thought: if I'm not going to marry her, what the hell am I doing here? Never thinking that if he was really that much in love with her, he would have proposed two-and-a-half years before. But by then it's too late—after all this time, he owed it to her, didn't he?

The over-priced white dress, the rented tuxedo, the ring worth two month's salary. The other friends getting married left and right. When are you two getting married? The question posed at every barbeque, birthday party, and other venue of excuse to get too drunk.

Then the kid. It's just time to have a kid, right? Then the dozen or so different ways to say: "I hate you." Why don't you spend more time with the baby? I hate you. Boy, you really gained a lot of weight. I hate you, fat ass. Can you please fill the ice trays? I hate you. We should buy a house. I hate you (but I want you to be financially bound to me, so you can't leave, and I can hate you forever).

Kai reaches for her purse on the bed stand, and takes out a pen. "You don't see him except at the house, right?"

"Yea, only at the house. "

She puts the purse back, sits so that her back leans against Banyan's chest, and then grabs Banyan's cast and holds it out in front of her. "Stay still," she says.

She begins to write on the plaster. She's using a ballpoint, so it takes some effort to create a black line thick enough to stand out. "Where should we live, me, you, Josh, and Raimi?"

"Before we do anything, I have to work on some way of getting her back, at least part-time," he says.

As much as she adores his face, his humor, and his quirky imagination, his love for his daughter is his best trait. Banyan loves Raimi like Kai loved Xavier, like she should have loved Josh. She sees it again: the non-descript house, the small yard, the teenage step-brother and little step-sister playing in the sprinklers. Maybe a tree swing? Bliss is not bliss without a tree swing.

Kai retraces and darkens black lines. "I love swings."

As she draws, she feels Banyan's restlessness, like he desperately wants to go get a drink of water. She grabs onto his cast harder, presses the pen down on plaster, and digs.

"Haunted house in Mililani Mauka," Banyan says, "seems so unlikely."

"There has to be a first. You can't have a community without a haunted house."

She twists the cast a bit, forgetting that moving his forearm that way might hurt him. She gently brushes his fingers as if to say sorry. He doesn't seem to feel anything, though; he's just a man locked in his own thoughts.

"Wonder if you have to disclose that when you sell," he says. "You know, like asbestos or lead paint."

She's concentrating on her drawing. "They don't make houses with asbestos or lead paint anymore."

"Yea, didn't think they made houses with ghosts anymore either."

She finishes her picture and lets go of the cast. "Done," she says.

Banyan shifts so his head hangs over her shoulder. He looks down, chin pressing against her skin. It's a small house with a rickety wooden sign in front of it, "No ghosts allowed." There's a tree swing where a boy is pushing a little girl.

"I was afraid you were losing interest," says Banyan, hugging her.

Kai breaks the hug, turns back around and kisses him. She was. When Josh and Dan came back from the hospital still wearing their armor, and she saw how Josh fretted over Dan's broken collar bone, she was losing interest. The way Dan put his arm around Josh and let the kid drag him to bed just so Josh would feel better.... Kai had to admit, she felt a twinge of attraction for Dan, too.

She dozes off and dreams about the little house with the tree swing. A giant strides to the house. The little girl and teenage boy look up and run inside. The giant smirks at the "No ghosts allowed sign," yanks it up, and picks his teeth with it. The giant spots Kai and heads towards her. It lifts a foot that casts a shadow over Kai and Banyan, who don't seem to see the giant as they both grin at the swing, as if the little girl is still there.

Kai snaps up, awake. "What?" Banyan asks.

"Bad dream," she says.

"About what?"

"Let's not talk about that ghost crap again."

11

It's past noon as Dan hammers a steel cuirass left-handed. Josh sharpens the head of his first halberd, flinches each time the mallet hits steel. The high pitch ringing sends shivering waves to his inner ear. He turns around to look at Dan. Dan, whose right arm is still in a sling from the broken collar bone, puts a dent right in the middle of the chest guard. "You're ruining it," says Josh.

Dan looks up at Josh. "No shit," he says.

Dan throws the hammer on the ground and leaves the workroom. "I'll be right back," he says.

Josh looks up at the clock. One-thirty in the afternoon. Dan returns with a beer in hand. He hands it to Josh. "Be a pal and open this."

Josh wraps the top of the beer with the bottom of his shirt and twists the cap off the bottle. Dan takes a swig. It's the first time Josh has seen Dan drink alcohol. "Thought you don't drink?" says Josh.

Dan looks up at the clock. "Yea. My shoulder is killing me. The beer helps."

Kai didn't come home last night, and Josh can tell it's bothering Dan. Josh puts down the halberd head and the sharpening stone. "We should get out of here. Clear our heads."

Dan pulls his keys out of his pocket and tosses the keys to Josh. "Yea, you drive."

The sky is filled with smoky clouds floating slowly in opposite directions. They appear to be headed for collision; however, one cloud is higher and floats above the on-coming condensed vapor. Josh rolls down his window. It's November, but the air is still thick with salt and heat. They descend the drought-bleached mountain while Dan sips his beer. "Where to?" Josh asks.

"Just drive."

As they head down Farrington Highway, Josh feels the heat coming off Dan. He doesn't know where to take him—Wai'anae turns to Makaha, the last town at the end of the road. Beach parks to the left, houses and strip malls to the right. Dan tells Josh to pull over at Aloha Gas Station. He picks up a six pack and tells Josh to drive on.

They continue through Wai'anae, all the way to Makaha, where the yellow "Pavement Ends" sign is as far as they can go by car. "A long time ago, you could four-wheel though all of this, go around Ka'ena Point and end up on the North Shore," says Dan.

"What happened?" asks Josh.

"Rockslides, so they closed it."

Josh turns around. As they head back, Josh tries not to look at the beach, his past home. He wants to head for the mountains, so he turns up Cindy Chang's street, knowing it's a bad idea. Dan perks up. "Where we going?"

"I just wanna drive by this girl's house."

Dan nods and pops the cap off his beer with the car seatbelt latch.

Josh creeps by houses with peeling paint fronted by junkyard carports and chain link fences. He slows as they near Cindy's.

She's in the yard, shooting water on a plumeria tree. She's wearing a tank top and pink jogging shorts. The smooth tawny of her arms and legs make Josh want to cry. He steps on the gas, and the sound of the motor draws her attention. "The jig is up," says Dan.

Josh stops as Cindy, who puts down the hose and adjusts her bra strap, walks toward the car, her face a puzzled half-smile, glowing divine. "Kill the engine," says Dan. "Go out and talk to her."

Josh pulls to the side, and turns off the car. He gets out and walks across the street, hands in his pockets, already looking down. "Hey Josh," says Cindy.

He looks up. "Hey."

She drops the tailgate of a broken down truck in the carport and sits. He slides up by her. They sit there, quiet. "Where's your cell phone?" Josh asks, genuinely surprised he does not see it.

Cindy turns and smiles. "I don't use the phone when I'm watering plants, silly."

Although Josh wants to ask her a list of questions including whether he's a bad kisser, whether Lolo kisses better than he does, and if that was why she broke his heart, he sits there, quiet, both enjoying and dreading the electricity bouncing back and forth in the few inches between them. The quiet is broken as the high-pitched prattle of a dirt bike approaches. A shirtless dirt biker rides by, looks at Cindy, and pops a wheelie. "I saw you with Lolo the other day," Josh says.

Cindy sighs. It sounds like a practiced sigh, or at least a sigh that she's performed in earnest many times before. "I know. I'm sorry. But, like I'm fourteen. Too young to be tied down. I'm gonna break up with him next week, probably. It's like Carrie said, 'Maybe some women aren't meant to be tamed. Maybe they just need to run free till they find someone just as wild to run with them.'"

"Who's Carrie?"

"You know, the TV show."

"Oh."

Cindy swings her legs like two pendulums in sync, and her toenails, covered with chipped red polish, flash with each kick. "I like you more as a friend," she says.

Crushed, Josh jumps off the tailgate and heads back to the car. He's trying to put on a show of anger, but realizes he must look like a little kid who just isn't getting his way. By the time the dirt biker comes back up the road and stops in front of Cindy, gunning the engine, staring at Josh, smiling, Cindy doesn't even seem to notice Josh is there. He gets into the car and slams the door as hard as he can. He turns the key, revs the engine, and slams the gearshift into drive. The back tires screech, and the rear end does a mini fish tail, but for the most part Josh knows that the spectacle is like watching a baby lion growl for the first time. "Whoa, take it easy tiger," Dan says, humiliating him even further.

As Josh and Dan head back home, Dan's quiet disturbs Josh. "Hey," he says, "you've been giving me advice ever since I met you. Well, now is a good time to lay more on me."

Dan sips his beer. "What, about the girl you mean?"

"Yea."

Dan thinks about this. Finally, he says, "Does it seem like I know what the hell I'm doing when it comes to that?"

Josh switches on the radio and searches for a sad song to make him feel worse. He has no idea why, but feeling even more awful has appeal.

When they get home, Kai's cooking dinner. She stands over the stove, mixing a pot filled with canned green beans. It must be a special occasion, Josh thinks, because normally she'd just dump the canned vegetables in a plastic bowl and nuke them. A pot of green beans on the stove instead of in the microwave, this is Kai's idea of home cooking. "What's the occasion?" Josh asks.

"Good news," she says. She turns around and folds her arms. God, where'd she get that apron, Josh wonders. "Dan, we'll probably be out of your hair by next month. Thanks so much for letting us stay."

Josh and Dan look at each other and walk out of the kitchen. They head to their separate rooms and close the doors.

IV. Krill's Grace

1

As Banyan stands in his mother-in-law's study, he looks up at the book shelf and browses book titles that delve into local topics such as plantation heritage, pidgin, racial stereotypes, fishing, local music, surfing, indigenous flora, and even Spam recipes. He steps to the fiction section and sees more of the same, willing to bet there's more compulsive apostrophe use to depict the tone of local language in this section of books than in all of the Library of Congress. Somehow, ***Blood Meridian*** is sandwiched between one book about an effeminate Japanese hairdresser who grew up on Lānaʻi and was persecuted in the salon business because he spoke pidgin, and another book about a pudgy Filipino high schooler whose daddy took her fishing to pass pearls of wisdom, and who, incidentally, was persecuted in high school because she rolled her Rs.

Caley's mother enters, in full aloha print as usual. Extremely thin like Caley, she has large bony hands that are disconcerting, as if instead of writing books on flowers and Hawaiian quilts, she should be ferrying souls across the river Styx. "Caley and Raimi will be here shortly," she says. She points at the books. "You should write one."

"I am," Banyan says, the pain in his hand making him testy. "It's about a bouncer from Waiʻanae named Ikaika. He has an affinity for stand-up comics and Swarovski crystal Christmas ornaments. He goes to poetry slams and is booed offstage because his stand-up is not self-indulgent and doesn't rhyme. He goes nuts and kills a table of piercedeyebrowed college kids in the coffee house with a mic stand. The audience applauds."

She can't tell if he's serious. He isn't. "How can you type with a broken hand?" she asks.

"Slowly," he says, "very slowly."

She changes the subject. "That Carballo girl made the top three. I bet the hibiscus in the right ear becomes a fad that sweeps the nation."

He's bunking out in the room of a national celebrity. His mother-in-law reaches up to the top shelf of books. She's on one foot, tiptoed, and looks as if she's about to spin into a pirouette. She's thin like Caley, and has severe short blond hair, which makes him think half-spinster librarian, half ballerina. She pulls the book down and hands it to Banyan. It's "Chicken Soup for the Soul: A Tribute to Moms."

"You should write a self-help book. There's a lot of money in it."

The book cover has a photo of a mom in a closed eye embrace with her son. "Does it look like I'm in a position to give people advice?" asks Banyan. "Especially on how to treat moms?" he adds.

"I told her she should never have married a man like you," says Caley's mother.

Banyan, irritated, understands that now that Caley has left him, his mother-in-law has somehow obtained license to say what she wanted to say all these years. He bites his lip and holds back, knowing that Caley must catch the worst of the self-righteous babble. He puts the book back on the shelf. He's curious and can't help but ask. "What kind of man am I?"

"The kind who lives inside himself. So is it schizophrenia?"

"Is that what she's saying?" he asks, referring to Caley.

"No, but she says you were seeing things. Ghosts, other women. It surprised me. Sort of hard to see things with your head that far up your ass."

His mother-in-law heads out of the study before he can reply. "Want a sandwich or something?" she shouts from the other room.

Banyan follows her out, and passes through the vestibule—beautiful, marble, a spiral staircase, a chandelier—the home of a cantankerous old woman with thinning blond hair and bony hands who took her husband to the cleaners in a divorce and still can't handle the fact that her daughter chose nursing as a career and married a ***community college*** professor. She once told Banyan that those who instruct at the community college level should just be called teachers. Just as Banyan is about to clear the entry room and step into the kitchen to tell his mother-in-law where she can stick her sandwiches, the front door opens. "Daddy! Daddy!" Raimi yells, delighted.

Banyan steps back into the vestibule. Raimi runs to him, shoes pattering across the marble floor. He scoops her up and hugs her, fighting off tears. She pushes away. "What doing, Daddy?" she asks.

"I'm squeezing you," he says.

She throws her arms around his neck and yells, "I'm squeezing you!"

Her little hand pats his back, like she's trying to comfort him. Caley enters, avoiding his eyes. Still holding Raimi, he walks into the study. He wants her all to himself, away from her mother and grandmother, but Caley follows them. He sits on a chair with red velvet cushions. The room is filled with furniture like this, Victorian relics that his mother-in-law probably imagines he'd appreciate if he were a professor at a four year university instead of a teacher at a junior college. Caley looms at the doorway, waiting for him to say something, maybe apologize. Instead, holding Raimi in his lap, he says, "A restraining order? You got to be kidding."

"We can talk about it later," says Caley. "Take a look at her birthday invitation."

Banyan shifts Raimi over to one side. Caley walks to him and hands him an invitation. It's typical, one of those Costco ones, a picture of Raimi in pink, framed by pink, framed by flowers. Raimi's appetite for pink borders obsession. "It looks good," he says.

"That's me daddy!" Raimi says, pointing at the invitation.

Caley looks tired, on the verge of defeat against the will of a two-year-old. The cut on her cheekbone is now a white line with a few tiny chips of scab. She even heals faster than him. "You always hated those invitations," she says.

"Sure, except the ones with my daughter's picture on it."

Raimi scratches at Banyan's nose, looking for the stud. "Let me take her," he says.

"In that heap outside? Are you nuts?" She's referring to his pick up. "It doesn't even have a back seat."

Raimi goes for the cut on Banyan's forehead and rakes it. "Ow!" says Banyan.

Raimi laughs, never believing that her father has a nervous system. He enjoys it, though, his daughter thinking he's the toughest guy in the world even though it's far from the truth. "Just come to the party," says Caley. "We'll work something out later."

"I'm not letting you keep her solo," he says.

Caley's mother walks in, trying to beckon Raimi to her. Raimi buries her head in Banyan's shoulder, scared of those long, bony fingers, two rings set with big, obnoxious diamonds. "She doesn't have Raimi solo," says Caley's mother. "She's got me."

The mother and daughter stand beside each other, arms crossed, freckled forearms covered with tiny, almost transparent hairs. He looks down at Raimi and wonders if the pair were ever like her, full of wild-eyed, buck-toothed smiles.

"Just help with the party," says Caley. "You'll behave yourself, right?"

"Who me? Of course," says Banyan.

Caley and her mother look at each other skeptically. Banyan puts Raimi down. She climbs right back on him. Raimi notices the cast and slaps it with everything she's got.

"Ow!"

She laughs. Caley's mother shakes her head and leaves the room. "I'm going out with my mother to get coffee," says Caley.

"Fine," says Banyan, not looking up.

"It strikes me as funny," says Caley, back to him. "You say you want to split time with Raimi, and yet you buy a car that makes that impossible."

Banyan thinks about that. He wanted a truck so he could move stuff. His stuff out of the house, maybe Kai's and Josh's stuff off the beach as well. How did he forget that he'd need a back seat so that when he drove, Raimi would be safe? "I'll trade it in and get a new one," he says.

"I split our savings," says Caley. "I mailed you a check to the house. We've been staying here."

"Thanks," he says. They had about three grand in savings.

Caley stands at the doorway waiting for him to say something else. He ignores her and takes Raimi to the closet and pulls out the board game Candyland. Caley releases a guttural sigh and leaves.

Banyan tries to teach Raimi how to play Candyland, which turns out to be a dreadful yet wonderful experience he's sure he will never forget.

Banyan pulls up to the Carballo house right before dark. Bart is sitting in a lawn chair on the driveway with a pink blanket over his legs. Banyan, still high from his visit with Raimi, grabs a lawn chair from the garage and sits by his friend. He opens a beer. The street is quiet as families gather inside for dinner. "They coming back?" Banyan asks. His hand has been throbbing throughout the ride back to Mililani.

Bart pulls an open beer out from under the blanket. "She might win the whole damn thing. And she's only sixteen, so her mother needs to be there. She can't do without the little one, too."

"Can you?"

They look at each other, recognizing a common thought. The Carballo girls, all three of them, are never coming back. Banyan hands Bart a Raimi birthday party invitation. "You're coming, right?" Banyan says.

Bart nods and sips his beer. "I don't see this ending well for us," he says.

Banyan stands and tanks his beer. "I'm going to head to the store. Need anything?"

Bart shakes his head. Banyan looks across the street, the wall menacing as the sun sets. He's thankful that Caley and Raimi have been staying at Caley's mother's house. Banyan told her he'd check things out inside, maybe air it out a bit since the windows are closed and the air conditioner hasn't been on, but as he looks at the house, he doubts he'll go through with it. It's odd to imagine a haunted house with an automatic garage door opener, central air, and stain resistant carpet, but there it is, sending chills down his spine. He could even stay there if he wants, maybe even ask Kai and Josh if they want to live there until he and Caley figure out what they're going to do, but looking at the house now, that idea has bad written all over it. He forgot to ask Caley if she contacted a realtor.

The drive to the grocery store turns into a lonely two-hour circle island trip. There isn't much to see outside as the landscape turns from suburban, to urban, to suburban, to a long stretch of rural, a merry-go-round of sorts, with multi-colored breaking waves for borders and Mililani as a hub, the drive a slow revolution too weak to propel Banyan off any course but the one already set in motion.

2

Things you see at just about any baby lū'au in the state of Hawai'i: catered kālua pig, lomi salmon, tako and 'ahi poke, haupia, chicken long rice, squid lū'au, white rice, chafing dishes, boiled peanuts, light beer, a shave ice machine, a bouncer, a guy hired to make balloon animals, a piñata, live music, folding metal chairs, and of course an elaborately frosted birthday cake. Like the wedding receptions with their buffets, sappy bridesmaid speeches, slideshows, and fork-clanging water glasses, birthday parties for kids are melding into one event for Banyan, tame afternoon celebrations he is not sure who is more likely to forget—the baby guest of honor or himself. This one is different of course, it being Raimi's, but he can't help but notice that many of the guests walk around like zombies with permanent smiles plastered to their faces.

Banyan and the balloon-animal guy, Darrell, are on first-name basis as Darrell has been at the last four birthdays Banyan's been to, and now Banyan would be twisting a grey balloon, making a sword for his nephew, and the thing would have come out just as good as one of Darrell's, except his hand is broken. "Jesus, Darrell, I've been to too many of these things."

"At every party I do, there's a guy like you hanging out here learning to make balloon animals. Remember, that's what the light beer is for."

"Good point."

Banyan's family is here, even his parents, who flew down from Shaver Lake, California, baby-boomer retirees who spend most of their time fishing for trout and drinking gin martinis. They'd sent all of their children to private high schools, spent tens of thousands of dollars to end up with a butcher, a hair colorist, and a community college teacher. The depths of their disappointment drove them out of state. When Banyan and Caley house-shopped in Mililani, he was tempted to ask them for money for the down payment, but he felt too guilty. Throughout his childhood, there were conversations about politics, art, books, evolution, and Spanish-American War history at the dinner table. They were good parents, and not even Banyan knew how it was possible that two out of three children didn't complete college. The failed Mott children are hardly a catastrophe, but the Mott parents had had enough, and not even grandchildren could persuade them to maintain a Hawai'i residence.

Caley's parents, the ones who fronted fifty-thousand dollars to help with the down payment on the Mililani home, you couldn't kick them out of Hawai'i if you wanted to. They both have an insatiable appetite for things Hawaiian. Her father, a grey-haired, big-shot developer who spends most of his free time surfing and canoe paddling, is so well toned Banyan is sure the old man will outlive him. The mother has published three books—two on the indigenous flowers of Hawai'i, the other an instruction manual on Hawaiian quilting. Banyan likes the father, but never sees him, is not that fond of the mother, but as she's Raimi's chief babysitter, he's always seen her more than he'd like. The only one he despises is Caley's brother, heir-apparent to his father's development company and a living example of how the children of the wealthy often turn out to be ignorant assholes.

"Banyan," Caley's brother says. "You're looking old. What happened to the curly hair and pierced nose?" His name is Alex, but he'd decided that a Hawaiian name was cooler; he demanded to be addressed as Alika. Alika doesn't notice the most obvious change, the cast on Banyan's arm.

"Long time no see, Alika. Guess I'm trying to grow up."

"Hey, you're an English professor, right? I started up this magazine, a hobby of mine. It's sort of an activist thingy, you know, keep the country country in the North Shore. We have some good photographers, but we could use more writing talent."

Banyan's two nephews, dressed in Little League Boston Red Sox attire, approach, eyes glued to their Gameboys, navigating through the crowd with occasional furtive, peripheral glances. Banyan stops, extends a balloon sword to one of them, and the kid grabs it without breaking stride or looking up. "I think I've seen this magazine. I wanted to ask you something. Didn't your company have a hand in building most of the stuff on the North Shore?"

"Yea, what's your point?"

"You're a developer who is anti-development?"

"Yea, I'm trying to give back."

Banyan has in fact seen this magazine before. It's a thin, glossy rag filled with photographs of breaking waves and anti-development protesters and retellings of Hawaiian folklore. Half the magazine is advertisements for North Shore eateries and hotels. Even the resort there has a one-page ad, the resort that is planning the five-acre expansion that the people in the photographs are protesting. "Are you guys the ones expanding the resort up there?" Banyan asks.

"No way. That'd be hypocritical, no? Besides, we lost the bid."

Alex hands Banyan a business card before walking off, probably the thirtieth he has received from this millionaire whom Banyan is convinced is mildly retarded. On the card, Alex has given himself the title of Vice-President and Environmental Activist. Banyan feels bad for Caley, who should be the one running the company, but when her father left her mother for a beach-volleyball queen while Caley was in college, she'd made it clear that she didn't want anything to do with him outside of family get-togethers, even after her father admitted he was wrong, and divorced the volleyball queen a few years later. Banyan suspects that the father will never be able to retire, and he could be sizing up Raimi, wondering if she would have the capacity and interest in running a development company, wondering if he can hold out for another quarter of a century so that he does not have to turn over his life's work to the son whose acceptances into private schools and colleges were paid for with baseball fields and libraries. The thing that Banyan likes best about his father-in-law is how he seems to hold Alex in the same contempt as Banyan does, even occasionally addressing him as retard in public.

Banyan makes the rounds. There's the Luapele Street Posse. Then there are the old friends from high school and college, most local Japanese and into golf, some pregnant, many with kids of their own. His older brother Dexter, a man with hard hands that Banyan always envied, and his sister-in-law Judy, a Korean immigrant whose mother owns the biggest Korean supermarket in the state. His unmarried, older sister, Tammy, pretty but overweight, short hair dyed purple, who'd once sworn him to secrecy and told him she was a lesbian while she was piercing his nose. Caley's friends; his parents; the in-laws; every conversation distracted by children being fed or running beyond the sight of their parents. Banyan wonders what the spectacle would sound like without the man sitting in front of the mic with his acoustic guitar, droning out local favorites. It seems to Banyan that the music is not really entertainment, as no one is even looking at the musician, but is there to ease the pain of the mundane conversations and drown out the shrill voices of children.

The last stop is in front of the cake, where Caley, her mother, and her grandmother, who is holding Raimi, are all arguing about the tempo at which the birthday song should be played. "He should sing it fast," says the grandmother. "I hate when they play the song slow."

"They play it slow so the other children can participate," says Caley.

"That song was not meant to be played that slow," says Caley's mother. "It's supposed to be upbeat. The slow version lacks energy, like we are begrudgingly humoring the child."

"Raimi doesn't care, Mom. She probably won't even remember this party."

"She damn well better remember it," says the mother, looking at Banyan. "I forked over five grand for it."

"I remember my third birthday party," says the grandmother. "A stale cupcake with a single matchstick. It was the Depression, you know."

The women don't consult Banyan concerning the tempo of the birthday song. Raimi kicks out of her great-grandmother's grasp and runs to Banyan, scaling his cast like a mountain climber. "Such a daddy's girl," Caley's mother says. "It's not healthy."

"I never saw my father much," says the grandmother. "He was always looking for work. It was the Depression, you know."

"At least she looks like Banyan," says the mother. "No freckles, big eyes. Caley, you're lucky."

Caley nods, which infuriates Banyan. He thinks of one of the fonder memories of Caley, one night at the old duplex where he came home from work. Caley was sitting in the bathtub with Raimi, something she almost never did, popping bubbles with her daughter, letting the kid furiously splash water that soaked the bathroom floor. Banyan was struck by the beauty of a mother and daughter playing together recklessly, a vacation from the normal girl-on-girl conflict that to Banyan resembled regurgitated force-feeding, and he stepped out of the bathroom, feeling like an intruder. He remembers that night and wants to defend Caley. "I wish Raimi had freckles," he says to his mother-in-law. "I'm just hoping she didn't get that recessive retard gene that Alex has. I can't really afford to pay college tuition plus add a new wing for the law school."

His mother-in-law's body stiffens and facial muscles go to work, as if suppressing a long-ago, almost-forgotten, predisposition to bite. "You can't even afford college," she says. "And by the way, Alex didn't have to beg me for fifty thousand dollars for a down payment for a house. He's successful."

Banyan isn't angry, only amused, but the pain from his broken hand has made him grouchy. "He is. And it's all merit-based success, too. Just like yours is. I mean, the fifty grand came from a divorce settlement fund right? That's cash hard-earned on your back."

Caley and the grandmother listen in shock. The acoustic guitarist waves at Caley, awaiting pre-cake cutting-and-singing instruction. "Caley," the mother says, "get this boy out of my sight before I slap his face."

"Let me help you with that," says Banyan, as he scoops up a handful of birthday cake and plows it in his mother-in-law's face. Raimi laughs. Everyone is watching now, even the guitarist and Darrell, the balloon-animal guy. Caley grabs Raimi from Banyan just before he is tackled from behind by Alex. And now Alex is straddling Banyan's back, raining hardly-felt blows on the back of his head. There's a popping sound, a broken knuckle probably, followed by a scream. Alex is hoisted off Banyan by Ster-Roy, and the posse men are shoeing Alex; Roy is trying to keep him pinned down with just his foot, while Bart is overly zealous with his stomps. The women scream at the children to leave, as if the rec center is on fire, and Banyan and his father-in-law try to pull Bart off of Alex, who is on his knees throwing weak punches like an enraged octogenarian.

All told, the only guy who ends up with an emergency-room injury is Alex. He broke a knuckle on Banyan's head and is screaming threats of lawsuit from the other side of the room. There is no singing of the birthday song, fast or slow, and Banyan is sitting on the ground with Darrell the balloon animal maker, who smiles and says, "Now that's the best goddamn baby lūʻau I've ever been to."

Balloons trailing ribbons are already deflating, bobbing slowly off the ground when hit. The ground is littered with crumbs, juice stains, and crumpled napkins. There is also glitter from the favors Caley made, one-by-one, by hand. "Happen to see where my wife and kid went?" Banyan asks.

"Yea, they took off, man," Darrell says. "Good thing you folks aren't younger and in shape. Someone could have gotten hurt."

Banyan sips a warm beer as the Luapele Street Posse, the only people who stayed after the fight, are cleaning up. Ster-Roy stores metal folding chairs ten at a time as Jesse Suzuki loads up tables on a hand truck. Bart, who is packing food into freezer bags with metal tongs, answers his cell phone. It's a short conversation. He walks up to Banyan, cold kālua pig fat congealed on the tongs, and says, "Caley says she has divorce papers for you."

"Peachy keen," says Banyan as he pops a Vicodin. As the Posse tidy up with single-minded purpose, he cannot help but think that what he is witnessing is not all that unlike an ant colony at work. He suspects that all of Mililani Mauka works in this way. Bart, sitting next to Banyan says, "Let the labor catch the rest. With your cast, you're useless anyway. You should straighten this shit out with your wife."

Banyan nods.

"A face full of cake for your mother-in-law, didn't know you had it in you," says Bart.

"How long were you married?" Banyan asks.

"I'm not sure. Like seventeen years? Before you start, just to let you know, the Posse does not talk about our marriages, especially when they're in the shitter."

"Why is that?"

"I was one of the first guys to buy on Luapele Street. It's like you're playing a game for the first time, but somehow you already know all the rules."

"Where'd you live before that?"

"Grew up in Kalihi," says Bart. "Near where you teach. Wasn't going to raise my kids in that shithole. Look at Lianne now, all on TV, singing lessons since she was four. Man, she loved to sing."

The Carballo girl—Bart's immortality. "You should go up there," says Banyan.

"Fuck the mainland. Also, fuck flying."

Banyan remembers being exhilarated by turbulence as a child. Now, turbulence is just scary. Banyan is surprised that Bart would use fear as an excuse, but suspects it's not the real reason Bart won't try to get his family back. "What's so great about this place anyway?" Banyan says. "It's pretty much just like the mainland. Look at where we live. We got soccer moms for Christ's sake. I didn't even see a soccer ball till I was twelve."

"Yea, it's changing, fast too. Maybe I should dump the house while prices are still high and go live on a neighbor island or something. I don't know, man, this is just home. Also, fuck snow."

Bart does not really want his wife and children to come back. He will miss them, but he has already avoided death in his own, small way. The son in college will carry his name, the hibiscus-eared daughter on television is testament to his success, and the youngest, well, two out of three is not bad. All that is left is indulging in pleasure—drinking beer on his driveway with his neighbors and riding his motorcycle. It is why he can sit here with Banyan while Roy and Jesse pack up chairs and tables. Bart, as far as Banyan can tell, has built his pyramid and is done with life.

Banyan envies Bart. He's tired just thinking about everything he has to do before he's done.

3

In the annals of disastrous but non-fatal 21st-century Thanksgivings, there are stories such as that of the Garcias of Escondido, California, who as volunteers for a homeless shelter, undercooked twelve turkeys that sent one-hundred-and-twenty uninsured people, many of them illegals, to the emergency room. There are the Johnsons of Sun Valley, Idaho, whose anorexic daughter was on a feeding tube. They smuggled her out of the hospital and took her home, where her mother blended mashed potatoes, condensed milk, and turkey gizzards and force fed the daughter until vomit shot out of the tube like a water hose. There was Randall Benedict of Detroit, Michigan, who put a $40,000 bet on the Lions for the early Thanksgiving game, lost, and went double or nothing on the Cowboys versus the Broncos, who covered by a half-point in overtime. No one knows where Randall Benedict is today. Then there were the Wangs of Gaithersburg, Maryland, who decided to pop magic mushrooms while cooking Thanksgiving dinner, only to end up naked in the front yard, chasing imaginary turkeys. Mrs. Wang mistook Mr. Wang's erect penis for an unshucked corncob; a trip to the emergency room followed.

Kai makes up these stories while cooking her first Thanksgiving meal ever. She misses Banyan most when her imagination takes over and she thinks of him now as she chops shiitake mushrooms and Portuguese sausage for the stuffing.

Dan walks into the kitchen, his wounded posture preventing him from sticking his chest out as he strides to the cabinet. He removes all of his deep-frying turkey paraphernalia. Kai wonders if anyone just cooks turkey in the oven at 325 degrees anymore. It's the first anniversary of the turducken Thanksgiving, the three birds forced upon each other in the oven for nine hours, a two-day cooking marathon that started with the sharpening of kitchen knives and ended in a six-hour surgery. The thing had tasted like poorly cooked versions of all three birds. She and John got into an argument about it, because he swore it was the best damn bird he'd ever had.

Dan's arm brushes against hers. The sight of his wrapped-up figure-eight sling reminds her of the bottle necklace breastfeeding she'd done and how most things medical left a person with very little dignity. "How tall are you again, Dan?" she says.

"I'm five seven. Don't start with me on this again."

"I'm five six, and I swear you're exactly the same height," she says.

"I'm slumped over from the sling. Throw all of that in the mixing bowl, short stuff," he says.

She has yet to meet a man who is not engaged in a lifelong battle of self-delusion with a particular measurement: height, weight, or waist size, sometimes IQ, or time on the fifty-meter dash, and sometimes measurements below the waist. "Josh, come help the little guy take the deep fryer outside," she says. Josh enters the kitchen. He always hunches when he's next to Dan, like he doesn't want to be taller than the cop.

Josh convinced Dan to put a television in his living room, so he doesn't look like a freak. The suit of armor and other larger pieces of medieval gear, like the shield and jousting stick, are stored in the garage, against the wall, like forgotten tools. Kai feels guilty about this slow shift to a more domestic look, but Josh, despite his recent acid-reflux problems, hasn't seemed this normal since before the death of his father.

A Thanksgiving Day football game is on, the Ravens versus the Bengals, and she actually has an interest in it because Banyan, who told her about the divorce papers, said he needed to see her. She told him let the fates decide, pick a winner, Ravens or Bengals, and if his team wins, she will see him. He picked the Ravens, then informed her that linebacker Ray Lewis was going to prison rape quarterback Carson Palmer, which was unlike Banyan. He was staying with Bart Carballo, a fantasy football fanatic who occasionally slapped and screamed at his wife and kids when he drank too much Guinness, so she guessed it made sense. She is happy to see, and a bit envious, that the Carballo girl is about to win the nationally-televised karaoke contest. Poor girl should never come back.

Dan, almost unbelievably, is not a football fan. Nor does he drink much. He is, in fact, seemingly vice-free, which worries Kai. He sets up the propane tank in the work room, instructing Josh on where to put the gas burner. "You can't become a real man until you deep-fry a turkey of at least fifteen pounds," Josh says. It's the first day Josh has been showing signs of a sense of humor since she got back from the night with Banyan.

"Shut up, Krill," Dan says, laughing.

"Won't there be smoke?" Kai asks.

"Beats me. I'm a cop, not a fireman." Dan turns the knob on the propane tank while Josh hoists a pot full of oil onto the burner. Dan says, "Can you believe I got this for Christmas? Who the hell gives out turkey fryers for Christmas? I've never used it before. Josh, you play your cards right, I'll give you this one."

"Gee, thanks," says Josh. "A turkey fryer. What a dream come true."

They never talk about how this is a temporary living arrangement. Kai's efforts at finding a rental have doubled since quitting school and moving in here. Again, it seems all she qualifies for are near-condemned buildings with community restrooms. At this point, she has probably seen every ghetto rental on the island of Oahu. She has gotten one nibble though, and is just waiting to hear back. "I'm going to get Dan here a tape measure for Christmas, but he will probably cut off the bottom inch with one of his crazy swords."

"Big Krill, you keep it up, that's not the only thing I'm cutting," Dan says as the gas burner ignites. "Throw the pot on and let's watch the game."

"You don't even like football," says Kai.

"Or TV," says Josh.

"Well, I put the damned thing in the living room, might as well use it," Dan says.

They close the sliding glass door and sit on the curved couch in front of the television. The Ravens are winning. At halftime, Josh and Dan get up to put the turkey in the hot oil. Dan makes Josh wear covered shoes, jeans, rubber gloves, goggles, and a chain mail coif. Kai watches from the other side of the glass door. Josh lowers the turkey in with the sober severity of someone pulling the lever at a gas chamber. The oil bubbles then smokes. The two come inside.

Despite opened louvered windows, the workroom fills with smoke. The three of them now stand at the glass door, hands on hips, hoping that the smoke will fade, but soon they can't even see the fryer.

"Don't think it's going to get better," Kai says.

"Such a pessimist Big Krill, but yea, you're probably right," says Dan. "Stay here." He slides the door open and smoke floods into the living room. Eyes stinging, Kai can make out Dan standing over the fryer, lifting the bird out one-handed. He rushes past them to the sink. "Broke my collar bone again, I think," he says as he passes them.

He takes off his sling and goes for the big pot. Josh moves to help him, but Dan says, "Stay back. This is dangerous. Once I get the oil out the front door, turn off the tank, put on some gloves, and take the burner out front."

He strains, lifting the pot of oil, and waddles inside. Spilling oil sizzles as it hits the laminated floor. "Whoa, this is hot," Dan says, as some of the oil stains his jeans. He slides around like a kid learning to ice skate, and even when a little oil splashes on his hands, he does not let go of the pot. Kai sees what's going on now. She grabs the propane tank and follows, and tells Josh to put on his ridiculous safety outfit and get the turkey.

They manage to save the turkey at the cost of a re-broken collar bone and some third-degree burns on Dan's left hand. He refuses to let them take him to the hospital until they finish Thanksgiving dinner. They are sitting in front of the TV, Kai and Josh rushing through their food while Dan has his left hand in a Tupperware full of ice water, his right hand wrapped around a turkey drumstick. "Damn good turkey," he says. His eyes well up.

There's something familiar about this guy, Kai thinks, the memories of John taking a blade to the ribs and asking her if she's OK come flooding in.

Kai puts a hand on Dan's thigh and feels like crying. "You're such a moron," she says.

"Sir Josh, you're not a real man until you impress a woman with your single-mindedness and tolerance for pain," Dan says, mouth full of dark meat, a twig of cartilage dangling from his mouth.

Josh scrapes the last bit of stuffing from his paper plate into his mouth, "Let's go," he says.

"Take me to Queen's," Dan says.

"That's all the way in town," says Josh.

"I thought Straub was the one with the burn center?" Kai says as she runs off to throw the empty plates away.

"I like Queens," he says, winking at Josh. "Best emergency room on the island. I've been stabbed twelve times. I should know."

The biggest difference between the Queen's emergency room and the others on the island is that there is a fairly elaborate security check-in process, like the ones at the airport. There's a remodeled newness to the large, carpeted lobby, but otherwise it's fairly typical—grave faces and children watching television. It's full despite the holiday, but Kai thinks that maybe holidays are the busiest days of the year for people who care for people who are in the business of ruining their own lives. The nurses here recognize Dan, and after only a few minutes of waiting, Dan's nurse, a skinny, freckled Caucasian woman with an elbow brace, approaches the waiting room and sighs, although it sounds more like she is clearing her throat. "Ah, Mott," Dan says, hand still in ice water. "Long time no see."

"One day you will get hurt so badly, Dan, you'll go to the emergency room on your side of the island."

"I went to the emergency health center in Wai'anae when I broke the collar bone." Dan says. "I like it here better. There's carpet. Now that's class."

Caley Mott looks at Kai. Kai stares at the elbow brace. Banyan had talked about his wife's arthritis, how he'd felt bad about it at first, and then how difficult it became to feel sympathy for someone who does not sympathize for herself. Kai took the notion one step further—it was infuriating dealing with people who did not sympathize for themselves. People like that, people like John Krill, like Dan, they not only refused to feel self-pity but expected you to do the same.

"I didn't know you were married," says Caley.

"I'm not," Dan says. "Meet Krill and Big Krill. Hey, how's that kid of yours doing? And what's with all this arthritis shit?"

Caley is still looking at Kai, rubbing her good elbow. "It comes and goes. Not a big deal."

"Mott, you and I come from the same stock," says Dan, who looks now at Josh. "I once saw this skinny lady pin the arms of a man twice my size while he was having a seizure."

"Let's go take a look at that hand and collar bone," says Caley.

"Mom, I'm going to get a soda from the machine outside. You want anything?" says Josh.

Dan and Caley walk toward an examination room. Kai slumps in her chair. "No thanks," she says. "Hey, no soda, your stomach."

Josh ignores her and walks away.

Five chairs down, a mother is trying to comfort a crying baby. The old man in front of her has his head covered, like a boxer in his corner, with a blood-stained white towel. Kai wants to make up disastrous but non-fatal 21st-century Thanksgivings for them, but instead, two words pop into her head: nymphomaniac and adulteress. Nymphomaniac, she knows she is not one of those. She never felt like she needed sex anything close to on a daily basis. Adulteress, yes, that's her, might as well tattoo a big "A" on her forehead. Seeing Caley Mott rattled her, and maybe, besides the obvious reason, it's because she knows, just by looking at the woman, that Caley, though not much to look at, is strong in the way Kai's parents wanted their daughter to be strong. Caley looks steady, hardworking. If she knew all about Kai, maybe she'd despise Kai. And Kai would deserve it.

Kai wants to kill herself, then thinks: attempted suicide in an emergency room ... talk about dumb. As the man in front of her shifts his towel and more red spreads through the white, she realizes that all these years since Xavier's death, she's been attempting suicide. But her attempts have been as asinine as those of the man with the noose tied to the steering wheel at Pōka'ī Bay. She was equally ridiculous. She's ridiculous now, as she slouches and pounds the back of her head on the cushioned chair.

What she'd wanted all those years was her head on a pike in front of the Luapele Street house, courtesy of John.

He'd promised it when they talked about the penalties they would exact for adultery, and she deserved it.

And now she's ruining this arthritic nurse's marriage for reasons entirely different, for love, that tired word whose true definition should be delusional justification for selfish acts of desire.

Emergency room, that's about the right place to be when it dawns on you that for most of your life, you've been a rotten person, that this world would have been a better place if you hadn't been born, that no angel named Clarence is going to come down and show you otherwise, that at least other rotten people who wreck lives sometimes have the nerve to off themselves, that she is not only rotten but a coward, a coward who couldn't do it by herself, so instead she hurt her husband and hoped his hand was far more steady—which it was, but he aimed at himself instead of at her. Slouching and trying to force sound out of the seat cushion with her pounding, she wants to scream, is there a scalpel in this place?

Josh approaches, a bottle of Coke in his hand. She gets up and puts her hand around the bottle. She pulls, but he won't let it go. They are going at it now, like two kids fighting over the remote control. Josh looks surprised by her strength, but he is stronger, and he swings her around in circles while she is tethered to the soda bottle. "This is not good for your stomach!" she screams.

"And this is?" Josh says.

The security guard is coming now, and Caley steps out of the examination room. Kai lets go of the bottle and rushes toward Caley, aware of the security guard, racing him. It's not only Caley she sees now, but a translucent party of ghosts gathering behind the nurse, her parents and John—John holding a swaddled Xavier. Kai runs faster. Caley does not step back or away, but catches Kai, lower back arched like she's doing the limbo, holding Kai off her feet. "I'm so sorry," says Kai, hugging her.

Caley backs the guard off by raising a hand. Kai is still bear-hugging her. "Ms. Krill, what's wrong?"

"I'm Kai. Kai, Kai, Kai ..." she says.

The name, the word, the confession feels good so Kai says it over and over. She feels as if she is learning to swim again, flailing to the bottom of the ocean, digging up sand despite the fact that air is four feet above her. Someone sedates her, and the "Kais" become softer, something between a soothing mantra and the beat of a rogue shark horror movie.

4

Josh is thinking about Mililani Mauka when Dan, with a fresh sling and a wad of gauze wrapped around his hand, asks him if he is ready to drive all the way to Nānākuli from town. He is not thinking of his own former home, but the one across the street, the Carballo one that houses the girl he fantasized about for years—Lianne Carballo, next American singing sensation—and the guy Josh idolized, her older brother James, who joined the Army right after high school and went to Bosnia, then Afghanistan. He remembers when James came back from the Mid-East and told him about being in a helicopter and buzzing over sheep that were so startled by the copter, they ran straight off cliffs. Then there were the stories of the enemy taking pot shots at a military base, the French ducking for cover while the Afghan troops braced gunstocks on their thighs and fired automatic weapons into the mountains.

James got the hero's welcome when he returned, a barbeque in his honor, Costco pre-marinated steaks and Alaskan king crab legs, while the Carballo men swapped war stories, the grandfather ribbing his son and grandson, telling them that their wars, the good Iraq War and the war in Afghanistan, were nothing compared to his, the Korean War.

It was at this barbeque that Bart Carballo got really drunk and pulled John Krill to the side. Josh pretended to listen to the Carballo grandpa's advice about staying in school, going to college, and never joining the military, while overhearing Bart telling John, "I think Ster-Roy and your wife have something going on, and I'm pretty sure everyone else thinks the same."

John didn't say anything, just rubbed his chin, and Bart, drunk and not sure that John had heard him, said it again. This time Mrs. Carballo heard, and she passed off the barbeque tongs to Jesse Suzuki, and told her husband to go inside and get some coffee. By the time their argument had escalated into a slap to Mrs. Carballo's face, John was already across the street and inside the Krill garage.

While Ster-Roy was pulling Bart away from Mrs. Carballo, Josh went across the street to see his dad.

John was in the garage, crouching, staring at the empty eighty-gallon fish tank. He watched it with such interest that Josh had to blink to make sure fish weren't in there. There were no fish, only a prism of light extending in front of John's feet. "You okay, Dad?" Josh said.

John didn't look up. "Just tired man. Very tired."

There was a commotion outside the garage door. Josh pressed the button to open it, and as the chains pulled the door open, a neighbor's loose dog, a sandy Pom-Chi ran in, rolled on its stomach and peed all over itself, then ran right back out, one neighbor apologizing while the other chased the loose dog. John started to laugh hard. Josh, feeling good, laughed, too.

Josh breaks from the memory and takes the keys from Dan. "I can drive," he says.

"Good, good," says Dan.

They dump Kai, who is still foggy from sedation, in the backseat. Dan gets into the passenger side while Josh turns the key. He can't help thinking that it's funny how he has had to learn how to drive under duress, first Dan's broken collar bone, now Dan's broken collar bone, the sequel, and his catatonic mother. He's learning something sort of like how his parents learned how to swim. He's just getting tossed in. His catatonic mother—hasn't she been like that most of his life?

Josh follows a station wagon with a Darwin Jesus fish and a magnetic yellow ribbon on the bumper. They pass a building, 1960s blue-green, the Board of Water Supply. A sign notifies passersby that it's Detect A Leak Week.

"Don't follow so close," Dan says.

On the freeway, the driving gets much easier. There's a slow, but consistent flow of traffic. Dan must be feeling confident about Josh's driving, because he says, "Stay in the right lane. Let's stop off at Mililani Longs. Shortest wait of them all. We can pick up our prescriptions."

All three of them have prescriptions—AcipHex for Josh's heartburn, Percocet for Dan's pain, and Zoloft for his mother's depression. Josh can't help to think that she deserves the breakdown and wishes that his parents had been more like the Carballos, a soon-to-be superstar daughter, three generations of war participants, and a husband who occasionally slapped his wife. That's what Kai needed from John, an occasional slap in the face. The way she was looking at that poor skinny haole nurse with the elbow brace while they were wrestling over the Coke. What was up with that? It was as if she'd seen John Krill from beyond the grave, not some freckle-faced woman who shocked Josh by her ability to lift his mother completely off the ground. He knew that if it was that lady wrestling him for the Coke bottle, she would have won hands down.

"Maybe we should grab dinner, too," Dan says. "You seem to have the hang of this. Maybe Outback Steakhouse. Give me a place that serves steak and has the front page of the paper above the urinals, and I'm in hog heaven."

"Who was that nurse?" Josh says.

"Mott? Nice as hell. Poor thing must've caught hell growing up in Hawai'i with all those freckles. Jesus, my hand is killing me."

The air-conditioning is on, but the back of Josh's neck sweats. The nurse. Kai somehow knew the nurse.

The Mililani Town Center, the one that Josh's dad ran over, is a pleasantly pink cluster of shops that include a Borders and a 14-plex movie theater. His dad had brought him here all the time; the pet store was a sort of min-zoo, where they'd pick up their cichlids. They often hit Taco Bell, Burger King, or KFC drive-throughs after Little League practice and games, most of which John Krill had coached. There's the supermarket, City Mill, the Wal-Mart.... Josh wonders why his father chose to smash into Wal-Mart, rather than any of the other stores. Probably because it was the biggest store of all, the one that would make the biggest impression. Maybe he was being nice, because Wal-Mart was maybe one of the few stores that could take being out of business for several months. Longs Drugs is also here. Dan turns on the police light, and they leave the car running with Kai asleep in the back.

After they are notified that their prescriptions will take at least an hour, Josh suggests that they take a drive to his old house.

"Think that's a good idea with Big Krill like how she is?" Dan asks.

"She's in La la land. Doubt she'll even notice," says Josh.

"La la land. That's a good way to describe this town." Dan rubs his swaddled hand. With that and the figure-eight arm sling, he is starting to look like a mummy who had risen from the dead, having changed his mind about all this embalming business. His slow, careful stride and hanging shoulder do wonders to punctuate the image.

"Mummy in aisle ten," Josh says.

But Dan does not reply, and Josh does not find it funny anymore. If Dan had never gotten mixed up with Josh, he would probably be healthy, happy, and banging away at his armor, instead of dragging himself up aisle ten, looking at picnic supplies then greeting cards. Get-well cards—maybe Josh should buy Dan and his mother one, maybe even the nurse at Queen's, too many people need get-well cards. They exit Longs, greeted by the smell of baking from The Cookie Corner.

Kai is still asleep when they exit the parking lot. They pass the library—a small, one-story building with a mural out front—Hawaiian petroglyphs—an ali'i, old Hawaiian chief, petting a flower lei'd pig, the women, wide-waisted and topless, one holding a platter full of fish, an ukulele, and live chickens over her head.

They pass the Christ Lutheran Church, Josh's old preschool, when he realizes that he is taking his father's bulldozer route in reverse. Up Mehe'ula, under the shade of monkeypod tree branches hanging over the avenue. They pass the freeway overpass and are in Mililani Mauka now, where the suburban homes, some thirty years younger than the Mililani Town homes, line the street like the end products of an assembly line, packed neatly in light-colored wrapping and tied up with white ribbons. Despite living in Mauka just about his entire life, he takes two wrong left turns before he finds his old street. He has to admit that the Mililani critics at his old private high school were almost right—the houses do look the same. But no, it's not just that; it's the streets that look the same, as if he is moving through a lab-rat maze lined with infant wallpaper, with corner signs marking streets with unspellable Hawaiian names. Apparently, there is no such thing as an unkempt front yard in all of Mililani Mauka. Dan says nothing, just smiles each time Josh has to turn around at the end of a cul de sac.

After time spent in Wai'anae, he sees now the appeal of this place, that it's not just normal, which he always thought it was, but a place with little memory, where mistakes are trapped behind manicured lawns and automatic garage doors. Josh sees cul de sacs filled with bunkers like on his computer games, bunkers that hide middleclass soldiers armed with pressure-washers and soccer balls who are fighting the most boring war in the history of human existence—the war against ugly. It's funny because Josh is starting to think that ugly is much more interesting than pretty. He's already almost over Cindy Chang.

He heads up Luapele Street, most of the houses empty because of Thanksgiving family get-togethers, and he spots two bunker soldiers who seem to be losing the war, two men on lawn chairs outside the Carballo house. One is his calabash uncle, Bart, drunk as usual and rubbing his fish-hook pendant, the other a skinny man who looks like the type who wears jeans to the beach, a sulker who holds a gallon jug of wine in his lap, staring at Josh's old house across the street like a man trying to case a future break-in. It's Banyan, of course, the man who came looking for Josh at school, the man who was looking for Kai, the man who is probably the reason his mother lost it. Dan leans toward Josh. "The nurse at the hospital, Mott? That's her husband right there. Kai is sleeping with that poor woman's husband."

Josh stops the car in front of them. Banyan looks shaken by the police light and tries to conceal his jug of wine with his cast. Bart sees that it's Josh behind the wheel and gets up, staggering toward him. Josh gets out of the car.

"Holy shit, hey Josh," Bart says, embracing Josh. "Didn't know they let cops in the department so young."

Dan is out of the car now too. "My chauffeur," he says, lifting his swaddled hand in explanation. Both Dan and Banyan look at each other, then look down at their damaged arms.

"Hey Banyan, come here," says Bart. "This here is John Krill's son, Josh. Josh, this is the new neighbor, Banyan Mott."

Josh knows that skinny guy Banyan is messing with his mom just by looking at him. Besides Uncle Ster-Roy, it's the first he's encountered one of his mother's ... he doesn't even know what to call it. He is even more perplexed by Kai. Why would she choose a guy like that when she'd been with men like his father and Roy Heap? Maybe he's missing something, some lesson about manhood, because as far as he can tell it'd take about two Banyan Motts to equal a John Krill, a Roy Heap, or a Dan the Man.

It's dusk and a growing shadow looms over all of them. The night falls in fast as charcoal clouds fill the sky. The men all look at each other, confused by the sudden change of weather, as the neighborhood dogs howl. All four men face the mountain, stunned by the clouds rolling in. The hairs on Josh's forearms and neck rise. Then a single, horrible scream.

Josh turns and sees his mother's head sticking out of the car window. She's staring at the house, the old Krill house. Josh turns to face the house. Nothing there.

All the men face the house now. The peach street lights flicker then shut off. Kai screams again, pointing at the empty driveway. "You better get her out of here," says Banyan, talking about Kai, who is now out of the car, looking snake-charmed, as she stands in the middle of the street. Banyan seems to be the only one who knows what the hell is going on. Dan moves to grab Kai while Bart, shaken by Kai's screams, heads inside.

"Help him out, will you?" says Banyan.

Josh grabs at Kai, who slips out of Dan's grip. She charges the house. Josh manages to tackle her before she gets to the sidewalk. "You don't see him?!" she asks, pointing to the driveway. Josh yanks her up and looks. Nothing's there.

As he drags Kai from the house, he stops and turns around. "Dad?" Josh says. Kai nods. Josh squints his eyes. His mother's lost it. Banyan walks past them toward the driveway. He seems to see something, too.

Kai braces herself against the open car door, screaming, trying to fight her way back to the house. They finally get her in, Dan driving, and Josh in the back with his mom. Dan guns the engine, throws the car in reverse, and spins around. Josh kneels and peers through the rear window as they speed down Luapele Street. The last thing he sees is Banyan on the sidewalk, looking up at his roof as if a man is standing on it. Banyan spins and throws the gallon wine jug at his garage door, hollering at his house. "They're nuts," says Josh. "The both of them."

Dan looks back in the rear view mirror. "Or we're blind," he says. Josh trembles at the thought.

5

Night marchers—the ghosts of ancient Hawaiian warriors. Some say they are restless souls searching for the entrance to the next world, others describe them as guides for descendants who have recently passed, and yet others believe they come back with a thirst for vengeance. That sounds about right to Banyan, vengeance, but night marchers, it's always plural. John Krill is a night marcher who broke ranks and went AWOL—there are no drums, no torches, and Luapele Street is not an ancient battlefield site. Instead, it's lined with asphalt shingled homes that house the occasional duel between husbands, wives, and children; only one was a duel to the death. Banyan decides that John Krill is not a night marcher, just a singular, swaggering, savage spirit who won't fall for the old night marcher trick—lie face down and they won't see you. It doesn't matter though, Banyan has had enough of laying face down, and he won't do it again.

Heading across the street toward a pike-wielding demon twice his size, Banyan is feeling surprisingly chipper. First off, he's not crazy, is he? Or at least he's not alone. He knows Kai saw it, the ghost of John Krill, though more devilish demi-god than ghost now, a far cry from the tank-top wearing menehune. Second, though he is admittedly piss-his-pants scared, the pacing monster now before him seems to be shrinking as Banyan stands at the edge of the driveway, and he's thinking of the phrase "all show and no go" hoping it's true.

When Banyan takes the first step off the sidewalk and on the driveway, the street lights flicker on. Banyan looks from the lights to John Krill, who in that brief moment, shrank back down to menehune size, though he's still naked and holding a pike. The dark clouds begin to clear, revealing a night slightly lit by a just-set sun. "You can't leave the property can you?" Banyan asks.

John, a bit more relaxed, but still breathing heavily, stops pacing, puts a hand against the garage door and sighs. "Nope."

"I guess you never could."

"Never."

Banyan stays near the sidewalk in case he has to bolt. "After Kai, huh?"

"Close but no cigar," says John. "Wouldn't mind getting my hands on that cop, too."

Banyan walks back across the street to grab a lawn chair. He looks over his shoulder to see if John is growing back to monster size. John just looks tired, leaning against the garage, so Banyan grabs two lawn chairs and returns, unfolding both and inviting John to sit with him. They both sit, John's chubby feet barely hanging over the edge of the seat. "Plastic is sticking to my ass," John says.

"That was some spectacle."

"She was here. I can really get it up for her."

"That's the last time you'll see her," says Banyan.

"I know."

"Your son was here, too. You didn't see him?"

John lets out a sad sigh. "No."

The admission makes Banyan sad as well. "We forget about our kids sometimes, don't we?"

John sits there rubbing the bridge of his nose. "It's late. I better start heading back."

"I'm gonna wait around here. Caley might turn up. She said something the other day about grabbing the rest of her clothes after Thanksgiving dinner."

"Watch the traffic. It's murder," says John.

"Will do."

Banyan looks over to John, who has the same face that he probably had when he gunned the engine of the bulldozer and rolled it off the trailer. His tired eyes close as he inhales. He opens his eyes, still holding his breath. He exhales loudly and his puffed up chest flattens as the mass moves to his brown belly. Looking more sad than scary, Banyan reaches for John's shoulder, wondering if he will feel flesh, vapor, or nothing.

Before Banyan touches him, John scoots off the lawn chair, stands, and looks up. He jumps. Pathetic vertical. He jumps again and begins to float. He gets about ten feet up, his tiny feet kicking like he's swimming, It starts to rain. John is sucked down through the pavement. All that's left are little hands that grip the edge of a manhole cover. The fingers slip, and he's gone.

Banyan sits on a lawn chair on his driveway, waiting for Caley in the rain. He perks up at the sound of every approaching car, but it's just families returning from Thanksgiving dinners. His head and eye throb from getting hit and drinking too much wine while he wonders if he can run the table. If he can get Raimi and Kai, that'd really be something.

And Caley—he is surprised that guilt over the cheating evaporated when she pulled what she did. He's kept his distance after Raimi's birthday party, respected Caley's wishes, but when he approached her about Thanksgiving, telling her how much he wanted Raimi for the weekend, since he was still on sick leave and Caley was working, she'd stood there with her knee braces and elbow brace, like a suburban cyborg, and informed him that Raimi was spending Thanksgiving weekend with her mother. Banyan had heard the whistle blow, the tip-off of an ugly divorce, and as she carried Raimi inside, the kid screaming for daddy and reaching for him over her mother's shoulders, he wondered if fear of this scene right here was why John Krill had put up with Kai for so long. John would not have been able to bear it. The child seems to always go to the mother. So Banyan was stuck with Bart and a jug of wine for Thanksgiving.

Banyan rubs his eyes as a car approaches. The car comes up Luapele Street fast. The tires screech as Caley hooks the right turn into the driveway, but Banyan doesn't get up to move. The car stops, the bumper inches away from Banyan's knees, and he looks at Caley over the hood of the car. She doesn't kill the engine at first, like she is seriously considering the option of running him down and telling the police that it was an honest accident. Who expects a man sitting in a lawn chair on the driveway in the middle of the night? Both he and Caley face each other—a stand-off—she's gunning the Volvo engine while he shows her his resolve. He sits there practically daring her to do it.

But she kills the engine instead of Banyan and steps out in the rain.

"What do you want?" Caley says.

It strikes Banyan as sad that standing up for yourself always means hurting someone else. "I want Raimi," he says.

"I met your girlfriend at the hospital today."

"She was just here. A loon, just like me."

"You aren't getting Raimi."

"We split custody, fifty-fifty."

"Right now, I am utterly incapable of giving you what you want."

"If I don't get it, I'm here to take it."

"My knees are killing me," Caley says. She sits up on the hood, puts her feet on the bumper and rubs her knees. The headlights are still on, bright in Banyan's eyes. He stands. "My knees always worse when it rains."

"You and I both know you don't even want her full-time," says Banyan. "That if it's only you and her every single day, she'll drive you crazy."

"My mother is going to help me."

"No, no, no," he says.

"What if I forgave you?" says Caley.

Banyan faces the garage. He stands under the eave, puts his good arm against the garage door, and pushes hard until he feels the hollow metal flex under the pressure. For some people, telling the truth takes strength, but for people like Banyan, it takes more strength to keep his mouth shut, like a man trying to hold back a wave. So what Banyan says next is easier to say than it should be. "I don't want you to forgive me."

Caley stands and puts her arms on the garage door like Banyan. He feels that she is pushing too, like they are challenging each other to see who can put a bend in the surface first. "If I stay," Banyan says, "if I stay, well, I will stay if it means not losing Raimi. How hard are you going to make things for me?"

Caley laughs. "Oh, your life will be a living hell."

"Maybe I can take it," he says.

"Probably for a while, you could," she says.

They stand there, leaning against the garage door, quiet. Caley sighs and pushes herself off the door. "Get out of here. We will work out some kind of joint custody."

Banyan, surprised, turns to face her. "It was always joint custody anyway, wasn't it? One of us with her while the other was at work, hardly spending time together as three."

Caley shrugs as if there isn't anything remarkable about that. "It was," she says.

"Remember that first night we moved in here, you were unpacking boxes and I went for a drive to check Mililani out? Were we even happy that night? We should've been happy, right? A young family, first-home buyers, all of that. I remember just being worried."

Caley laughs again.

"What's so funny?" Banyan asks.

"This is the best conversation we've had for two years."

It's true. Banyan is in awe—he admires this woman. "How are your knees?" he asks.

Caley smiles. "That's the first time you've asked in months."

Banyan feels like a jerk, and does the right thing by not making an excuse for being such an asshole. "Why'd you marry a selfish prick like me anyway?"

"I thought we'd have smart, imaginative, good-looking kids. You weren't really offering much more than that."

They are both laughing now, laughing so hard that tears flow. Both plop their backs on the garage door and slide down until they are sitting side by side. "You are such an asshole," she says. "When a man leaves a wife, he's looking fit and prime, while we women can only feel as if we wasted our bodies and time on the whole ordeal. It's not fair."

"No, it isn't," Banyan says. "If it makes you feel any better, I'm not so fit and prime. I just saw a fifteen-foot ghost pace our driveway."

"Wish he got you."

"He had a pike. I'd have been done for."

"And I'm supposed to let Raimi stay with you?"

"This is the only place I see him. Right here."

"Well, I'm going inside and getting drunk," she says, standing up. "Maybe he'll keep me company."

"Don't go in there," he says. "Just do me a favor and stay away from this house. Keep Raimi away, too."

She studies Banyan's face. "OK," she says. "But what are we going to do with it?"

"I'd burn it to the ground if we could afford it," he says.

He stands up. Banyan feels like crying, so he talks to stop the tears. "Were you really going to run me over earlier?"

She walks to the car and opens the door. "I bet I would've gotten away with it, too."

"Thanks, Caley," he says.

"Up yours, Banyan," she says as she steps inside the car.

Banyan is stumped as to why a conversation like that, a good conversation, despite ending with some hard feelings and colorful language, is so hard to have. What if John and Kai Krill had had a similar conversation? What if the Carballos had the conversation instead of slapping each other in the face like the Three Stooges? But for some reason, often, marriage, ideally a life-long relationship, is mute, and instead functions on the principles of silence and subterfuge, a quiet battle between two wills escalating into a sort of small-scale cold war that results in wicked acts and broken hearts.

6

As Josh, Kai, and Dan speed down Mehe'ula, Josh turns to look at Kai. He knows she saw something utterly terrifying. "You OK mom?" he asks, even though he knows the answer.

She buries her head in his shoulder and whispers. "I should've been dead a long time ago. Why didn't you guys let me die?"

This crazy talk has Josh even more worried now, and he promises himself he will not let his mother slip away like his father. His father—did she really see him? Josh is not sure, but he's never letting her near that house again—even though a part of him wanted to see a giant ghost of John Krill grab Kai by the throat and rip out her spine. She kind of deserved it.

Dan swerves into Mililani Town Center and stops in front of Star Market. "You OK?" he asks, leaving the engine running. Josh nods. Kai is practically on his lap, her fingers wrapped around the back of his neck.

"I want to drive," says Josh, wanting to get his mother off him. He feels like a roach in a glue trap, every time he tries to free a limb from Kai, it's as if another gets tangled up.

"I better drive," says Dan. "Plus, it's night. It's storming."

Torrential rains pelt the car. "No, you sit back here with her. I pretty much hate her right now."

And with that, Kai releases Josh and moves to the other side of the seat. He feels bad, but it's true, he'll protect her, but pretty much hates her. Why couldn't he see what she saw? It was like John building the bulldozer in secret all over again. "No such thing as ghosts," says Dan, sounding as if he's reassuring himself, too.

"I know," says Josh.

Dan turns up the radio. "See, storm."

Dan pulls out of the parking lot. As they head toward Nānākuli, Josh thinks about all the unconditional love bullshit, about children and parents, that he was fed all his life. Love without limits or conditions—there was no such thing. If there were, Josh's dad would not have built the goddamn bulldozer to begin with. If there were, Kai would not have done the dozens of wrong things she'd done since he was born. If there were, the ghost of John Krill would have talked to ***him.*** It was worse than finding out Santa didn't really exist, because these asshole adults still sold this unconditional shit as if it were true. Josh feels the sudden urge to open Kai's door and let her slip out onto the freeway.

But then he thinks, maybe he owes her one. She never did peddle that unconditional bullshit. It was his father who sold it and betrayed it. "We forgot to get the medicine," says Josh. "We were just there, too. Should've picked it up."

Dan looks into the rear view mirror. "I ain't going out in that rain," he says. "Plus, after tonight," he says, "I don't think there's a medicine in the world that'll help her."

"We didn't get our steak dinner at Outback either," Josh says.

A minute of silence passes. "You didn't see nothing, right?" says Dan.

Josh looks at his mother, who is now sleeping. "No," he says. "But that's not what's bothering me."

"What is?"

"That if it was real, if she really saw him, he didn't see me."

7

It seems to Kai that when you start to lose it, non-narcotic self-prescribed therapy beats anything a shrink can tell you. She wasn't a kooky anti-psychiatry scientologist, or a stoic, or anything like that—if psychiatry helps a person, if religion helps a person, whatever; that's great; it's just that these are things that will not help her. She doesn't need someone to tell her why she is the way she is. One thing that always shocked her about John Krill was his lack of self-knowledge, how he'd thought his intellect was weak, but it really wasn't, or how he'd forced himself to believe that if he set the example, his family would turn out okay. She's always found other peoples' capacity for self-delusion funny, but now, as she drives to the beach in the middle of the night, she is shocked to realize that she is one of the crowd. That image of her and Banyan and her children on a porch—it was about as possible as selling pyramid scheme juice and making millions. Caley Mott and the ghost of John Krill with pike in hand showed her that.

It's late, long past midnight, as Kai sneaks out of the house and gets into her car. When Kai gets to Ulehawa Beach Park, she parks and gets out. The wind is really swirling, and it kicks up sand from the asphalt and whirls it into her face. She wipes her eyes as she strips down to a one-piece and wonders where she should leave the keys to her car. She figures no one will go out of their way to steal an '89 POS, so she leaves the keys on the driver's side seat and heads out to shore.

The once-evicted homeless are making a comeback. There are three tents to the right, one with a generator and water hose outside, another with a hibachi made from a beer keg sawed in half. By now she recognizes the difference between those who were forced into homelessness and those who are actually living on the beach as a sort of permanent arrangement. Those who have been forced onto the beach sleep in their cars and lack cooking devices. Those who are in for the long haul—generators, water hoses, hibachis, picnic tables and laundry lines—these are the ones who have accepted their fate.

Kai steps into the water. The coldness jars her. She figures the human race can be divided into two types: those who are exhilarated by jumping into water and those who find only discomfort in it. Her body tightens with each step, water inching up her legs in assault. The next step will put her neck high, so she closes her eyes and jumps in.

Somehow she believed the ocean would cure her, that learning to tread water would cure her. Now, as the current tugs, she realizes she's been duped by self-delusion again. The horizon pulls her like a magnet and seeing a psychiatrist starts to look like a good idea, as does religion. The tips of her toes don't sink into sand anymore and the only way to keep her head above water is to hold her breath, sink, then pop up again.

Soon, Kai has to use her arms to get deep enough for her feet to touch the sand. The sand dimples she makes are erased with each push of the tide. As the water deepens, thoughts disappear. There is only the will to get back to shore. She holds her breath and cups her hands. The strokes and kicks are frantic but effective. She is back to the spot where she can hop on one foot and catch breaths as her head breaks the surface of the water. But she does not stop there. She moves closer and closer to shore until she can feel the sand beneath her.

As she lies on the sand, she notices a burning in her nasal passage. Goosebumps cover her skin as her body now longs for the warmth of the water. She stands and presses her fingers against a nostril and blows out snot and water. She heads back out into the ocean, this time staying where her feet can touch ground. After ten minutes, she is doggie paddling parallel with the shore. The worst thirty-five-year-old swimmer in the world is feeling good about herself.

When her muscles, lungs, and burning eyes have had about enough, she walks up to the parking lot. Her car is gone. She sits on the knee-high stone wall and laughs. Kai walks to Nānākuli in a one-piece and no shoes, and for the first time in her life realizes that sometimes having nothing is the best feeling in the world.

When she gets about a mile up Farrington Highway, her car is there, motor running, an open driver's side door, hazards blinking. She leans in, checking if anyone is inside. It's empty. Kai climbs in, sits, and slams the door shut. Fingers wrapped around steering wheel, she laughs so hard she cries.

8

Banyan and Bart sit on barstools in the Carballo kitchen. Banyan has a stack of frozen blueberry waffles in front of him. He presses one against the purple patch under his eye. After one waffle warms, he eats it then grabs another. "You know what's sick?" Bart says. "When I have erotic dreams, I don't dream about some hot model or actress. I dream about my wife every time." Bart has already made it clear he does not want to talk about what Kai and Banyan supposedly saw on the driveway.

"You need your head examined," says Banyan, pressing a new waffle against his swelling skin.

"Seriously. And it's not some super-young version of her, not when I first met her at my cousin's grad party, but that forty-year-old woman, mother of three. Actually, that's a lie. Maybe she looks younger, long hair, smoking body stuffed in a tight red dress, but yea, it's always her. I didn't even really notice this until like our tenth anniversary, sometime around there. Not sure what it means."

"Either you really dig your wife or lack imagination, maybe both," Banyan says. "I thought we don't talk about marriage here?"

"It's better than talking about that other thing, you crazy fuck. Besides, we're not talking marriage," Bart says. "Just dreams."

"Kai told me you beat up your wife."

"Bullshit."

"You never hit her?"

"Slapped her a few times, but not as many times as she slapped me. Hell, if anything, she's Mo and I'm Curly. Sometimes, we have to wake each other up. Last time it happened, it happened in public, when my oldest came home from Afghanistan. That's probably why I'm known as the Luapele Street Wife Beater. But yea, it was in public, so for her, it was unforgivable."

"Would've been fine if it was in the bedroom?"

"Yea. Plus, it was me who should've gotten slapped that time. I was the one running my mouth."

"About what?"

"Was telling John about Kai and Ster-Roy. Man, I figured he would have whooped one of their asses, and both of them deserved it. You ever watch Chris Rock's stand-up? He has this great line about how no one is above an ass whooping. As we get older, we forget that. Being old is no license for acting like an asshole."

Banyan nods.

"No one is above an ass-whooping, indeed," says Bart. "Didn't think John would build a bulldozer. But I'm sitting here now and thinking about it for obvious reasons. Wife and two daughters in the mainland, probably not coming back, and I'm thinking I want to do the same damn thing, and I have no idea why."

"I remember being in school," Banyan says, "learning about stress. We got this list of the most stressful situations in a person's life, and at the top was death of a spouse or child, of course, but the second one was divorce. I remember thinking, how is that even possible? I'd broken up with girls before. How can that even be in the same ballpark as getting your legs bit off by a shark, or losing your arms in an industrial accident."

"What do you think now?"

"I'd still rather get a divorce than lose my arms," Banyan says.

'Yea, maybe divorce is third then, because I'd rather have my arms too."

"Maybe fourth, because I'd rather get a divorce than say, get terminal cancer."

"Yea," says Bart, "same here. I'm starting to feel better."

The conversation strikes Banyan as weak in comparison to one he'd have with Kai, where she would match his terminal cancer with twenty years of Chinese water torture, then he'd say something like getting ass-raped for twenty years in prison, then she'd say falling in love with a different person every day, then he'd say finding out hell really exists, and she'd say it doesn't really matter what's second place, because she experienced the world champions of stress two times in her life, the deaths of child and spouse, and, well, he is not sure what she'd say after that. But he wants to find out.

Bart chews a frozen waffle. "These aren't bad."

"The Posse up to helping me one more time?" says Banyan.

"It's Thanksgiving, so I know Jesse is off tomorrow, and I bet Roy is too. What did you have in mind?"

"I'm going to get Kai," Banyan says.

"Why?" asks Bart.

"She needs me."

"Sure you don't got that the other way around?"

"Maybe. Probably. Who knows."

"Know where they're staying?" asks Bart.

"Nope. But I figure Ster-Roy can find out. He's a firefighter in Wai'anae, and the firefighters and cops all know each other, right?"

"What about your wife and kid?"

The kid. People always use a kid's well-being as an excuse to stay married. But that wasn't it at all. They just didn't want to live in another place, without their children, or he didn't at least. Maybe that's why textbook psychologists listed divorce as the second most stressful situation a person can face. It was because of what came with divorce—either the guilt over giving up a child for a shot at selfish happiness, or becoming a single parent, which must be a variation of Chinese water torture in itself. Anyway, divorce without kids was just breaking up. With kids it was an irreversible severing of more than one thing.

"We're done," says Banyan.

"Same here," says Bart, with a mouthful of waffles. "We ride out at sunrise?"

"I don't know about sunrise," says Banyan. "Maybe high noon?"

"Mmm, high noon. Yea, I like that."

"The first time I met the cop, he said that if he ever catches me with Kai, he'd kill me."

"He seemed nice to me. Rational."

"We all looked rational next to her. Even me."

"Yea. Don't worry, man. I got your back. I'll call Jesse, too. Maybe we can borrow a nuclear submarine."

Banyan thinks about what Bart said about having erotic dreams about his wife. He never dreamed about Caley like that. Most of his dreams starring Caley involved her dissecting him like a frog in a sophomore biology class. It was a mean thing to dream even if he had no control over it. Poor Bart. The guy really loves his wife. "Sorry about your wife and the kids," says Banyan.

Bart gets off the stool and stretches. "Do me a favor. If it actually works between you and Kai, no slapping. A good wife—that's the only person above an ass-whooping."

Bart heads upstairs. He stops and turns around. "That cop. Right before he grabbed Kai, I saw him looking at the driveway, almost like there was something there out to get him."

"He was the one who shot John."

"No shit?" Bart says. "Well, I guess that makes sense."

"He loves the kid." Banyan thinks back to the first time he met Dan, how it wasn't Kai he was protecting in front of Wai'anae High School. It was Josh. "The kid is with me now. Her too." That's exactly what Dan said, as if Kai was an afterthought.

"Yea, I think it's the kid," says Bart. "But he knows that without the mother, there is no kid. They come in pairs. Don't think he's going to let her go without a fight."

Banyan heads upstairs for bed. He thinks about popping a Vicodin as he looks out the window, rain assaulting the neighborhood. Aside from the paint job (olive-grey, maroon, and dark-brown trim), the house under the peach light looks just like the houses next to it. When he and Caley put it on the market, he does not see how a prospective buyer will even guess at what went on in there: the menehune named John, the destruction of two marriages, the battle over the wall that now needs some patching up, but is within MTA regulations. No, a prospective buyer will just see a two-story 3/2 1400-square-foot home with central air, priced to move, children riding their bicycles in cul de sac figure eights, the smiling parents chatting together on smoothly paved driveways.

They will look up Mililani Mauka on the Internet and discover that the top-rated public elementary school is nearby, that the community has the fewest registered sex offenders on the island, and decide that the nasty morning and early evening traffic is a price worth paying. They will buy. They will hang pictures their child drew at three years old, stick figures without torsos, arms, and legs attached to a bulbous head. They will put up pictures on the fridge with magnets—custom Costco Christmas cards and birthday invitations, pictures of children with smiling parents mass produced on glossy photo paper.

Whether John Krill ever returns and haunts them will depend on the couple. When Banyan looked up how to get rid of ghosts, he found out that ghosts only appear if the people who live in the house create negative energy, oxygen for the spirits. Along with furniture, appliances, toys, framed pictures, and decorative koi figurines, Banyan and Caley brought enough of this energy to feed John, each negative thought and action a meal packed with nutrients, and boy did John Krill thrive and grow.

Banyan draws the curtain over the window, gets in bed, and dreams about Xavier Teve Musashi Krill, and wonders if he will ever swoop down and take his father, both their kicking feet propelling them up in the air.

9

"We need to see something real," says Dan.

It's ten AM when Josh and Dan head into town, leaving a sleeping Kai at home, to check out "Bodies ... The Exhibition," a showcase of real human bodies preserved with acetone, silicone rubber, polyester, and epoxy resin. The exhibit is at Ala Moana Shopping Center, next to Nordstrom. Josh is pretty sure he'll be grossed out, but something real sounds good to him, too.

Josh and Dan walk into a room with avocado green drywall and track lights. Dan pays the kamaʻāina rate, twenty-three fifty a ticket. They hand over their tickets and enter a room with lighted display cases containing human bones. Little signs posted on the walls point out interesting factoids, like "children's bones grow faster in the springtime." This first room is rather tame, so Josh and Dan head over to the next display area. "Not very crowded," Dan says.

The next room is more gruesome. A severed arm and leg, flesh still on the bone, in a large rectangular display case. Two intact male bodies, one shooting a basketball, the other in mid-stride with a football. Josh and Dan stand in front of the football player, examining muscles closely. "Looks like dried out prime rib or something," says Josh.

"Supposedly these bodies were donated by the Chinese government," says Dan. "Like dead prisoners or something."

"You can do that, just give bodies away like that?"

"I guess, in China."

A curator in a white lab coat asks if Josh and Dan need help with anything, like they're out shopping or something. They don't. The curator heads to three girls arguing whether these are real human bodies or all this is a sham. The curator ensures them that the bodies are indeed real human cadavers. "That's not too cool, that these were real people," says Josh.

"Ah fuck um," Dan says. "Probably murderers and rapists and shit."

Josh reads a sign that says, "If all the muscles in your body worked together, you could lift more than ten tons."

The next few rooms are organ displays—brains sliced in halves and quarters like fruit. The nervous system growing from the brain like long strands of dry grass. Dimmer lights further in, accompanied by a stronger formaldehyde smell—hearts in display cases, bright blue and red blood vessels in clear liquid, like coral with string thin branches in aquariums. Dan looks as bored as Josh. Josh expected to be sickened, these being real people and all, but he can't see them as anything but objects in a rather tame freak show.

The last few rooms are more amusing, to Dan at least. Two display cases, one with the blackened lungs of a smoker, the other the white lungs of a non-smoker, a glass disposal case in between them where smokers are supposed to dump their cigarettes after being thoroughly disgusted. Dan laughs. Next, they stand in front of a full female body. "Look at the size of that camel-toe," says Dan.

"Man, it's like I'm here with a kid," says Josh.

"Dude, look at those tits. A-cups tops."

Josh shakes his head and walks to the embryo and fetus display, Dan following him. More formaldehyde—tiny bodies, from eighteen days to twenty-four weeks old, in glass cylinders. "Damn, look at this one," says Dan. He's standing by the twenty-four week old fetus. "It has a head of hair."

Josh looks at the hair and thinks of Xavier. His brother was a lot bigger than this fetus when he died, but he always imagines his older brother as a diaper-wearing baby. It's the only display that shakes Josh. A dead baby on display—pretty sick stuff. His father's shoulder tattoo of Xavier, it used to give him the same feeling he's feeling now, like he's looking at something he shouldn't be looking at.

Josh sits on a bench in the last display room, by the biggest case in the exhibit, an entire male body sliced in thin pieces, like ham in a butcher's shop. Dan sits by him. "Not that great, huh," Dan says.

"Seriously. It could be cows or something, and to me it'd be the same."

"I wonder why."

Josh shrugs. Other customers walk by in twos and threes, mostly women. Dan's cell phone rings. One of the lab coated curators approaches him as he answers the phone. "Sir, you were supposed to turn off your phone," says the curator.

"Josh, I'm gonna head outside and wait for you." Dan walks off, talking into the phone.

Josh knows why he's not wowed by all of this. All he sees is slabs of meat and bone, the stuff he's made of. These may have been real people once, but they aren't anymore. Real bodies are in constant motion or emotion, and these dead things, well, ghosts didn't come from these. They came from something else.

Josh passes through the last room, a gift shop that sells "Bodies ... The Exhibition" tee shirts, coffee mugs, soaps, body lotion, and honey cinnamon almonds. He pushes through the door where Dan waits for him. "We gotta head back," says Dan.

"What's up?"

"Friend at the station called. Banyan, and a couple of the other Mililani knuckleheads are headed to our house to try to spring Kai or something. Guess that was a courtesy call."

They jog back to Dan's car and get in. As Dan reverses out of the parking space, Josh says, "Wait a minute. Spring her? It's not like she's in jail."

"No shit," Dan says.

"Well?" Josh asks.

"I don't even know what the fuck I'm doing anymore," says Dan, clearly frustrated.

But as Dan flips on the siren and speeds towards the Wai'anae Coast, Josh wonders, if she isn't in jail, why the hell are they rushing back as if she's about to escape?

10

USA: 80% white, 4% Asian, 13% black, 1.5% two or more races, .2% Native Hawaiian or Pacific Islander, 1% American Indian or Native Alaskan.

Hawai'i: 24% white, 42% Asian, 2% black, 22% two or more races, 9% Native Hawaiian or Pacific Islander, .3% American Indian or Native Alaskan.

Mililani: 20% white, 47% Asian, 3% black, 24% two or more races, 5% Native Hawaiian or Pacific Islander, .2% American Indian or Native Alaskan.

Wai'anae: 9% white, 19% Asian, .8% black, 42% two or more races, 27% Native Hawaiian or Pacific Islander, .3% American Indian or Native Alaskan.

According to Wikipedia, Latino is a separate question, and Banyan has no clue why.

Banyan has never seen as many 4x4 trucks, Hawai'i state flags, tents, and cars with missing hubcaps as he does on the Wai'anae Coast. He always feels like a tourist here, and the place, unlike Mililani, blows away his notion that Hawai'i is more American than anything else. The Luapele Street Posse passes a sign that says, among other things:

The Government which our
Queen and Ancestors Died

Protesting against the Theft
by the American Govt.!
Koho ʻole mai namunamu

The beach is a surreal rural ghetto, because behind the tent communities is a coast that can stand up aesthetically to any other beach on the island. The water is a pure, expansive blue that conceals the depths below. The poverty seems like a CGI special effect Photoshopped over a picture of tropical paradise. But the tents aren't the ugliest part—it's the cars, oxidized, rusted, or both, that line Farrington Highway, and the highway itself with its steady traffic that is like graffiti on a Frederic Church painting. When people, locals and tourists alike, drive around the island, they do not drive through the Waiʻanae Coast because it is a sixteen-mile tangent off the beaten path and dead ends at Makaha.

"Interesting place," says Banyan from the backseat of Bart Carballos' maroon SUV.

Roy turns around from the front passenger side, propping his huge, veiny arm on the seat. "I've been stationed here for four years, and let me tell you, this place has the most action on the island. Just last week a drug dealer dropped a jacked-up car on another guy. Brush fires, stabbings, shark bites, gambling, drugs, I'll probably never leave. I actually like to work for a living."

"More interesting than Mililani," says Banyan.

"Don't know what's so bad about Mililani," says Bart, who is driving. "I just wanted a place that's relatively affordable, a nice place to raise kids."

It's a simple sentiment, but so true. No one in their right mind moves to Mililani unless they are parents. John Krill—he bulldozed Mililani because it went back on its promise, the promise of healthy, well-adjusted GT (Gifted and Talented) kids, a stable marriage, and swell neighbors who shared tools and coupons. Instead, what he got was what he could've gotten easily enough if he'd stayed in his hometown, Wai'anae—a marriage riddled with problems, and neighbors who break into your house when you're not home, stealing pussy instead of jewelry. He could've gotten all that shit anywhere, and Mililani Mauka, that hypocritical son-of-a-bitch, was the ultimate in false advertising, so John Krill spent months cementing sheets of steel to a bulldozer, and took his futile revenge.

"Remember that news story?" says Roy. "The haole kid from the mainland was going to start college here. He decides to camp on the beach before the semester starts and starts taking pictures of people on the beach and gets himself killed."

The three other men nod. "The government once dumped like 4000 tons of chemical munitions in the ocean here," says Jesse. "Like right after World War II."

"Aren't most of the sumo wrestlers from Hawai'i from Wai'anae?" says Bart.

"Think Akebono was from Waimanalo," says Roy. "Konishiki was from Nānākuli, I think. Musashimaru went to Wai'anae High. Two yokozunas and an ozeki. Not bad at all."

The drive up sixteen miles of Wai'anae Coast begins to feel like a train ride to Banyan, but the scenery lacks the repetitive vastness of a train ride on the mainland—Mililani is only about twenty miles behind him. Oahu is a 600-square-mile island stuffed with 900,000 people and over 700,000 cars that busy themselves like ants on a bologna sandwich floating out to sea. Banyan is right there with them, digging through the moist, enriched middle, chasing a taste of meat before the sandwich takes in too much water and is sucked under or ripped apart by waves.

"Farrington Highway," says Roy. "Who was Farrington again?"

"He was one of the first governors of Hawai'i when it was a territory," says Jesse. "He was from Maine or something."

They stop in front of Wai'anae Police Station, a pink, single-story building the size of a 7-Eleven. There is a flag pole out front; the American and Hawai'i state flags flutter like laundry in the wind. "Like I said," says Roy. "I know Dan, know all these guys. I'll find out where he lives, but everyone needs to behave. We just want to talk to Kai. Nothing is going to spiral out of control."

Banyan doesn't want to talk to her. He wants to spirit her and her son away. "I guess I should've just come by myself," says Banyan. "But I needed you to get the address."

"Didn't he threaten to shoot you if he saw you around Kai?" asks Roy.

"Not shoot, just kill."

"Like I said, I know him," says Roy. "He means it."

As Roy enters the station, Banyan can't get over the smallness of it. Wai'anae is a well-publicized frontline of the war on ice, violence in general, and the homeless. Cops in this small station should be coming out of a two story compound dressed in fatigues and armed with M-16s.

After about fifteen minutes, Roy comes back out. "Back up to Nānākuli," he says.

"How'd it go?" asks Bart.

"I talked to the captain, asked if maybe a couple of them wanted to come with us to make sure things went smoothly," says Roy. "He just laughed and said, 'I don't wanna get myself killed.'"

"Jesus," says Jesse. "He knows we are coming, right?"

"He does," says Bart.

"Give me the address, and I'll go alone," says Banyan.

After a few seconds of silence, Bart says, "No, it's fine. He's a rational adult, right? I mean, to become a cop, you need to take some sort of psychological exam, right? We just want to talk."

As they drive back up the coast, Banyan feels like they are meandering up a rough trail in a covered wagon while shirtless Comanches hide in the brush, knives in mouths, drooling to cut off some tourist nuts.

11

Kai, still in her one piece bathing suit, wakes up, glad yet surprised that she has the house to herself. She showers, changes, then steps out of her room to grab the morning paper. She takes out the classifieds and begins her search for a place to rent. She thinks of Josh as she sips coffee and circles affordable listings with a pen, thrown by the idea that there was a time that he actually lived and grew in her belly, from embryo, to webbed-finger lima bean, to three-pound preemie, all that time, fingerprints etched on, eyelids unfusing, and rubbery cartilage hardening to bone—he'd been like a parasite feeding off her, and now he hated her. It was the first coherent thing she heard in the car after seeing John's ghost, "I pretty much hate her," he said.

The coffee table that Josh made with the two koi intertwined. It was her and Josh wasn't it, the two koi, one trying to get away from the other? Too fucking bad, she thinks, circling one listing hard, ripping the newspaper, you're my son, you're a kid, and you're stuck with me for a few more years. You hate me, and I deserve it, but I'm your mother and I'm going to take care of you, like it or not. As for the fifteen-foot, pike-wielding ghost of John Krill, she's sorry, but he can go to hell.

A car approaches outside, so Kai gets up and looks out the window. It's a maroon SUV. The car stops and four men come out, Ster-Roy, Bart, Jesse, and Banyan. She thinks about love and its chronic bad timing as she rolls up the classified section, puts it in her pocket along with the pen, and steps out. "What's this?" she says. "The posse come to hang me?"

"We came to spring you," says Banyan, winking. "You and the kid."

And Kai can see that the kid, Josh, is an afterthought. She knows too well how that works. She pulls the classified section from her pocket and holds it up. "I'm going to spring myself."

Banyan looks at the others, who catch the hint, and climb back into the SUV. He puts his hands in his pockets, and looks up at the sky. The brightness of the day turns his hair from light brown to amber. She wonders if he knows how beautiful he looks with his head up like that. "Let's find a place together," he says.

"Think I need to do this alone," she says.

"Is this some sort of feminist awakening?" he asks. "I'm not being an ass; it's a serious question." Sweat builds on his brow. "And why do you think you can all of a sudden find a place now after all these months?"

She's not sure why, but she ***knows*** she can. Teaching herself to swim the night before made her feel like she can do anything. "I still want to see you," she says. "But I need to do this alone."

Banyan nods. "Well, let's go then. The least I can do is help you look. Hell, I need to look for a place myself. We can work together."

She feels like she's being suckered into something, but it does make sense. She looks at his cast. The picture she drew, the one with the porch, the no ghosts allowed sign, and the boy pushing the girl sitting on the tree swing, has faded to the point where if she didn't draw it herself, she would have no idea what the picture was supposed to be. Banyan turns to wave to the posse. The maroon SUV starts up. "They're gonna go," says Banyan. He grabs the classifieds from Kai and looks down at the circled listings. "Let's go take a look at some of these," he says while grabbing her hand and gently tugging. The SUV reverses and turns, pointing downhill. Kai takes the pen out of her pocket and grabs Banyan's cast. She scribbles on it. Banyan reads it, nods, and smiles.

That's when the blaring of the police siren nears, and the three men in the SUV get out, looking like a group of boys who are about to get busted for stealing a bicycle or something.

12

Josh half expects Dan to stop the car, rip off his sling, throw on a suit of armor, and jump on a white horse with shield and sword in hand. Instead, he drives up to the maroon SUV, stops, removes his gun from its holster, steps out of the car, and fires twice, shooting out two tires. The rapport of the gunfire shocks Josh with two sharp, ear-splitting cracks. His ears ring as he gets out of the car and follows Dan to the group of men running towards the house, ducking, as if giant mythological birds are going to sweep down, grab them, and carry them off. Banyan is the only one not running. He's standing there with his hands up. Kai takes one look at Dan and heads inside, slamming the door before anyone else can get in. Typical, thinks Josh.

Bart, Jesse, and Roy stop scrambling and put their hands up like Banyan. "What did I tell you," says Dan, putting the gun back in the holster. "You come around the kid and his mom, I'm gonna kill you."

The other men, Bart, a fifty-year-old who looks like he is pushing sixty, Jesse, with his premature grey hair and body by Bud, even Roy, with his absent neck and mounds of muscle, all look deflated, despite the fact that there are four of them and they are looking at a man who has one arm in a sling, and a hand sloppily wrapped in gauze, looking like a pile of toilet paper. But yea, he does have a gun.

A couple of neighbors crack open their doors to take a look. Dan looks at both of them and the doors close. "All of you, put your hands behind your head and lie on the driveway," Dan says. "Bad timing, boys. I'm sick of all this shit."

As Josh heads inside to his mother's room, he can see the headlines: Psycho cop kills four suburbanites. He is reminded of his old fish tank, and that foot-long Tiger Oscar, El Toro, and how it seems he has finally found the little cichlid that can replace it as the bull of the tank. Only he finds no satisfaction in his discovery, as it's only causing heartburn, and for the first time in a long time, all he wants is his mommy. Before he gets to the hallway, he crashes into Kai. They are tangled up for a second, and she puts down the two packed suitcases she's carrying, grabs his shoulders and moves him to the side. He loses his balance and falls to the floor flat on his back. He looks up as she looks down.

"Get your stuff together," she says. "We're out of here."

"I don't want to go back to the beach," he says.

"We aren't. Never again. Get your stuff. **Now.**"

He heads to his room and starts to pack, flinching at imaginary gun shots. He fills a duffel bag with clothes and takes it out to the living room. He places the bag on Kai's suitcases, which sit under the inspirational poster of a man dangling from a snowy cliff. He peeks outside the window. The men are no longer there, but the crippled SUV still is, slightly leaning to the right. Josh heads back to his room to pack more stuff. As he packs, his mother rolls her coffee table past his doorway like a wheel.

Josh finishes up packing a cooler with the last of his things—more clothes and a toothbrush. Kai waits for him at the front door. She doesn't even seem the least bit curious about what's going on outside. "You got everything?" she asks.

"My bike," he says. "It's in the garage."

"Let's load this stuff in the car," she says as she opens the door.

Josh carries the cooler outside. What he sees next, he will never forget.

Banyan stands facing Dan in the middle of the street, twirling a one-handed war hammer. Both are in full suits of steel French plate armor, burgonets, cuirasses, vambraces, greaves, sabatons and all, except for their right arms, Dan's in a sling, Banyan's in a cast. Roy, Bart, and Jesse watch with the intense interest of sports fans, sitting on the tailgate of the SUV, grinning. Dan raises a flail, and twirls the spiked iron morning star around and around. "You're going down, professor," he says.

Banyan crouches defensively and grips his hammer. The plate greaves are a bit short on him, making him look like he's wearing clam diggers. Kai bumps into Josh, distracted by the spectacle of the two men in metal suits. "Put the cooler in our car," she says, shaking her head.

"Do you see this?" he asks.

"Yes," Kai says, not really looking, grabbing the cooler from him. "We're out of here as soon as I finish packing up."

Josh can't believe his mother isn't interested in watching. Dan charges Banyan and swings downward. Banyan ducks and slides, but the flail head hits his shoulder. He struggles up, the weight of the suit almost bringing him down. Dan chases and swings again. This time he hits Banyan's back, the strike setting off a loud ping of metal against metal. Banyan tumbles, pings on asphalt this time, but manages to squat back up.

"Jesus, he's swinging hard," says Roy. "This isn't all that funny anymore."

It goes like this for awhile, Dan catching Banyan with a hard blow, the spikes of the morning star planting tiny dents in Banyan's breastplate, Banyan tumbling and retreating, but he gets back up each time. Both are panting. "Yield, motherfucker," says Dan between gasps. But Banyan is back up. He swings his hammer for the first time, and the head ricochets off the breastplate, almost fumbling out of Banyan's hand.

Dan backs up, giving Banyan more respect after that blow. Banyan drops the hammer and takes off his helm. He tugs at the rest of the armor. Sweat drips from his face. He removes the gauntlet first and wipes his brow.

"You give up then, pussy?" asks Dan, panting.

"Nope," says Banyan. After all the armor is off, he picks up the hammer and charges Dan, who backs up slowly. It's Dan who's taking a beating now, Banyan much too fast and steady without armor. It's a risky ploy, but Josh respects him for doing it. One hit from the flail, and Banyan will be done for.

Kai taps Josh on the shoulder. "It's time to go," she says.

"Dan's going to kill your boyfriend," he says.

Kai watches for the first time as Banyan dances around Dan, who is dragging around his own body as if it's a ton of bricks. Kai walks to the hood of Dan's car and pulls his gun out of the holster. Josh feels sick as she points it at Dan. "Is this the gun?" she asks.

Dan pulls off his helm, revealing a face gasping and sweating like there's no tomorrow. "No," he says. "I got rid of that one."

"You saved him," she says. "You saved my boy."

Dan nods. "But he's ***mine,***" she says.

Dan drops the morning star on the pavement. "We're fine, OK?" she says as she puts the gun back in the holster.

Dan looks at Banyan, who is also panting, and Banyan puts his hands up, indicating he's had enough. Dan looks at Kai, then at Josh. He stares at Josh.

"Jesus fuck," says Dan.

He walks to the house, chest jutted, shoulders back, metal armor clanging, and he doesn't look back.

Banyan walks up to Kai and Josh. "So I'll see you around?" he says while bending down, holding his knees, trying to catch his breath. Kai points to his cast. He nods. Josh reads it. It's a simple math equation. "Kids > all."

"You're right," says Banyan.

"I know," says Kai.

As Josh and Kai head down the mountain in their luggage-piled '89 Sentra, Josh thinks about his father, and how sad it was that he could not leave this world gracefully. That was the thing about John Krill nobody got, that the death of Xavier Teve Musashi Krill was just as hard on him as it was on Kai, and that although he tried to face the tragedy with grace, grace was not the same thing as taking abuse with a shit-eating grin. It amazes Josh that people get the two mixed up, considering that one brings up images of a gazelle fleeing while the other conjures images of a live gazelle getting its guts pulled out by a lion. You can watch the Discovery channel anytime and know those two things aren't similar at all. Maybe his father thought he'd learned grace from the sick and dying Xavier Teve Musashi Krill, who John told Josh, every year on Xavier's birthday, hardly complained as he lay dying. But Josh now knows that grace is impossible when inevitability is involved. Grace is something that can only occur when a body trying to survive expresses its self-love through motion. What Banyan did back there, that was grace. What Kai is doing now, grace.

"Let's go get some food before we check out some rentals," says Kai.

"I'm with you," says Josh.

And for the first time in fifteen years, he is.

v. Mele Kalikimaka

Josh sees the hole as he pounds a nail into the eave. When he hammers the nail, a buzzing comes from inside the dime-sized hole. He leans forward, a carpenter bee shoots out, and Josh almost falls off the ladder.

"Mom!"

Kai's going through a string of Christmas lights, looking for the burnt out bulb.

"What?"

"There's like bees in the wood."

Kai puts down the lights and looks up. She grabs a broom and approaches Josh. "Get off the ladder."

Josh gets down. Kai whacks the eave with the broomstick. Another bee shoots out, buzzing, angry. Josh jumps back. "Jesus, they can dig through wood?"

"Yea."

"Do they sting?"

"Only the female, I think, the queen."

Josh smirks. "I got an idea."

Josh returns with a net. Kai hits the wood while Josh catches the bees. His mom's smiling even after nine bees. It's been awhile.

Kai and Josh managed to qualify for a 2/1 805-square-foot rental in Wai'anae. The iron bars over the windows are a bit disconcerting, as is the neon-green exterior, but the stove and fridge work and the roof doesn't leak.

Josh places each live bee in a large bottle. "Why are you saving them?" Kai asks.

"Figure Raimi would like it."

Raimi and Banyan come out of the house. Raimi runs to the bottle, almost stumbling twice before she gets there. "What's with all the banging?" Banyan asks. Just as he says it, Josh nets another one. Raimi, excited, watches, as Josh puts the bee in the bottle. "Need help?" asks Banyan.

"Nah, I got it," says Josh.

"Don't think your landlord will be too happy about the nails," Banyan says to Kai.

Kai knocks on the wood. "It's dead. This eave doesn't have too much life left in it anyway."

Banyan nods. Raimi shakes the bottle vigorously and squeals when the bees erupt.

Dan pulls up. He's carrying a casserole dish. "Pineapple Spam," he says.

"What the hell is pineapple Spam?"

"Jesus, Krill, plantation food." He looks and Banyan. "How're these kids? Good thing I made it. It'll teach them some culture."

Dan puts the dish on the picnic table and shakes Banyan's hand. "They'll miss out on a lot," says Banyan.

"Like how to pick 'opihi," says Dan.

"Like never turn your back on the ocean," says Banyan. "So when did Hawai'i stop being Hawai'i?" he asks Kai.

Kai lifts the foil off the casserole dish and sneaks a peak. "Hmm, maybe in the 70s when they went all out to criminalize pot?"

"When kids stopped sitting in the back of pick ups?" Banyan says.

"When kids stopped putting their slippers on their hands to run faster."

"When they began building houses without jalousie windows."

"When plate lunches came with a choice of tossed salad."

"When the fishing became better in Waikīkī than Kahalu'u."

"When they translated the Bible into pidgin," says Kai.

"Good one," says Banyan.

They do this a lot, go back and forth, like it's a contest only the two of them are fit to play. Sometimes Josh thinks of one or two to add, but he doesn't interrupt. It'd be like walking in on them when they're making out or something. Josh thinks Banyan is trying to get Kai to marry him, but for some reason, she's not into it. Josh wouldn't mind. Banyan's a pretty cool guy. He digs the little girl, too. Neither of them live in the Mililani Mauka house anymore. In fact, Banyan says someone is buying it. They supposedly laughed when Banyan told them about the ghost. Josh can't help himself. "When people in Hawai'i stopped believing in ghosts."

Both Banyan and Kai look away, quiet. Dan climbs the ladder and crams his pinky into one of the holes. "Don't think that's a good idea," says Josh.

"Relax, Krill. I'm a professional."

Sure enough, Dan leaps off the ladder after the queen stings him. He almost falls on Raimi, who drops the bottle full of bees. The glass shatters, and the bees hover above the house for a moment before heading back into their home. Banyan holds a crying Raimi in his arms. Dan looks as if he's on the verge of tears as well. "Sorry, little girl," he says.

"Go inside before you inflict more damage," says Kai.

"What's for dinner?" Dan asks.

"Just your traditional turkey, stuffing, and mashed potatoes," says Banyan, comforting Raimi, checking her clothes and hair for tiny shards of glass.

"And pineapple Spam," says Josh.

"Josh, I brought the deep fryer," says Dan. "Just for you."

"Never again," says Josh.

Kai sweeps up the broken glass as Banyan, Dan, and Raimi head inside. Josh picks up the big pieces and puts them on the picnic table. "Be careful," she says.

"So what about these bees?"

"Doubt we can get rid of them. Even if we kill them." Kai's smiling as she says it.

Josh looks at the house and thinks what a strange extended family this is. He supposes it's an American thing, the divorces, the step-children, the children posing as adults raising real children on a bare-bones budget where utilities like cable TV and broadband Internet access are nonetheless necessities, and as he looks out, amazed to be living in a house with a view of the ocean, he thinks about the inevitability of suburbia and how it is imperceptibly sprawling towards them now. It's pavement, not lava, that flows from the mountains as the warming planet's sea level rises. Josh figures that one day the asphalt and ocean will meet, and a new city, lacking native things, will rise out of the brackish Pacific waters.

An interview with the Author

1. **Bamboo Ridge is well known for its cadre of local writers whose collective conscious brought what it means to be local into the mainstream back when no one was defining it. There's a shared experience there, a shared background, and they wear the label "local writer" as a badge of honor. Do you consider yourself a local writer?**

   No. I consider myself someone who writes about Hawai'i by default. There's that writing cliché, "write what you know." I write about Hawai'i because Hawai'i is what I know. I don't know if I'm a local writer. I think about Hawai'i, but it's more coincidental than anything else.

2. **Your books blow up all the usual clichés about Hawai'i—the countryside in your books is ugly, proverty stricken and violent. Hawai'i isn't about the aloha spirit, it's about hatred. How did you get past all the clichés?**

   Country living has been romanticized since the invention of the city. The clichés revolve around the concept that country offers what a city can't: a quiet, laid back, pastoral life. There's truth in this. However, it is also true that many people live country because it's the only place they can afford to live, which means poverty often trumps pastoral. And whether urban or rural, poverty comes with the same trappings—anger, ingnorance, violence, the ugly. It was impossible not to see this where I grew up.

3. **Often your novels contain characters doing bad—occasionally reprehensible—things, yet somehow they manage to remain sympathetic. How are you able to create such deeply flawed, deeply troubled characters that still manage to engage readers' empathy?**

My major compulsion is to be realistic when creating characters (sometimes, maybe even to a fault). Couple that with informing a reader on what makes each character tick, the characters should ultimately resemble, in at least some ways, people every reader knows. Like everyone, each character wants something. Oftentimes, these wants are desires that the reader can easily identify with. I'm not saying that every reader will react to desire in the same way as the characters do, but chances are they've at least been tempted to at some point in their lives.

4. **All of your novels explore Hawai'i's underworld of sex, drugs, crime, and prison, and your depiction is awfully realistic—or, at least, believable. How familiar are you with this world, and do your characters come from real people who inhabit this world?**

I have second-hand knowledge. Thankfully, I've never been to prison. The stuff that the character experienced in prison comes from research and from knowing people who have experienced those things. I have a cousin who's been in and out of prison—he filled me in on certain things. When I was doing ***The Tattoo,*** I had the opportunity to go to a prison and do a tour, because I knew a corrections officer there. That's where I got the physical detail.

Fiction writers create characters out of thin air and have to give these characters both physical and personality traits. They sometimes borrow traits from real life people, [but] I have never created a character thinking, hey, my friend Bob would be perfect for this.
Strip bars and jail—I seem to have a definite problem avoiding these two places in my writing. I made a promise to myself that neither place will make an appearance in my next book, and they haven't in *Mililani Mauka*.

5. **Were you surprised by the reaction in *The Tattoo,* how popular the book seemed to get quite quickly? Did you get any negative response or backlash?**

The Tattoo originally started off as my master's thesis. So there was a certain demographic that seemed not to like my novel, which made me like my novel more. When older Caucasian women complained about the amount of profanity and the amount of violence, well, that's what I was doing with the book—shoving this in your face. The negative reactions only encouraged me to make it gritty, to make it honest.

6. **Infidelity is a theme of *Mililani Mauka*—Kai is unfaithful to her husband, Banyan is unfaithful to his wife—rather than treat the topic as salacious or as a means to make some thunderous moral pronouncement, however, this novel treats the subject with a great deal of maturity. Banyan and Kai's mutual indiscretions might ultimately be destructive, yet together they manage to find a humaneness and connection that they've lacked in other relationships. Given this approach do you worry about alienating readers who might not be willing to accept**

this depiction? Did you set out to challenge commonly held perceptions of infidelity?

I try really hard to avoid making moral judgments when writing (like most people, I do enough of this in real life). My approach is more journalistic—try to report what happens with some objectivity. Kai cheated. Here's how it happened. Banyan cheated. Here's how it happened. Now when it comes to the fact that they might build a more positive relationship than their previous ones, I'm sure it happens. There's probably millions of people out there who made a better go at it the second or maybe even the third time around. If a reader is unable to accept this depiction, they are unwilling to accept reality. That's fine. There's certainly fiction out there that satisfies those kinds of needs. I don't think I challenge perceptions of infidelity. I challenge the desire to see a cheater burn in hell for eternity.

7. **The other relationship in the novel is the one between Josh and Dan, the police officer. Josh, the son of John Krill and Kai, has lost a father, is distant from his mother, and at the beginning of the novel is homeless. Dan, then, becomes something of a surrogate parent, feeding, clothing, and looking out for the boy, but more importantly he becomes a friend. Through Dan, Josh finds a means of re-integrating himself in the world, of reclaiming some sense of normalcy. The reader begins to understand what this friendship represents for Josh, but what does it mean for Dan?**

Josh becomes all Dan's got. He's divorced, no significant other, no real friends, he's lost passion for work, though I guess he does have a hobby. Josh becomes Dan's next project. The next thing he carves from wood, the next piece of armor he smiths. And of course, more than that. Ultimately, like any father, he is taking a son and trying to make him a man. Dan's unwillingness to let go of Josh is understandable. The problem is, like most of the adults in this book, he's still kind of a child himself.

8. John Krill is a strong character--when he's alive and, greater still, when he's dead. He's emotionally and physically larger than life, and his exit from this world illustrates that. Why did you decide to make him half-Samoan given that Samoans make up a small portion of Hawai'i's population? Were you concerned about making him a cliché and how did you avoid doing that? Is there a reason why his last name isn't Samoan?

Unlike my other books, when it comes to ethnic identity, this one is ambiguous. Banyan, Kai, Josh, Dan, and John are all mixed ethnically and little time is spent dwelling on their racial backgrounds. These characters represent a new Hawai'i, one far removed from its plantation roots, and one where "local" doesn't quite fit either. The quickly expanding suburbs—there isn't a Chinese block, a Japanese block, a Hawaiian cul-de-sac. It's mixed. It's American. It's where I see Hawai'i heading, fast. When I was a kid, I remember learning how to tie double hooked leader line to troll for pāpio. I don't foresee my daughter or my nephews learning such things. Instead, I see them walking around with Nintendo DSs and iPods, and playing soccer. Growing up, no one I knew in Kahalu'u played soccer.

John just happens to be part-Samoan. Therefore, so is his son, Josh. Neither are stereotypical Samoans because these local stereotypes wither as each generation grows further from its immigrant ancestral roots. So I took an ethnicity that carries a lot of stereotype baggage and avoided attaching the stereotypes to these characters. John's last name, Krill, also works towards this end. Ultimately, John starts off as a tall, lean, handsome, majestic man who from the outside, looks like he's got everything going for him. The only way Samoan really fits is a) he's originally from Wai'anae, so there's a believability issue b) he becomes a menehune, and seeing say, a pure Japanese menehune might be taking things too far for the reader c) he's really tall.

I guess the real question being asked here is why isn't he Hawaiian. My answer is, because in this story, he doesn't have to be. That's part of the point.

8. **Flannery O'Connor, once wrote, "In my own stories I have found that violence is strangely capable of returning my characters to reality and preparing them to accept their moment of grace." Certainly your novels frequently feature scenes of violence—*Mililani Mauka,* in fact, opens with a particularly memorable scene as John Krill rides a bulldozer around and through his hometown—but not just physical violence, there's a great deal of emotional violence as well. Do you find O'Connor's statement to be true as it relates to your own fiction? Through violence, are you hoping to help your characters achieve their moments of grace?**

I'm a big O'Connor fan. Yes, a person may enter a moment of grace in the midst of violence. Violence, in fact, can bring about all sorts of moments—shocking, predictable, humorous, melancholy, beautiful, ugly, electric, etc. John

Krill's exit is not particularly graceful. Other violent moments are plain clownish. And yes, a violent moment here and there might be graceful. Violence is often simply the last straw. Characters at their last straw, for me, are the most interesting to watch.

9. **Your writing often contains elements of fantasy and the supernatural—this novel even features a sardonic menehune. Is this influenced by your own reading? If so, are there any particular authors who've influenced you? Does it derive from living in Hawai'i with its rich mythology and imported folktales?**
   Yes to all of the above. Like most lit nerds, I'm an admirer of Gabriel Garcia Marquez. It's tough to resist playing around with the supernatural once you read something by him that tickles your fancy. And it can't be thrown in frivolously. It has to mean something. For example, in my book, I'm asking two things. First, the common question: Do ghosts even exist or are they a result of psychological problems? Second: Does a twenty-first century ghost even look like, say, a nineteenth century ghost? I doubt it. Like, if I saw a menehune in a malo playing with my Wii, I don't know what I'd make of it. Hawai'i's changing. Seems possible that its ghosts are changing or maybe even going extinct, too.

10. **The scenes along the Wai'anae coast in *Mililani Mauka* feel particularly timely. Readers will no doubt be familiar with scenes that have appeared in newspapers and on television of the homeless being rousted from encampments. Aside from providing contrast to the scenes among the manicured lawns and obligatory social gatherings in Mililani, were you attempting to**

convey any particular message or idea by setting part of the novel's action along the Waianae coast?

I don't know about conveying a message, but it seems impossible to ignore if you're talking about present day Hawai'i. In fact, I'd go so far to say that it's possibly the biggest issue in Hawai'i today, and to ignore it would be a disingenuous portrayal of current Hawai'i, in a contemporary novel at least. I mean, if you go out there, you're not really going to see white or Asian faces. And talking about Hawai'i and ignoring Hawaiians is like talking about the ocean and ignoring water. Hawaiians don't show up in my books because I'm some kind of wannabe Hawaiian or political commentator. Hawaiians show up in my books because, in this state, their issues are the most compelling.

11. **Suburban living has proven a rich subject for writers. John Cheever, Richard Yates, John Updike, and more recently, Tom Perrotta and Jeffrey Eugenides, have all written extensively on life in the suburbs. Their works, however, often center on how these bedroom communities are really a catch-all for barely sublimated rage and disaffected dreamers with disappointment lurking just around the corner. Now that you've written your own suburban novel, can you think of anything good, other than great fiction, that comes from living in the suburbs?**

Ha ha, yea, the suburbs often get treated rather roughly in fiction. I wouldn't enjoy living in Perotta's suburbs, but I'd take it over Richard Price's New York City and even Richard Russo's fun but economically depressed working class neighborhoods. In other words, the suburbs aren't that bad. Sure, I'd rather live in Diamond Head, but really, the suburbs are only as bad as the baggage you bring with you. If the suburbs reflect personal dreams unfulfilled, you'll hate them. If the suburbs represent promise of the good life, you'll be disappointed. For me, it's just a house. I don't have to drive through traffic to get groceries. My kid won't get cleaned out if she takes one step off the sidewalk in front of our house. Those are the biggest pluses, and if you think about it, they aren't half bad.

I think that people who've known me, for most of my life, will probably tell you I'm a lot more mellow now, than I was, say, ten years ago. I'm married, got a kid. I got your pretty much standard middle class life.

Questions and responses were compiled from interviews by John Heckathorn for ***Honolulu Magazine,*** Michelle White for ***Ka Leo O Hawai'i,*** and the publisher.

About the Author

Chris McKinney follows his groundbreaking earlier novels, ***The Tattoo, The Queen of Tears,*** and ***Bolohead Row,*** with another in-depth look at the "other" side of Hawai'i. Winner of the Ka Palapala Po'okela Award for Excellence in Literature and the Cades Award for Literature, he grew up in Kahalu'u and currently resides in Mililani with his wife and daughter. McKinney received both his B.A. and M.A. in English at the University of Hawai'i at Mānoa, and is currently teaching at Honolulu Community College.